The Broken Place

The Broken Place

BY MICHAEL SHAARA

McGraw-Hill Book Company

New York St. Louis San Francisco Hamburg
Mexico Toronto

1 2 3 4 5 6 7 8 9 D O D O 8 7 6 5 4 3 2 1

LIBRARY OF CONGRESS CATALOGING IN PUBLICATION DATA

Shaara, Michael.
  The broken place.
  I. Title.
[PS3569.H2B7 1981]   813'.54   80-29351
ISBN 0-07-056377-2

Books by Michael Shaara

The Killer Angels
The Herald

To Helen

The world breaks everyone and afterward many are strong at the broken places. But those that will not break it kills. It kills the very good and the very gentle and the very brave impartially. If you are none of these you can be sure it will kill you too but there will be no special hurry.

ERNEST HEMINGWAY
A Farewell to Arms

HOMECOMING: SPRING, 1953

ONE

WILSON LAY STARING down a long gray slope into the rising dark.
Nothing moved. There was light in the sky, red light in the tops of
the trees. But down there the night was coming up out of the
ground. Soft darkness flooded the bushes, flowed in under the trees.
Wilson shivered, looked to the sunset. A rich bloody glow, thin
wet streams of purple and rose. In a clear space to the north he saw
three white contrails; three jets up high, coming south, going home.
He thought: *they're* safe. An odor, something thick and rotten,
drifted slowly up the ridge. He nearly gagged; he had never gotten
used to it.

The lieutenant crawled up behind him. The lieutenant was a thin
tall man, without brains. He was very nervous.

"Where the hell is McClain?" the lieutenant said.

"He went down there." Wilson pointed down the slope.

"Well goddamit," the lieutenant said.

The man next to Wilson, a tubby man with a high fuzzy voice,
like an ex-fighter, said anxiously:

"What you hear, lieutenant? What's the word?"

"Listen," the lieutenant said to Wilson, "you go down there and
get him. McClain. You tell him I got to see him."

"He said he'd be back in a while. He said—"

"You just git him, that's all. Christ." The lieutenant shook his head.

Wilson rose slowly to his hands and knees; his rifle fell in the dirt. He felt a small spasm of weary anger.

"But didn't you git no word?" the tubby man said. "What the hell they gonna do? They gonna come git us?"

"You just get ready to pull out. When I give the word, we pull out, is that clear? But nobody pulls out till I say we pull out."

"Right," the tubby man said. "That's right. That's great. Let's get the hell out."

"Did you see anything down there?" the lieutenant said. He leaned forward, stretching his neck like a swan, staring. It was darker now, the trees and the bushes were gone, there was only the gray slope into darkness.

Wilson shook his head.

"Why the hell did he go down there?" the lieutenant complained.

"He took down another BAR, sir. He said they wouldn't be coming straight up the hill, they'd probably filter around to the rear and cut the road. He said somebody ought to protect the road."

The lieutenant was silent.

"Well," the lieutenant said. He took his helmet off and scratched his head. "Well, he's probably right. Only we won't be here that long."

"When do we pull out?"

"Not for a while." The lieutenant grinned. He had glistening, immaculate teeth. He scrubbed them every morning and every evening. Wilson had seen him. "Jesus," the lieutenant said. He shook his head again, like a man bothered by a persistent fly. "Christ," he added.

"Dint they send somebody?" the tubby man said. "Ain't no goddam body gonna come help us?"

"Oh, they sent somebody." The lieutenant grinned. "They sent one whole company, Love Company. Only Love Company got lost and not only don't know where the hell we are, they don't know where the hell *they* are. Christ. Christ all goddam mighty. So we'll hang in here for a while. But"—he lifted a finger, pointed it at Wilson—"but if any goddam attack starts, and they're not here by then, we pull out. So you get ready. I already passed the word. Now you get down there and get McClain, and tell him to shag-ass up here."

Wilson stood up and saw McClain coming. He was walking up out of the darkness. He was moving along slowly, too slowly. Wilson sensed danger. McClain came up into the gray light, stopped, looked at the sunset. He stood there looking at the sunset. Wilson started to call, but the world was too still. He held his breath. McClain went on gazing at the sunset.

"What the hell is he doing?" the lieutenant hissed. No one said anything. The three men on the ridge waited, watching the quiet man below. Wilson expected a shot, a scream. McClain went on standing in the stunned, darkening silence. Wilson realized suddenly that McClain was bareheaded—he'd taken off his helmet. At that moment another wave of that same appalling stench came flowing across the ridge. Wilson picked up his rifle, about to go down. McClain turned and came on up the ridge. He was still moving too slowly. He was moving as if there was all the time in the world and no place to go. Wilson knew something was wrong.

The lieutenant was up on his hands and knees.

"Goddamit," he said, "what were you lookin' at?"

McClain stepped down into Wilson's hole. It was not much of a hole, just a scraped depression in the gray dirt. McClain sat down. Still slowly, very slowly, not like a man who was tired, more like a man in a dream. He looked up at the lieutenant. The lieutenant had to repeat the question. "What were you lookin' at?"

"The sun," McClain said.

"Jesus." The lieutenant raised his hands. "Where's your helmet? Why'd you take off your helmet? Listen." He hunched forward, peering into McClain's face. "Listen, boy. Are you all right?"

"Fine," McClain said.

"Did something happen down there?"

"Nothing happened."

"Who was down there with you?"

"Becker. Indrisano."

"Are they all right?"

"They're fine."

"Then why the hell'd you leave your helmet?"

"Everything's fine," McClain said.

Wilson, watching, was afraid. But the lieutenant seemed temporarily satisfied. "Well, when you go back there you make sure you get into that goddam helmet. Listen, maybe we'll pull out of here.

I don't know yet. Love Company was supposed to be here, but they got lost. If they don't show soon, I'm on my own. We'll wait a while, but if they don't show, or somebody starts shootin', the hell with it. All right?"

"Fine," McClain nodded.

"You sure you're all right?"

McClain nodded. Wilson could not see his eyes.

"When do you think they'll come?" the lieutenant said.

"Who?"

"Who!" the lieutenant waved his arms with exasperation. "*Them*, goddamit." He pointed down the slope.

"Oh, they'll wait a bit." McClain turned and looked down into the swelling black. "They'll let it get good and dark. And it's going to rain anyway, they'll wait for that."

"You think it's going to rain?"

"Didn't you see it coming?"

"No."

"Behind us. Coming up from the south. You can smell it. It'll rain any time."

"You think they'll move around through that gulley, and cut the road?"

McClain nodded again.

"All right, here's what you do." The lieutenant paused. McClain had a gift for this kind of thing. He would know exactly what to do. And though the lieutenant was not very bright, he was bright enough to know that. "You go on back down there," the lieutenant said. "You get your helmet on. Then you hang in there until you hear something coming. Then you start shooting and get the hell out, and when we hear you shoot we'll start pulling out, only we'll wait for you, all right? Only it'll be black as hell, so come in a hurry. All right?"

McClain nodded peacefully.

"And if you hear any shooting start anywhere, up here, over on the right, you come back up. Because that's when we pull out. You got that?"

"Right."

"And make sure you get your helmet on. For Christ's sake."

The lieutenant left, crawling across the ridge. The tubby man, whose name was Finnegan, sat belching unconsciously, taking deep breaths. McClain turned and leaned back, his arms behind his head, facing the last dull rose in the western sky.

"That was a damn fool thing," Wilson said.

McClain was watching the sky. In the last soft light Wilson could see his face: the eyes wide and black, sunken in darkness, the head round and hard like eroded stone. McClain's mouth was slightly open, open and black; there was something in the face, an extraordinary silence, a tension. Something terrible had happened. Was happening.

"What's the matter?" Wilson said.

McClain turned to face him. The head moved like a stone idol. The face was in darkness.

"Tom. You all right?"

The head nodded.

"You look . . . you don't look good."

"It's going to rain," McClain said.

Wilson thought: he's gone crazy.

"Can't hear worth a damn in the rain," McClain said. "I used to hunt deer. You can't hunt in the rain."

"He ought to pull out *now*," Finnegan said suddenly, bitterly. "Why the hell is he waitin'? First thing you know, you can't see nothin'."

"Tom," Wilson said. "Stay here. Will you stay here?"

"Uh-uh," McClain shook his head decisively.

"Listen, I'll go on down and tell those two guys what to do—"

"No," McClain said. He loomed forward, he stood up. He looked down the slope into the darkness. Wilson stood up with him.

Finnegan said: "Will you two guys for Christ's sake sit down?"

"We still goin' to Singapore?" Wilson said.

McClain turned to look at him.

"Hell yes," McClain said.

"Well, then take care of yourself," Wilson said.

"It'll be all right," McClain said.

"Let me tell you frankly, man, you worry me."

"There's no problem," McClain said. He reached out and touched Wilson on the arm. "You bloody limey," he said.

"You want me to come down with you?"

"No. You stay here." McClain looked up into the sky. "It ought to start pretty soon now." He turned back to Wilson and grinned. "Let it come down."

Wilson was reassured.

"Just keep your mind on Singapore," Wilson said.

"All right."

"And put your goddam helmet on."

"Well," McClain said. A wind picked up behind them: Wilson smelled oil and cut grass and wet, open earth. McClain said: "When you hear the shooting, pull out. Don't wait. I'll be along. But don't you wait."

"Hell," Wilson said. "I'm not going to wait even for the shooting."

"All right, but you get moving. And I'll see you. You'll be all right."

He went off into the darkness. He was still moving slowly, like an old man. Wilson knew he was going to die. He had known from the first moment he saw him stop to watch the sunset, bareheaded, in the gathering dark. Wilson did not quite accept it, but he knew it. He sat back in the depression, felt his own fear begin to suck at his stomach: He's going to die. He knows it. Maybe we're all. But what does he know? Too damn dark. Oh God, I've got to get out. He's going to die. He's going to die.

"What do you think was the matter?" Wilson said. He had to talk.

"With what?"

"With McClain."

"Him? Nothin' was the matter with *him*. I should have nerves like him. That goddam idiot lieutenant, what's he waitin' for?"

"Didn't you see anything wrong with him?"

"I just as soon start movin' back right now. You wanna? We just shove back here off this goddam line. They prolly know where this line is anyways. Maybe we move back it'll fake 'em out. If they throw grenades. . . ."

Wilson did not move.

"We ought to move back a little," Finnegan said. "Get a head start."

Sometime after that the rain began. Very light, very fine, a soft wet rustling in among the rocks. Wilson thought: the quality of mercy. The rain increased. Finnegan crawled up out of the hole and perched on the back of it like a fat frightened bird. There was firing from down in the gully. A sprinkling of rifle fire, the heavier thump of the BAR. Grenades. One. Two. Then many grenades.

Wilson heard a voice call behind him. Finnegan was gone. He

heard boots slipping on rock. The BAR began again. The sound was mindless, impersonal; Wilson could feel holes appearing all around him in the air. He isn't coming. He's going to stay. Wilson stood up. A flare screamed silently in the falling rain, Wilson convulsed back into the rock. Now it was time to go. McClain wasn't coming up, had planned on not coming up, would stay down there and let it roll over him, the flares, the thunder. Wilson could still hear the BAR firing in short bursts, the light popping of rifles spreading around it, and more grenades. Wilson stayed. And then he could hear feet coming up the rocks toward him, a crawling, pattering doom, and that pushed him away. He broke back across the ridge and down into the darkness.

The hilltop was empty. The rain fell softly, steadily. Men came up and crouched on the hilltop. In the dark of the gulley the BAR was suddenly still. There was a moment of silence. The men on the hilltop waited. The first shell came in behind them, passing on overhead and exploding down the hill. The men lay down in the rocks. The shells came in clusters, thickening. They fell on the hilltop and down in the gulley, and when the first one came down in the gulley the BAR began firing again, from a new place, and went on firing steadily for a long while, firing back at the rocks, at invisible men, firing blindly into the dark, the falling shells, the ripped and mindless rain.

WILSON PASSED THE NIGHT in a wooded ravine. The rain fell all night long. He was exhausted, but he did not sleep. He sat wrapped in his poncho, tucked under a bush, listening to the rain. He felt the presence of an obscure vacancy somewhere in his brain, a rounded hole of emptiness, not a fog, not a mistiness, just nothing, nothing at all. He dreamed vacantly. He had never accepted death. He had seen it quite often but he had never seen it happen to anyone who mattered to him personally, and there was still something about it he had never quite believed, just as you never quite believe in some new scientific marvel; even though you've seen it and know theoretically exactly how it works, there is still in the mind that one small reactionary unconvinced area which hangs back from complete acceptance, that unique and stubborn human regret. His own parents had died in the war, the big war, killed by a bomb in London. He had not seen that happen. When he heard about it he did not quite believe it, and he did not really believe now, even though he knew absolutely and for certain that it was true—he had his mother's gold locket to prove it, her locket taken from her body—and when it happened they shipped him off to America, a boy in his teens, to live with his sole relative, and to become an American. And he had grown up and gone into another war all the while knowing for certain that they were dead, and yet continuing to have these same dreams that they were not, or at least one of them wasn't, it had all been a terrible mistake, common in wartime, and one of them had not been killed at all but had been badly wounded, and had amnesia, and could not be identified, and so had wandered hopelessly years after, and then suddenly the memory had returned.

And so he dreamed of his father standing in the door, holding his arms out, tears on his cheeks, a big big man with a red face and bright blue eyes. He dreamed sometimes of his mother, but less often, because there was, after all, the locket. And he did truly believe in the back of his mind, especially when he was alone late at night, that it *was* possible—after all, there was always that one chance, nothing was ever that certain, it *had* happened, and not even the locket was proof, if you thought about it, because it could have blown off one and onto another, and in all that mess you couldn't tell one from another.

He thought about them that night, sitting in the ravine. He knew they were dead, he tried to picture them as dead. They were dead all right. But he could not picture it. He felt a peculiar weariness. He felt not so much tired as suddenly old, his muscles thin, his mouth dusty, his hair falling out. He thought about McClain, but he could not picture him dead either. Yet he was dead, of course. But it was impossible to imagine it. He thought of dead bodies he'd seen and thought of McClain like that, but it didn't work, and he realized that he'd never looked on a dead man as real, and that was because most people were not real anyway. Nobody was real, they were just there. He peered off into the dark, trying to see somebody. He wondered if anyone was real but him. And then he felt unreal himself. Empty, a thin weak thing, cold, trembling, a weak, ticking, functioning machine. Vacant.

He had never known anyone who made up his mind to die. He could understand that a man could want to do that. He did not quite know why, but he could understand. He had a faint glimpse of the darkness, the weariness. Someday it was possible that he would do it himself. But he had not expected it of McClain. He remembered McClain as silent, as different. McClain was not a complainer. McClain was too calm and too tough to do a thing like that. And now with him gone it was going to be a different company. McClain would leave a hole. The lieutenant. Oh God, the lieutenant.

He shouldn't have done it, Wilson thought. He should have talked to somebody. If he'd told somebody. They might have helped him.

Never go to Singapore.

He thought about Singapore. Overland to Singapore. You pick up the car in London, cheap, you buy a Rover. It'll go anywhere. And you get out of Europe as fast as you can, heading east. Get through Germany quick, and then across Italy into Yugoslavia. And Greece and Turkey, and then you set foot in Asia. Mosques and domes, camels, girls in black veils. The wide white blinding desert. Overland. Singapore. He had planned to go with McClain. McClain had promised. You could trust old Tom. Dead Tom. Dead of his own hand. Why? Why did he have to do that? Why didn't he talk to me?

Wilson fell asleep just before dawn, but the guns jerked him awake. They were shelling the hill. The company was reassembling: they were to go back up. The men moved into position with thick dumb groping motions, mouths open, blinking into the dawn with pale exhausted eyes. Wilson moved. He had to strain to see. The rain had stopped; the morning had begun to clear. Some jets came over, flying low. The men down the line flopped into puddles. Wilson stared. The morning light hurt his eyes.

The planes dropped napalm on the hill. When they were gone, turning high up into the sun with the wings shining silver like wet laughter, the guns began again, and the company moved out. Wilson moved, one foot and another, and then tucked himself back down inside himself and let the body work, and functioned, tick tick tick, out of order and thick with mud, but functioning, mindless, up the hill. The guns let up. He made it to a hollow in the rocks and dropped there. He closed his eyes and breathed, and breathed. He began to smell the thick mud vapor, blasted rock, the warm wet stink of burned meat. He lay there for a long while, and there was no shooting. He crawled to a sitting position and put his head down and slept.

Somebody came by with coffee. He opened his eyes and stared. He was not hungry. He wanted to sleep. Men moved by him, somebody tripped over him, swore. He drank the coffee. After a while he woke up. He was alive. He looked at the raw ground, the soft blue sky. Things came into focus, the world became real. Two men sat near him, weary, bearded, trimmed with mud like gray cake frosting, unrecognizable. Wilson sat alone.

He did not recognize where he was. Somewhere off to the left was the gulley. The ridge to his right was scorched, still smoking where the napalm had flooded the ground with that appalling force. Wilson saw no bodies. He could not remember any shooting. All that shelling all that night and all that morning. They must have pulled out.

McClain.

Wilson stood up. From the ridge he had a clear view. The sky was patched with small white clots of broken cloud. The sun was high and warm, the ground was steaming; down in the brush a white mist was floating. The company was spread out all down the ridge in small exhausted clusters; gray flies along a dead spine. Wilson began to walk along the ridge toward the gulley.

The lieutenant was sitting with his back against a rock, talking into a telephone. There was dried blood on the hand that held the phone. Wilson heard: "Not till I get an order. I ain't moving one goddam muscle. Right. Fine. We're all tapped out. You tell 'em. Right." He handed the phone to a small man sitting near him, leaned his head back against the rock, blew out one long deep breath.

"Sir," Wilson said.

The lieutenant looked up at him. His mouth was open, his eyes were blank.

"Did anybody find McClain?" Wilson said.

The lieutenant stared. After a moment he shook his head.

The man next to him looked up at Wilson, then at the lieutenant. Wilson recognized him. A small silent college boy. His name was Dover. "What happened to McClain?" he said.

"He didn't pull out," the lieutenant said. He rubbed his eyes: gray flakes of mud drifted down over his chin.

"Oh," Dover said.

"What about the two guys who were with him?" Wilson said.

"They got back." The lieutenant looked up at Wilson, began to remember him.

"What'd they say?" Wilson asked.

"They didn't say nothin'." The lieutenant blinked, began plucking at his pocket, searching for a cigarette.

Wilson looked off down toward the gulley. He thought he might as well walk down there.

"You knew him pretty well," the lieutenant said.

Wilson nodded.

"You know anybody to write to?" The lieutenant sat forward, took a long puff on the cigarette. "He's got no next of kin."

Wilson shook his head. He remembered once, a long time ago, McClain with a letter from a girl. Pale blue pages, a baby scrawl. Picture of a scrubbed, dark-haired face.

The lieutenant sat back. He would not have to write a letter. The college boy, Dover, was staring at the ground. He said suddenly: "Well. That's a damn shame."

"I think I'll just walk down there," Wilson said.

The lieutenant watched him for a minute thoughtfully.

"There's people already there," he said.

Wilson walked off along the ridge. He was thinking about Singapore. Then he thought: you never can tell. He moved down past the place where they had sat the night before, looked out over the rock where McClain had stood watching the last sunset. There were shell holes all down the slope; the brush along the gulley was shredded, destroyed. He came around a mound of steaming rock, saw troops moving up the gulley. On the far slope he saw two corpsmen bending over something on the ground.

Wilson waited for a moment. The line of troops moved slowly by, looking at him without interest. Wilson crossed the gulley and went up the other side. He recognized McClain's face from a long way away. He looked like he'd just been dug out of the earth. Wilson came up and stood over him.

The two corpsmen were digging the dirt from around his legs. One looked up cheerfully at Wilson, went back to work.

McClain was lying turned on his right side, his right arm under him. There was dirt in his eyes, dried blood over the round top of his head. His legs looked like they'd been partially shot away.

One of the corpsmen said to Wilson: "You know this fella?"

Wilson nodded. He was looking at McClain's open mouth. The chin was clean, untouched, a bearded island in the bloody face.

The other corpsman, his back to Wilson, said gruffly: "C'mon, Jake, get a move on. He may make it."

"You think so?" Jake said. He looked down and shrugged, amazed. To Wilson he said: "You ought to get an officer over here, to see what this guy done." He motioned over his shoulder. "Looka that."

Wilson looked. He saw bodies in a row, laid out behind a rock, feet stacked straight, at attention.

Then he understood what the first corpsman had said. "He's still alive?" Wilson said.

"He is right now," the first corpsman said. "But if we don't get'm to an aid station goddam fast. . . ."

"There's a truck comin', man, take it easy."

"He'll never make it without plasma."

"Well I'm doin' the best I can."

Wilson knelt. He could see it himself: the slow silent breathing. "Tom," he said.

"He's pretty bad off, man," the first corpsman said. "But there should be an officer around here, to see what he done."

They finished digging McClain out. They cleaned off his face. He had bled a lot from a wound in the skull but the wound was not deep. The legs were bad. McClain lay with his mouth open. After a while some officers came up, and then McClain's lieutenant, and a jeep came up to get McClain and carry him back to the aid station. Wilson walked with him to the jeep, but McClain never opened his eyes.

The lieutenant looked over what McClain had done and put him in for a medal. The Silver Star. Wilson stood by and listened. The lieutenant had forgotten all about the way McClain had looked at the sunset. None of that mattered to Wilson. He walked back up on the ridge into the steaming light and sat by himself and thought about after the war, the great steppes of Asia, overland to Singapore.

TWO

MCCLAIN WENT INTO THE HOSPITAL during the late spring of the year, during a time of heavy rain. They put him in a room overlooking black rocks and the sea. The first thing he saw was the rain blowing against the window, but he could not see clearly. The next time he looked there was sun in the window, yellow and clean.

During the first month he was almost totally deaf. They worked on his legs and his head and smiled down at him and moved their mouths. Through most of that time he had pain in his legs, pain moving slowly through him like fire burning in a vein of coal. In the nights he had nightmares and people came in and turned on the lights: he saw faces above him, yellow nostrils, gleaming eyes. There was a toothless orderly who brought him cigarettes and cleaned up the room, talking, the mouth opening and lips sucking soundlessly, and McClain watched him and nodded whenever the man talked. McClain did not try to speak.

In the mornings they wheeled him out onto a balcony overlooking the sea. He began to hear the first sounds: a birdcall, a crow, the clean starched scratching of a nurse's dress. For a long while he did not let anyone know he could hear. He sat by himself all morning and sometimes all afternoon, watching the clouds, the sea, the white lines of waves breaking on the rocks. There was a doctor who came to see him, a pleasant man with the saintly smiling face of a minister. The doctor wrote down questions and McClain answered them, trying to show the doctor that everything was all right. The doctor watched McClain throughout the first month and then listed him as a mild case of combat fatigue. The beauty of combat fatigue was that McClain was not going back to war, and therefore the causative factor was now removed and McClain would get better. Sometimes McClain would cry, silently. That would stop. His heart would flutter, skip, flutter. That would end. He would be able to sleep nights and the feelings of terror would depart gradually, and he would begin to move around. He would be as good as new. The doctor wrote down the news that McClain would not have to go back. McClain smiled and nodded. In July the doctor brought in a newspaper showing him that the war had ended. McClain smiled and nodded. After that the doctor wrote in his report that Sergeant McClain seemed much improved.

They left him alone, and McClain liked the silence. The silence matched something in himself: an absence, a darkness. Something had died. Most of the time he was all right. He would sit and watch the waves and the rain, and the colors of the sky. Every now and then there would seep through him like a spreading stain this wet thick feeling of despair, this appalling feeling of the most terrible despair. That was when he cried. When he had trouble sleeping at night, there was a trick he used. He would imagine himself boarding a boat, a small white cabin boat. He would lie in the dark and start the engine and cast off the moorings and move out onto a flat black river. He would move down the river slowly and it was always night with a full moon, and he would follow the river in the moonlight as it widened on out to the open sea. When he reached the sea he usually fell asleep, but sometimes he went a long way out.

ONE DAY there was a new doctor. He came out on the balcony and smiled at McClain, raising one hand slightly in greeting, and stood for a moment with his hands on his hips, looking out to sea. The day was flat and gray, there was a thick wet wind coming in off the sea. The doctor's white coat fluttered; he shoved his hands into his pockets. He was a short man with a square, weary face. He needed a shave.

"My name's Kashka," he said. He glanced down at McClain, shoved out a pack of cigarettes. McClain shook his head. Kashka looked him over cheerfully, thoughtfully, leaned back against the railing.

"I've been assigned to you," Kashka said.

McClain nodded. He had been perfectly comfortable alone on the balcony, and he hoped this one would not talk too much.

"I've just been reading your record," Kashka said. "You have one hell of a record." He folded his arms, smiled pleasantly. McClain noticed that his face looked very tired. His collar was open, his tie had been pulled loose.

"Do you feel like talking?" Kashka said.

"Sure."

"Good. I want to get together with you one of these days. How's everything coming along?"

"Fine."

"You need anything?"

"No." McClain did not say 'sir.' Kashka, a captain, did not notice.

"If you need anything—" Kashka said.

McClain shook his head.

"You like it here?"

"It's fine."

"Um," Kashka grunted absently. He lighted a cigarette. After a while he said: "I see they're giving you a medal."

McClain waited patiently.

"Very interesting thing," Kashka said. "How do you feel about that?"

"About what?"

"Medals."

McClain did not know what to say.

"I'm just curious," Kashka said. "I'd like to know why you did it. I read up on it." His face was cheerful and calm, his eyes had the lively silent quality of a gambler at a poker table.

McClain shrugged.

"You don't feel like talking?"

"No. I feel fine."

"It's a curious thing. I read the report on you at the aid station where they brought you in. Do you know how close you came to dying? You almost bled to death. You were lucky. Fella there made a note. He said you were a classic example of the will to live."

McClain said nothing. He wished the doctor would go away.

"Another thing," Kashka said cheerily, curiously, "why'd you take the helmet off?"

McClain took a deep breath.

"Are you a psychiatrist?"

"No," Kashka said. He grinned slightly. "No, as a matter of fact, I'm actually in internal medicine." He chuckled. "They put me in here because they say I have a feel for it. The Army. They move in

wondrous ways. I have some training, though, in combat fatigue.
You ever take any psychology?"

"Yes."

"You had one year of college? Or two?"

"Two."

"What was your major?"

"No major."

"Oh? I thought you indicated a feeling for pre-med."

"Not any more," McClain said.

"Um. They tell me you used to fight. In the ring."

"Yes."

"Professionally?"

"Yes."

"How'd you make out?"

"I did all right."

"Are you going back to it?"

"It wasn't a career."

"Did you like it?"

"Sure."

"Um. What are you going to do now?"

McClain shook his head.

"You ought to go back to school. How old are you? Twenty-
three. Hell's bells. What was wrong with pre-med?"

"Nothing wrong with it."

"None of my business?" Kashka was smiling.

McClain looked at him.

"Sorry. No offense," Kashka said. He stood up. The wind was
blowing his hair over his eyes. McClain saw again that he looked
very tired. Kashka looked down at McClain silently. He seemed to
be trying to make up his mind. After a moment he said: "You ought
to talk about it, son."

McClain said: "I wish I could."

"You ought not leave here without talking about it."

"I guess not."

"I'll be around," Kashka said.

He waited, but McClain said nothing. Kashka went away.

McClain sat looking at the wide gray sky. For the first time he
felt an urge to speak. But no words came. He was too tired for
words. He lay back into the silence and closed his eyes. Now in the
darkness he was detached from the earth.

ONE DAY they gave him the medal. By that time he was able to walk, but it was somebody's idea that it would look better for him to get the medal while sitting in a wheelchair. He shaved and they gave him a new bathrobe, velvet, bright red. Orderlies were all over his room all that morning scrubbing and polishing. A Gray Lady came in and put books and flowers and magazines by his bed. Then he sat waiting alone for a long while, staring out the window. The day was bright but windy; he could see huge waves breaking on the rocks. It was pleasant to be in the hospital. He almost fell asleep.

Then a nurse came rushing in and fussed around him, propping him up, sitting him at attention. Then the rest of them, so many that they crowded the room. The man who gave him the medal was a colonel from McClain's old regiment. McClain did not remember him. He was a tall, grim, sad-looking man, heavily sunburned. Behind him was the old hospital colonel who kept popping his eyes open like watery flashbulbs. There were several other officers, and Kashka. Kashka had to stand on tiptoe to smile at him over somebody's shoulder. The infantry colonel said hello and asked him how he was getting on, and said he came from a fine body of men. There was an Army photographer with a loose tie and a sloppy hat who patiently arranged the group for pictures. The infantry colonel stood at the foot of McClain's bed and read the citation. McClain sat through it with his head lowered, staring at his hands and his knees. He did not recognize what the colonel said as having much to do with that day on the hill. He thought of the rest of them, remembering the dead ones. Dead meat underground, rot buried in slime. Bone and metal. He felt his own life beating in his chest.

The colonel finished and bent down and took the medal out of a black box and pinned it on the front of his bathrobe. McClain was startled to smell whiskey on the colonel's breath. The colonel's face was proud and firm. McClain knew that the colonel was experiencing a strong emotion. He shook McClain's hand with a mighty grip.

"Congratulations, soldier."

"Thank you, sir."

"Want to see you get out of here, soon as you can."

"Yes, sir."

"That was a very fine thing."

"Thank you, sir."

"I was up there that day. I was over to your right, on Sunrise. You were in Lieutenant Hubble's platoon."

"Yes, sir."

"I knew him. Son of a friend. I was very sorry about that."

McClain looked up. "Sir?"

"Oh." The colonel blinked. "I guess you haven't heard. Lieutenant Hubble was killed. Shortly after you left."

"Oh," McClain said. He was thinking, but his mind was a blank. The colonel went on talking, but McClain was trying to remember. All the names, all the faces. He could not see the faces.

"You don't plan on staying in the Army, do you, sergeant?"

"No, sir."

"Going to be a doctor, they tell me."

McClain looked up at Kashka, couldn't see him.

"Well, you have a lot to be proud of. We want you to know that the Army is proud to have had you with us." He put out a hand. The photographer took a picture. They all came by and shook his hand, although he knew none of them but Kashka. After that they all left except the nurse and Kashka.

Kashka went to the door and peered craftily down the hall. Then he beckoned to the nurse.

"Maybelle, you go round up some ice. Okay?" The nurse looked at him and simpered. Kashka patted her absently as she went by. When she was gone, he pulled a shining silver flask from under the white coat.

"Cheers?"

"Cheers," McClain said.

Kashka came around to the side of the bed and poured some whiskey into two water glasses.

"What the hell," he said, "a man ought to celebrate these things." He handed one glass to McClain. "Do you mind it straight?"

"No. Not 'tall."

"Shall we wait for the ice?"

"Cheers," McClain said. He held up the glass. Kashka joined him.

"Ah!" Kashka said.

McClain blinked. He looked down into the glass. "What is it?"

"What is it? Why, boy, it's Scotch. Real Scotch. What's the matter?"

"Hoo!" McClain said.

"Don't you drink?"

"Oh yes. Only, not recently."

"That's a damn shame. More? There's a mite left."

"Fine."

Kashka filled the glass half full. McClain looked up at him thoughtfully.

"Let me see the medal," Kashka said. McClain handed it over. Kashka stared at it.

"Courage has never much impressed me," Kashka said. "I never much believed in it."

McClain stared at the whiskey in the glass. He thought that it would be better if he did not drink much.

"It's always a question of what a man fears most," Kashka said. He held it against his own chest. "Do I look brave? Oh. Excuse me. This is very nice." He handed it back.

McClain looked at it for the first time. The ribbon was blue and white around a thick stripe of bright red; the medal itself was small and bronze, the bright silver star tiny in the center, enclosed in a bronze wreath. He put it in the black box and put the box on the table. He had a quick bright vision of the night and the firing and the shells beginning to come in. He shuddered and shook his head. He looked up to see Kashka watching him.

"You're a crafty bastard," McClain said.

At that moment the nurse came in with the ice. She reminded the doctor that he was very busy this morning. Kashka offered her a drink: she coyly refused. She departed.

"Good egg," Kashka said, staring after her. "Reminds me a bit of my wife. Charming." He swished the whiskey around over the ice, looked down at McClain.

"One of these days, you ought to let me know what the hell's going on."

"Right!" McClain said.

Kashka reached out and picked up the medal again. He held the Star in the palm of his hand. "Don't you feel anything?" he said.

"About what?"

"The medal."

"Oh. Sure," McClain said, obligingly.

"Then why did you do it?"

"I was tired," McClain said.

Kashka dangled the medal. "Tired of what?"

"I was just tired," McClain said. He looked out the window at the bright flickering light of sunlight off the sea. He held the glass up to the light and watched the color of the whiskey, watched his own unsteady hand and the whiskey rippling and fluttering along the edges of the glass.

"Tired of the war?" Kashka said.

"No. It had nothing to do with the war."

Kashka watched him, waiting. McClain stared dreamily at the whiskey. After a moment McClain said: "As a matter of fact, the war probably postponed it."

Kashka went on waiting. McClain drank, held up the glass to Kashka.

"This was very nice of you," McClain said.

"No charge."

"Do you really give a rap?"

Kashka tucked the medal back into his palm, closed his fingers over it.

"I mean," McClain said, "you look at me like I was a busted watch."

"Sorry. Occupational hazard."

"I don't mind," McClain said. "But sometimes it's uncomfortable."

"Sorry."

"Will I be out of here soon?"

"Soon as you can walk around."

"I better not have any more of this," McClain said. He rolled the wheelchair one-handedly to the window, set the glass on the sill. When the glass touched the tile, it chattered and nearly fell. McClain was aware of how much his hand was shaking. He looked up at Kashka with embarrassment.

Kashka said: "I've never seen any combat."

"Good for you," McClain said.

"I wish I had. You feel . . . left out. Some people get patronizing about it."

"I'm not," McClain said. He was suddenly tired, and the whiskey was making him sad.

"What are you thinking?"

"Nothing."

"You had an interesting look on your face just then."

"I wasn't thinking anything." McClain's body began to shudder suddenly, all over. He put his hands together in his lap and held on. Kashka watched him. McClain couldn't stop the shuddering. He felt ridiculous.

"Can I get you something?" Kashka said gently.

"Leave me alone," McClain said.

"I better get you something." Kashka started to rise.

"Leave me alone." The shuddering began to ease. And now Mc-Clain was deeply, terribly tired. His head was too heavy. God damn the whiskey. He closed his eyes and the dark terrified him. He opened them and stared at Kashka.

"You can't go home like this," Kashka said.

McClain stared at him. A nurse had come into the room. Kashka was saying: "You'll be all right, kid. You're going to be fine."

He slept.

"YOU HAVE A VISITOR," the nurse said. McClain looked up out of a peaceful silence and saw the grinning, silly face of Tony Wilson.

"Howdy, Thomas. How goes the soul?"

Wilson came into the room and stood awkwardly, happily clutching his hat. He looked thinner, much younger, his hair was messy.

"I'm on my way home. Can't stay but a minute. But I thought I'd drop by for a moment and check on the old progress. My God, you're all to yourself. Oh, lovely. How'd you work that? Listen, old soul, how goes it?"

"Hey," McClain said. He smiled, sat up, stuck out his hand. Wilson took it, grinning foolishly, embarrassed. McClain remembered: fumbling, stumbling boy. An appalling soldier. Trace of the English accent. No parents. Something aloof and ridiculous, anxious, graceless, eager to please. Guns came apart in Wilson's hands, cars would not start. There was something about him that was pathetic and vulnerable. But he'd lived through it. He'd stumbled through it. England will muddle through. McClain grinned.

"Well, when do they let you out of here? Are you up and about?"

"I'm beginning to walk now."

"Well, you're a lovely sight. Christ!" He shook his head. He was remembering the morning in the gulley.

"I'm glad to see you," McClain said.

"Well." Wilson sat down on the edge of the bed. "Well, I've only got a few minutes. Damn train. Well. When do we head for Singapore?"

McClain had forgotten.

"Singapore," Wilson said.

"Well, I don't know."

"Here's the drill: I'm going on home now and spend the fall in indolence and drink. Right through Christmas. But this winter I'm hopping on over to London and I'll pick up the car there, and shop around for the stuff we'll need, you know, parts and all, and get everything set up, and if you can get over by early spring we can push off. Good idea to get an early start, get through the desert before the summer."

McClain began to remember. But he had made no plans. When they had talked about Singapore he had already known he was not going anywhere. That seemed ridiculous now. The world was beginning again; he looked away from Wilson toward the window. Wilson watched him anxiously.

"Do you think you can make it by early spring?" Wilson asked.

McClain shrugged. He tried to think ahead. Nothing happened. His mind saw nothing, no visions, no roads. He blinked, shook his head.

"That'll give you seven or eight months," Wilson said hopefully. "By that time the legs will be jolly, um? You won't have to prepare a thing, I'll get the whole show going. But you've got to come, old soul, I'm counting on you."

"Well," McClain said. "I'll try."

"Ha," Wilson breathed out a deep, joyous breath. He flicked his hat into the air, caught it, dropped it, picked it up from under the bed, grinning, rapped a hand on the nightstand, babbled about the trip. McClain sat smiling, bewildered.

"You've got to give me your address, old friend. Now where will you be?" Wilson fumbled in his shirt pocket, extracted a small green notepad, a long blue pen, said with feeling: "I hope I don't lose this, damn it. Lost half my damn gear already. Goddam thieves. Now, where can I get in touch?"

"I don't . . . you'd better leave me yours."

Wilson blinked at him anxiously.

"No home address?"

McClain shook his head. Wilson suddenly remembered.

"Oh, that's right. Well listen, what about the school? You'll be dropping back by the school?"

"Yes."

"Well, how about that?"

McClain gave him the address of the school. Wilson said he would write care of the Dean of Men, then wrote his own New York address and gave it to McClain and asked if there wasn't somewhere safe he could put it. McClain told him to put it in the top drawer of the night table. When that was all done, Wilson was vastly relieved. He sat grinning cherubically and said: "My God. We're on our ruddy way. A little rest first, yes, but after that, we're off. E'en as the big-ass bird. One of the things I'm going to get, a good camera."

After a while McClain asked about the company.

"You heard about the lieutenant?" Wilson said.

"Yes. How'd that happen?"

"Damn fool, as usual. Although I suppose I shouldn't say that. Got caught out in the open, machine gun. Died instantly. We had quite a few casualties, after you left. I got nicked once myself." He started to unbutton his sleeve, then stopped, embarrassed. "Really nothing. Cut about an inch long. Something whizzed by. Well, at least I can say I gave my blood." He paused, turned, looked out the window. "Christ!" he said with sudden force. "I'm glad *that's* over." He turned back to McClain. "We missed you after you left, you know. You were the only one in the whole damn outfit who knew what he was doing."

He paused, looked at McClain with an eager, grateful joy. McClain said nothing.

"I must say," Wilson said, shaking his head, "you gave us a nasty shock. I thought for sure . . . well," he grinned again, "the whole thing's done. As Othello once said: no more of that. Now. What are your plans?"

"Going to take it easy," McClain said.

"No more fighting for a bit, ah? Good. School later on, I suppose. I don't know. I should, I suppose. But the time is ripe for Singapore. Oh, by the way, I heard about the medal. Want to congratulate, and all that."

McClain nodded.

"Don't suppose you'd let me borrow it sometime? Might be handy to charm a few troops this winter. Funny. I don't feel like a veteran. Do you?"

"Yep," McClain said.

"You are all right, old soul? You look a bit gray. Not enough sun. Well, there'll be plenty of sun. Oh Christ!" He looked at his watch, jumped from the bed, banged his knee on a chair. "I've got to push off."

He stuck out a hand. McClain took it.

"You will keep in touch?"

"Sure," McClain said.

"Maybe I can drop in on you, sometime this fall."

"Fine," McClain said.

"Well, I've got to run."

"I'm glad you came by."

"Damn good to see you. You will keep in touch?"

McClain nodded. Wilson smiled, hung in the doorway, waved, then exited, bumping into a nurse.

McClain sat alone in the silence. Wilson had been a breath of air. The summer ahead, the steppes of Asia. It was unreal. McClain looked out on the still air of this summer's afternoon. Nothing ahead was real. You went one step at a time. Summer, then fall. Then winter. Snow. Leave here soon. All that ahead.

But the future was all unreal. He had planned for nothing. He had come to the Judgment Day. And had passed through the gate and found himself on the other side, and he had thought you just went to sleep and it was all over, but it wasn't, it was beginning again.

HE STAYED IN THE HOSPITAL through most of that summer. When he could walk by himself they let him wander. He was very quiet and got in nobody's way, and he passed his time wandering along the wards looking into the rooms or walking along the grass by the sea. He began to stay up late at night, reading, watching the moon. It was all very pleasant. Everyone knew him. They were beginning to treat him with that special warmth that hospital people give to a long-term patient. He could feel the fall coming, the cooler weather. He knew it was almost time to leave.

The one person he got to know well, other than Kashka, was the night nurse, Lieutenant Ida Mae Cherry. She was young and fat, always messy, a Negress. The hospital was silent at night and sometimes she would come into his room, and sometimes he would wander down to her office. She would tell him funny family stories about life on the farm back in South Carolina. She had a sweet tooth and there was always candy near her, candy bars and cups of hot chocolate. She brought him coffee and orange juice in his room late at night, and he never touched her, and she knew he wouldn't. He thought about it. She was never a careful dresser, and sometimes the buttons of her blouse were open and he could see the rich chocolate skin above the white slip, and he had not had a woman in a long time. Sometimes when he was thinking about her she came into the room, and she could see it in his face, and she always politely went away. Because of that he could not touch her. He had never been able to touch any woman who did not want to be touched.

He talked to her in the evenings, and he talked to Kashka. He never knew when Kashka was coming, the man was always on duty. Kashka liked to come by in the late evening and drink coffee and kid Lieutenant Cherry, and talk to McClain about fighting. During the day he was busy, but at night he could sit long enough to relax. McClain knew he was waiting. He did not probe any more, but he was always waiting. For a long time McClain could not say anything. It was as if he had a bandage on the wound and if you took off the bandage the wound would begin to bleed. He wanted to let it alone. But it was getting on toward the end of the summer and he was going home.

ONE NIGHT in August there was a violent storm. McClain sat enjoying the sound of the rain and hail against the window. Lightning struck a tree nearby, McClain's eyes were blinded: he could feel the building ripple under him, the walls flinch inward from the white hot bursting stroke. When it was all over he sat watching it move on out over the ocean, the lightning still flaring in the cloud-tops, and then he sensed something new in the air, something cool and northern. He went outside onto the wet lawn, limped through fresh heavy grass out to the stone fence above the sea. The air was definitely colder, but there was something else: dark raw smell of something cold and far away. Pine trees. Maple. Canadian air. The first faint wave of winter.

He found a wet bench and sat down, not minding the wet. He began to think of Vermont. He had not been home for a long time and he had not thought of it. He remembered the sledding and the hunting, everything as it was before his mother had died. He tried to remember her, but it was too long ago. He remembered the presence, the voice speaking to him, soft, high above. He could not remember anything she said. But the presence was there like a fragrance, warm strong flowers. He thought of her death but he could not remember anything about that. He remembered trying to go up the mountain, and getting lost, and getting found by Dan Buller. He thought of his father: a voice of raw anger. He remembered being cold. He moved on in memory, leaving Vermont, and then the moon came out and he thought about the war, the moon in the sky like a silver searchlight, and attacks coming up out of the dark. He thought about nothing and watched the moonlight on the sea. Sometime later on Kashka found him.

"What the hell are you doing?"

McClain grinned.

"Christ. You make one hell of a patient. Ida Mae was scared out of seven years' growth."

"Sorry," McClain said.

"Well." Kashka regarded him carefully, sensed nothing, relaxed. "Well, it's been a hell of a night."

"Smell the air," McClain said.

Kashka sniffed.

"Do you smell anything?"

Kashka shook his head.

"Sure you do. Don't you smell that? It's come all the way from Canada."

"I'll have to take your word for it. I smoke too much. Which reminds me." He reached for a cigarette. "Well," he said, looking back to the hospital. "The hell with it." He sat down. They sat silently watching the lightning and the moonlight.

Kashka said suddenly, unexpectedly: "I wish to Christ I was home."

Kashka's face was in darkness. There was a light on the patio behind them, but Kashka was looking out to sea. They sat for a long while saying nothing.

McClain saw lightning strike the sea. He thought of what it would be like to be under it when it came down, and the way it came down, mindless, that awful power. Miles in an instant. To kill a tree here, a dog there, a man here. To kill a squirrel. Luck. The way it came down like the finger of God, but no mind behind it, it struck whatever was there. He respected the power of it, the beauty. He remembered the last night and the rain and the way the shells came in overhead just before the last dark. He remembered himself as he was that night. Luck. The lightning had missed. Mindless?

"What are you thinking about?" Kashka said.

"Luck."

Kashka grunted. "Ignore me. I'm in no mood tonight."

"Letter from home?" McClain said.

Kashka squinted at him. "You should have *my* job," he said.

"Why don't you tell her to come here?" McClain said.

"I did."

McClain looked back out to sea.

"She's a good egg," Kashka said. "But she's young." He drew in on the cigarette, an orange glow lighted the black eyes. "You were saying?"

"I was just wondering how much of it is luck," McClain said.

"Good point."

"It all has to be luck. But sometimes. . . ," McClain paused. It was dark, dark enough to talk. He could still smell the horror of that last night. "You can get trapped. You bend down at just the right moment and one goes by where your head was and takes off the head of the guy behind you and naturally you think about it. You wonder if there isn't somebody looking on. But of course, you're a rational man. You know nobody's looking on. Nobody told you to duck. But you have to think about it."

"I would," Kashka agreed.

"I was on a patrol once," McClain said, speaking out toward the sea. He paused. "You know, I had a certain amount of pride in being a soldier. That's foolish too. This is no longer the age for it." He paused again. Then he said: "I was on a patrol once. It was very early morning and we heard them coming and we lay down in the tall grass. I was on the point. There were only a few of them. There was this Chinaman coming up along the path; he didn't see me. Very cold day it was; he was all bundled up looking fat and cold. He was easy, there were only three of them and I was on the point and could have let them go by in the grass. I slid the rifle out and he was there for about three seconds, five, and right then I thought of that little boy and Pasteur—you remember?—the boy who got hydrophobia, Jacques somebody, and Pasteur cured it, so the boy was the first one ever to be cured of that, happening to get sick with it at just the right moment, when Pasteur had the cure, the first to be cured after God knows how many millions had died. And the little boy lived to be something like ninety years old and just died a few years ago. And I was thinking about that gook there, that this was his moment, like the little boy. If he got past this one moment in front of me he might live on and on into the next century and have all those years. If I didn't shoot." McClain paused. "So I shot. It was only the thinking of a second. It was the only thing to do. There were too many of them. I hit him in the chest. The other two ran and we got them too. But you know, I almost didn't shoot."

He could see the body: quilted bloody meat.

Kashka said nothing.

"Of course, you think about it," McClain said.

"What do you think?"

"You just think."

Kashka nodded. McClain could not tell what he was thinking. After a moment Kashka said: "Do you go to church?"

"No."

"Nobody's looking down?"

McClain sat in the midst of a huge silence. Lightning blazed a long way off. "No," McClain said.

"What will you do now?" Kashka asked.

"Go back East."

"To do what?"

"I don't know."

"What about your folks?"

"My mother's dead. She died a long time ago. My father and I don't get along. There's nobody else."

"You ought to go to school," Kashka said gravely. "There's always the GI Bill. They'll even pay you."

"There's this guy I know, he wants to wander. He wants to go to Singapore."

"Singapore? Why Singapore?"

"Don't really know. Except that he has this great urge to see Asia. I wouldn't mind. I'd like to see Jerusalem."

"Why?"

McClain shrugged.

"It seems an odd choice," Kashka said. "What do you expect to find?"

"Arabs. Some dry bones."

"You're a rare bird, do you know that?"

"I am indeed." McClain grinned.

"A very nearly resurrected bird, do you know that?"

McClain nodded.

"I wish I knew where the break was."

McClain looked up.

"You have a vacancy in you a mile wide," Kashka said. "I don't know what put it there, do you?"

"No," McClain said.

"The folks possibly. Your father? They're often responsible, if you go by the book. What do you think?"

"I don't know."

"What happened?"

"I got tired."

"You said that before."

"I mean very tired. I mean as tired as you can get." He looked at Kashka. The cigarette sparked feebly. McClain had never told this to anyone, but it was dark and cool and he would soon be moving on.

"I get very dark sometimes," McClain said. "There's this sensation of darkness. I'm not sure if it's a sickness. I don't know if I can explain it. But I get very tired. Years ago I began to get tired, when I was still a kid. There was never any point. Everybody dies; but there's never any point. It's all to no purpose, all the pain, all the dying. You hang on, hoping, but you know all along that none of it has a point. You move, you move. You move on and on, and every now and then you see it clearly and you get tired of it, but you hang on, you move."

He stopped. The moon was full up. The air was marvelously clear. He could see craters, one huge gray stain.

"I used to be very religious," McClain said. "But I'm not any more. I wish I could pray, but I can't any more. It's like talking to yourself in a noisy noisy room. I don't know what it is. It may be a sickness. Do you think it's a sickness?" He did not wait for an answer. "There's nobody looking down. But if there's all this dying . . . I seem to need a point. I'll do anything they ask, if they'd only tell me what. But of course, there's nobody there. There's no point. But I seem to need one. It must be a sickness. The war gave me a way to fight. You can't quit, but you can go out fighting. Do you see? I couldn't kill myself but I could let them kill me, if they wanted to, even though I knew all along that there was nobody there and nobody gave a damn. Do you see?"

McClain took a deep breath. Now that it was out he felt an acute shame; everything he had said sounded absurd. But Kashka in the dark flicked the cigarette out over the stone and sat quietly with his arms in his lap. McClain was expecting something professional, clinical, but Kashka said nothing. He sat there and McClain could not see his face. After a moment he said: "I know the disease."

McClain did not understand.

"We all get tired that way," Kashka said. "I used to get very tired."

"What did you do?"

"I waited."

"Does it happen now?"

"Oh yes. Sometimes. But not that bad."

"What do you do now?"

"I work," Kashka said.

He stood up. He seemed embarrassed. He looked up at the sky. A shattered cloud rushed down at the moon.

"But Christ!" Kashka said suddenly, "isn't it a lovely world?"

They went back to the hospital. There was nothing else to say that night. They planned on getting together the next week but abruptly Kashka was put on orders. He saw McClain briefly, once, over a cup of coffee. He was worried; it was obvious that he did not think McClain would make it, but there was nothing he could do. At the end he tried to say something philosophical and optimistic, and McClain appreciated the gesture. They wished each other luck.

Kashka was shipped east, and for a week McClain was left alone. The next doctor assigned to him was a man named Simmons, who had very poor eyesight and an intense interest in cancer. A month after that McClain was discharged from the Army.

THREE

THE TRAIN began slowing on the far side of the river. McClain looked ahead through a dirty window and saw the white spire of the chapel rising fragile and clean beyond the trees. He began to remember it all in a series of small pleasant shocks: the bluff across the river, the white houses of the girls, black rocks in the river. He rose: time to get off. He had come all the way across the country.

He was the only one to leave the train. He stood for a moment by the black iron railing looking down across the town. He had been away for two years. Nothing down there had changed. The platform was level with the rooftops and he could see down the main street to the movie house, the Rialto, and on the other side of the platform there was the college road going up a steep hill, and an ancient car was puffing straight up, the top down, five boys packed in the back, waving their arms. McClain waited until the train went away. It was a fine day, cloudless, with a warm south wind. He could smell the musty odor of burning leaves.

He heaved the duffle bag up on his shoulder and walked slowly toward the school. Statues and stone, huge spreading trees. It was all old and silent and permanent. He remembered a field trip with a geology instructor a long time ago, the man saying with a certain sense of pride that this was all old country, rounded hills, a middle-aged river. Permanent. McClain felt his own fragility: like dry light glass vacant in the wind.

He came around the bend by the science building and looked out across the long green Common. There were couples sitting on the benches, under the trees, flocks of girls strolling in light summer dresses. He went down the walk, beginning to feel pain in his leg, a slow growth up the bone like a hot fungus. He sat down on a bench and rested. Silently, from a great distance, he watched the girls go by. He did not recognize anyone. The faces were very young.

Three of them came, walking all together, lovely, self-conscious. He watched their awkward walk and dropped his eyes and watched them again after they passed, smelled the perfume, watched the light skirts flow around clean white legs. He felt a spasm of animal hunger. But he felt suddenly old. He saw one with long blonde hair coming, the face pink and innocent, innocence in the mouth and eyes. Beneath the face a woman's body, breasts tight against the white blouse. It was the innocence that inflamed him. He sat wrapped in a silent mindless longing. And then he began to remember all the struggles, the games: the need to kiss her good night, fraternity pins, her breast achieved in a car in the moonlight, the long lies of courting, all aimed at the warm wet center between the white thighs, under the dress, sweet goal of youth. He saw himself standing waiting, corsage in hand, fixing his tie in a mirror. His mind recoiled. He could not do that. He could no longer join in. He had gone too far away and now that he was back he did not belong, he could not fit in. The blackness in his brain warned him away: this was not his world. But he thought of it. To hold a hand. To walk under the trees, along the river, to touch and to hold. To make plans.

He sat on the bench thinking, well, I'll stay here for a while and rest, and then I'll move on.

THE ADDRESS he had for Ravenel was a room in the upper back of a dingy white building just off the campus. He dragged the duffle bag up the long flight of splintering wooden stairs and rapped on the door. Silence from within, then the rattle and crash of things falling.

"Just a goddam minute!" A high muffled annoyed screech. McClain grinned. Charley Ravenel was at home.

Ravenel opened the door, peered out unwillingly like an extracted mole, the light hurting his eyes. He was smaller than McClain remembered, hairy, scrawny, face bony and bright red, twisted with fierce concern. His hair was a pale fuzz; he was getting quite bald. He stood in the door in a white tee shirt and white shorts, blinking, bony, annoyed. He focused on McClain. His face opened up into the old joyous crafty leprechaun grin.

"Well Jesus Kay Rist. The Big M!"

"Hey, Charley."

"Well. Be god*damned*—" He shoved out the small delicate hand.

He was so obviously delighted that McClain became suddenly enormously shy. Ravenel dragged him happily into the grand disorder of the room.

"Jesus, TR, I'm glad to see you. Take a chair somewhere. Put the goddam bag down. How the hell are you? I wrote that goddam hospital, but by the time I found out you were in it you were already out of it. How was it, hey? How's the leg? Christ, I wish you'd wrote and tole me. I got to go over to the goddam hospital. Well. How the hell *are* you?"

Ravenel righted an exotic lamp which had fallen off an end table, swept a clump of books off of a sickly crimson couch and sat McClain in the vacancy, surrounded by more books, notebooks, stacks of paper, a guitar. He crunched himself down directly on top of a mass of magazines and sat grinning all over his face, waving the bony arms then hopped up suddenly, frantically and dashed into the cave of a kitchen to get McClain a drink. He came back with four fingers of warm Scotch in a cloudy glass, apologized for the lack of ice.

"Drunk it all up," he said gloomily. "Goddam refrigerator only works union hours. Say listen, lemme see the leg."

He got down on all fours and tugged at McClain's pants leg. McClain obliged cheerfully and pulled it up high enough for Ravenel to inspect the knee.

"Um," Ravenel said. His face was critical, professional, then quickly soft, then critical again. "Well, they did a decent job on the outside anyhow. No master craftsmen, *that's* for sure, but you walk all right, I guess, hey? But, how about fightin'. You gonna give it up?"

"I don't know. Haven't thought about it."

"Well, Jesus, good to see you." Ravenel grinned again the delighted chipmunk smile, then hopped off to get himself a drink. He toasted McClain in warm Scotch.

"God bless."

"Cheers."

"I almost said 'absent friends' "—Ravenel grinned—"like some goddam fink movie. But Jesus. That hospital jazz, that shook me. I thought you might be real bad off."

"How'd you know about that?"

"The paper. Hey. You got a medal. Be damned. It was in the

paper here and they said you were in a hospital, recovering from wounds. That's when I wrote. They didn't say what the wounds were so I was a little nervous."

He paused for the first time, looked at McClain inquiringly. "That's all?" He pointed at the leg.

McClain nodded.

"They didn't get you nowheres else?"

"In the leg only."

"Well," Ravenel nodded, heavy with satisfaction. "Cheers again." He drank. Then: "You look tired."

McClain nodded.

"You sure they didn't get you anywheres else?"

"In the leg. Only."

Ravenel was watching him with a careful fatherly look. McClain suddenly grinned.

"Why didn't you write," Ravenel said, "you bastard?"

"I couldn't, Charley."

Now Ravenel was watching him, grading him, trying to see what it was, what had changed. But he said only: "You got a place to stay?"

"I figured I'd put up over at the house. The frat house."

Ravenel grimaced. "Balls. That place has gone all to seed. The Mickey Mouse Club, with beer. All the older guys have gone, all the vets. They have nothing there but the rah-rah set. You won't like it there now."

"Well. It doesn't matter."

"You want to stay here? I could put you up on the couch if you want."

Ravenel said this apologetically, as if he were intruding too far, presuming too much. McClain realized that he must have seemed more distant than he really felt.

"I'd like to, Charley. Thank you."

Ravenel said nothing. He sat smiling oddly, was careful not to be too watchful.

"You back in school yet?"

"No."

"Are you comin' back?"

"I don't know."

"But no more med school?" Ravenel was looking down at the Scotch.

"Not right now. There's this fella I know, he wants to take a trip. From London to Singapore. It won't cost much, I've got the money. I thought I might try that. I'm not ready for this yet. I could use a rest."

"Balls!" Ravenel said. "Where else can you get the rest you can get in this goddam school? With the government paying for it. Especially you. You never studied much anyway. If you got to rest —well, they've got no girls in the goddam desert, and . . . well, what the hell. You do what you want."

They said nothing. Ravenel looked up slowly, grinned. "Jesus. Two years."

"Long time."

"I wish to Christ you'd learn to write."

"How're you doing?"

"The second year," Ravenel sighed. "It's getting heavy. Virology. And one goddam course in the history of medicine. Laugh yourself to death. Except for Semmelweiss. But it's getting interesting. Only thing, no time for much action. I'm withering on the vine."

"Me too," McClain said.

"Hey," Ravenel sat upright. "My God. Let's have a party."

"Okay."

"I mean, it ain't every day that old buddies come home from the wars. Like goddam Danny Boy. Let's have a blast."

"I'm with you," McClain said. "But don't you have to go to the hospital?"

"Hell with that. One day, I can sneak out. Listen, how're you fixed for broads?"

"Fresh out," McClain said.

Ravenel put a hand to his brow, concentrating. "Whatever happened to that, ah, Joann. The one that painted with glue?"

"She got married."

"That so?" Ravenel sighed. "Ah, that was very nice. I don't know anything like that."

"That's all right."

"Too bad. I got all kinds of stuff stashed away around here, up at the hospital. You know what? It gets easier, the older you get. You acquire a certain polish. Only it's a little *hard*, most of it. And you never did go for the brassy stuff. I could never figure that in you. I mean what the hell, when you got a problem, you go to a specialist. When you need a broad, what do you need with a virgin? But that's your problem. Let's blast, okay? Let's really fling one. I'll find something. 'Tis time for it. Can feel it in the ruddy air. Full moon tonight, I bet. My follicles have been twitching all day."

He fished in stacks of paper for the phone, found it, made several sweetly professional phone calls, grinning at McClain with the dark, gleeful smile of the hunter. McClain sat back on the couch. He thought: once more into the breach, dear friends. And smiled. He was glad to see Charley Ravenel.

RAVENEL set up two girls, like bowling pins, for later that evening. McClain had a premonition—Ravenel's taste in women was sometimes grim—but he said nothing. He warned himself about drinking. He did not want to take enough to go over the edge. They went out to Ravenel's car, a spattered and gastric Ford, and drove on across town to Harry's, down in the dark end of town. Harry's was good and dark and served hot pastrami on rye, and Harry himself was an enormous man with a bad temper. Harry did not like too many people, and those he did not like he culled—without perceptible discrimination—leaving the bar a place of peace and silence to the chosen few. Ravenel was one of the chosen. Harry had an upsetting habit of leaning gloomily across the bar like a great mean Buddha and staring at Ravenel for long minutes. Then abruptly he would guffaw, shake his head thickly, mirthfully, and wander off to brood by the window. Ravenel did not know why.

"There's just something about you," McClain said, "that seems to fracture him."

"But you know, goddam it, that's kind of insulting." Ravenel was injured. "I think one of these days, by God, I'll swat him one. Big bastard. Hey, big bastard. 'Nother beer."

Harry brought it down, grinning with repressed mirth.

"Listen Harry, you bastard, why the hell are you always laughing at me? Like I was goddam Jerry Lewis?"

"I don't know, Doc, I swear. Honest."

"Well, you better cut it the hell out."

Harry guffawed. "Yes sir, Doc, I sure will."

"Because if you keep doing that," Ravenel said dangerously, "one of these days I will strike back. I will go call down the health department on your lice-infested person."

"Hee," Harry bellowed, overcome. He staggered off, shaking his head.

"Now what the hell"—Ravenel was mystified—"is so goddam funny?"

McClain was grinning. Injured Ravenel, roostery Ravenel. He *was* funny. Three sad men playing darts were watching, also grinning. Ravenel glared, then abruptly relaxed. "The hell with it. This crazy goddam world. Filled with brigands and cutpurses. Hey, you know? Clawson is still here. Jack Clawson. Hee." He laughed with a lecherous leer.

"Jack Clawson? I thought he'd graduated."

"Oh, he did. But, haw, he's in graduate school now working for his doctorate. In *English*, for Christ's sake. And he's teaching classes in Freshman English and screwing his students."

"He's what?"

"Yes sir," Ravenel nodded vigorously. "He has all these little broads in spasms, rolling over like fat puppies. God. You never saw anything like it. The bastard. He's going through this school like a scythe."

"Hm," McClain said. "I always thought he was the poetical type."

"Oh, he is, he is." Ravenel chuckled. "Only nowadays he's giving that talent a somewhat more practical application."

"But isn't that dangerous?"

"Damn right. They ever catch him, they put him *under* the jail. For twenty years. But you ought to talk to him. He's thinner, and faintly bewildered. Insists they call him up at home, follow him around, says it's *them* doing the seducing. Says the morals of our century are a snare and a delusion. Very funny, no kidding. You'll have to go see him."

McClain smiled.

"Wassat?"

"I was just thinking." McClain grinned. "Clawson used to be president of the Woman Hater's Club."

"Oh he did," Ravenel chortled, "that he did, indeed."

"You remember? We had four officers, and one member?"

"You were the member."

"And then it occurred to me that I didn't want to be a 'member.' "

"So we passed a rule. The officers couldn't vote. Only the membership could vote."

"And I always abstained."

"Hee," Ravenel said.

"Long time ago."

"Another world," Ravenel said.

"What ever happened to Joe Collins?"

"You wouldn't believe it. He works for a goddam bank. Pillar of the community. Married some girl—ah, the horsefaced one. They make an interesting couple. With his face and hers, visiting them is like a trip to the zoo. I swear. They have a kid I'm ashamed to tell you what it looks like."

"He was a good man," McClain said.

"That he was," Ravenel said stubbornly. "I would be the last to deny it. He can have the shirt off, filth and all. He can have my last. But he had a face like a collie, and there's no getting away from it. We have to face these things, laddie, look 'em square in the eye. 'Nother beer?"

"And where's ole Malone?"

"Malone?"

"Is he still around?"

Ravenel waved to Harry.

"You didn't hear about that," Ravenel said.

"About what?"

"Malone got killed."

McClain turned to look at Ravenel. Ravenel was looking down into his beer.

"I thought you knew. Car accident, last year. Right around Christmas. He was in upstate New York somewhere."

McClain blinked, remembering Malone. Little man, like Ravenel. Bad temper. Very bad eyes. Always hungry. Moody, inarticulate, poetic when drunk. Malone?

"He was in some kind of trouble," Ravenel said.

"What kind?"

"You knew him. He was always in trouble." Ravenel paused. "About a week before that he dropped out of school. I saw him belt a cop. I never did find out why."

"Well," McClain said.

"Way it goes," Ravenel said.

"You think he did it on purpose?"

Ravenel shrugged. "You never know. Maybe so. He was . . . vulnerable, you know? He could be goddam mean when he wanted to. And then he'd turn around, and give you anything he had. He was too moody. I thought he'd get over it."

McClain remembered the face of Malone, struggling to explain, black eyes, wild hair, words locked in his throat.

"Cheers," Ravenel said.

They sat for a while in silence. The three men in the back went on playing darts. A young couple came in—a pink-faced boy in an expensive blazer, a girl with her hair arranged fashionably, delicately, over her eyes. They sat in a dark booth and were bored. Ravenel did not notice them.

"You ben back to Vermont?" Ravenel said.

"No."

"I went back this summer," Ravenel said. "I'm thinkin' I'll go back there to practice. If I ever get the hell out."

"It's nice there in the fall," McClain said.

"Listen. Thomas"—Ravenel put both hands on his beer—"Christ knows I don't want to pry. But you sure there's nothing else bothering you? Nothing but the leg?"

"I'm a little shook," McClain said.

"I can see that."

"Is it obvious?"

"Hell, you're all right. You just look a little . . . spacy. But the goddam war. Nobody has to explain after a goddam war. I remember when I came back. None of this"—he gestured vaguely—"was real."

McClain listened.

"Why don't you come on back? Go through the motions for a while. You'll settle down. You were good, you know that? You were damn good. This is only temporary."

McClain shook his head. Ravenel watched him.

"It's still the blacks, isn't it?" Ravenel said.

McClain nodded.

"Worse now?" Ravenel watched him. "Well, what you need is a rest."

"I ought to move on," McClain said.

"Why?"

"I get the feeling . . . I've got to look around."

"And no more med school?"

"Maybe someday. If I ever . . . hell, Charley, I'm not stable enough."

"You're a hell of a lot tougher than you think."

"During the war it was all right. You stayed busy keeping alive, you didn't have to think. Here it's . . . too quiet. I don't want to play games. It's like you say. It isn't real."

"You got to remember, everybody gets over it."

"Not everybody," McClain said. He was thinking: Malone.

THE GIRLS were a pleasant surprise. Ravenel's was tall and grave, somewhat matronly, unsmiling. Her face was plain and unpainted, but she had a truly remarkable figure. Her name was Meg, she was in her late twenties. She looked at Ravenel with a look that was cynical, baffled, unmistakably hungry. It was obvious that she had slept with him. McClain sensed tragedy: an ex-husband? She was carefully, tastefully dressed, a nurse.

McClain's girl was unexpected. She was small and young, dressed in a quiet blue suit with white edging along the neck. She was thin, but rather pretty, much prettier than Meg, shy, scared, had a clean shy smile. She was nineteen, still a student. McClain gathered that she was not one of Meg's close friends, but only a girl selected to order, plucked pink and trembling from one of the rooms in the sophomore dorm, bathed and dressed and preened for presentation, a girl who had not been anywhere yet and was therefore exactly what the doctor ordered: old Doc Ravenel. McClain sympathized with her. He set himself to be as much of a gentleman as possible. Dark sexual visions receded into the back of his mind. The girl's name was Ruth.

Ravenel introduced him loudly as a soldier back from the war. They took a booth in the gloomy cavernous back room of Harry's. The older one, Meg, regarded McClain carefully, judgingly, without friendliness. What she thought was not apparent. She turned back to Ravenel and there again was the hungry look, and Ravenel began being very funny and purposefully lovable, leaning forward across the table to gaze foolishly, soulfully into Meg's eyes, until he finally got her to grin. The young one, Ruth, hesitantly ordered rye and ginger, which Harry happily and illegally provided. Then he stood staring down at Ravenel and the big girl, who was slightly larger and perhaps even older than Ravenel and who certainly had a respectable body, and Harry stood there grinning with mysterious jubilance, and then wandered off, guffawing. Meg stared after him, amazed.

"The bastard," Ravenel fumed. "I swear, I'm going to pop him one."

"What's so funny?" Meg said suspiciously. "What have you told him?"

"Him?" Ravenel gasped, incredulous, touching his gaunt breast in outraged innocence, "what would I tell the likes of *him?* My God, the big bastard."

"Why do you come here anyway?"

"A good question," Ravenel gloomed. He turned and bawled at Harry: "Harry, you fink, why the hell does anybody come here?"

Harry gasped, collapsed, laid his head on the bar, and giggled tearfully, out of control.

Ravenel turned back bewildered, grinning. "You see? I really think the guy's got a screw loose. I really do." He looked back at Harry and chuckled, shaking his head.

"You pick the oddest places," Meg said.

"I'm doing you a favor. I'd hate for you to be seen with anybody of my reputation."

"That's the living truth."

McClain sat silently enjoying it, glanced down at Ruth beside him and smiled. Her eyelashes fluttered; she stared at her glass. McClain caught Ravenel watching her critically.

"He's got a medal," Ravenel said.

"Who?" Meg said. "For what?"

"Charley," McClain said, "for Christ's sake."

"No, really. This is a welcome-home-type blast. He just got out of the goddam Army." When Ravenel was profane, McClain could feel the wince in the small shocked girl beside him. At every "goddam" her body fluttered, like a small light car on a bumpy road. He peeked at her: she was bearing up bravely.

"And he really did get a medal," Ravenel was saying. "For

bravery. Honest to God. Come on, Tom, you got the medal with you?"

"Of course," McClain said. "I keep it pinned to me shorts."

Meg suddenly, unexpectedly laughed out loud. Little Ruth screwed up her courage.

"Were you really in the war? Or is he just kidding?"

McClain nodded.

"Were you in the fighting?"

McClain nodded again. He felt completely ridiculous. The girl said: "Oh my"—honestly, sincerely. McClain looked at Ravenel. Ravenel chortled.

"Tell them, Roberto, how thou didst blow the bridge."

"Oh my God," McClain said.

"How thou didst blow the bridge well and truly."

Meg was grinning, but Ruth was confused.

"Well, I blew it all right," McClain said, surrendering. "I blew it well and truly. It was a rare bridge."

"What bridge was that?" Ruth said.

"Hee," Ravenel giggled.

"Ask me when I didst blow the bridge," McClain said.

"All right," Ravenel said, "when didst thou blow the bridge?"

"I blew it," McClain said grandly, "in the doomed and dying summer."

"And you shall not only endure—"

"I shall prevail."

"Amen."

"All right, boys," Meg said. She explained it to Ruth. Ruth never quite grasped it.

"I'm sorry," McClain said. "It's just an old joke."

"Well. Was he joking about the medal?"

"No."

"Well, I'm glad of that. I don't like fellas who joke. About medals"—she added hastily—"and things like that."

"How much have you had to drink?" Meg interrupted. She asked the question of Ravenel but she was looking at McClain.

"Jesus," Ravenel said unhappily, "you had to remind me. Not near enough. I'm way behind on this year. That goddam school has really slowed me up." He called to Harry. Meg was regarding him with wifely disapproval.

"You know, they're beginning to talk about you at school. The drinking. You ought to watch it."

"What you mean?" Ravenel was offended. "*Who* drinks too much? Whose goddam business is it anyway?"

"Well, you know how it is." Meg was defensive. "You really ought to watch it."

"The thing is," Ravenel said sadly, happily, "I'm a troubled man. A man of many sorrows."

McClain laughed. Harry arrived, bearing a tray with four more drinks, although only Ravenel's glass was empty. Harry was under severe control. He plopped down the drinks with a stony silence, expressionless, turned mechanically and walked away. Ravenel stared.

"Well. I will be truly goddamned."

Ruth tried dutifully to finish her drink, as she would have tackled the milk when ordered by mother, although nobody had ordered her, or even mentioned it. She gasped, grimaced, turned to McClain. "Would you like to play some music?"

There was a jukebox in the corner of the room, the room's only light. It stood winking gaudily with colored bubbles burping along up glassy tubes, Martian, mechanical. Ravenel sighed but said nothing.

"Okay," McClain said. "What would you like?"

He did not know any of the popular tunes. She told him what to play and then asked, self-consciously, if he would like to dance. He took her out to the center of the floor; they danced alone. No one else was in the room. Ravenel sat in deep conversation with Meg, who was saying something insistent and serious in his ear.

McClain understood why Ruth wanted to dance. She was good at it, light and easy to hold, and she knew it and was immediately more sure of herself, on her home ground. He did not try to pull her in close, but she came in of her own will and lay all the way in against him, her forehead just reaching his chin. Not thin at all, not as thin as she seemed, skin soft and deep under the delicate scented blouse. They danced silently and then she tilted her head back and started asking him questions about the war. When she did that her pelvis came in against him and his leg went between her thighs, but she did not seem to notice. He talked.

They broke finally: he felt her take his hand and lead him to the table. She was flushed, much surer. She smiled and sat down still holding his hand and the others noted that, Ravenel and Meg, and Meg smiled a faint knowing smile. What McClain was thinking about was sex.

She went on holding his hand until it began to perspire. He could not avoid the nearness of sex, the sweet thick perfumed cloud. She looked up at him and smiled confidently and had absolutely no idea of what he was thinking, and he went quickly through another Scotch. He said to himself: Welcome home, Thomas. Then he decided to get seriously drunk. They were all getting drunk, except Meg. He eyed her critically. She was one of the ones who never got drunk, not any more. Not that one.

In a very short time little Ruth was crocked. They danced again and this time it was slowly and with great tenderness, and McClain began to feel welling up out of his own private darkness not only the sex but something else much finer, more delicate, an appalling plucking tenderness. He bent his head so that he could sense her hair, let it brush across his cheek. He closed his eyes, got slowly lost in the feel of her, in the music, in the pressure of the round belly. He opened his eyes and saw Ravenel smiling at him like a fond parent, Meg gazing sadly at Ravenel.

The worst thing about getting drunk was that after a while he couldn't help the sadness. He fought it by saying nothing. He sat at the table with his arm around Ruth and she leaned in against him, blurred, dreamy, not shy any more, beginning to say softly into his ear that she was so glad she had come, when she didn't even know at supper tonight that she would ever meet anyone like him. And he sat nodding and feeling slowly colder, chilled, and suddenly heard lines in the blur of his mind: In the desert of the heart, let the healing fountain start. He said nothing. He wound up being mothered in the back seat of the car on the way home. He kissed her, she kissed him back carefully, politely, then when the formality was done, she kissed him again, meaning it, turning her body against his, neither of them saying anything, and then she opened her mouth once and let him into her there, but that was all. She withdrew, but squeezed his hand. He felt like a schoolboy. He wished it had not begun.

They dropped off the girls. Ravenel had to help him up the stairs.

"You and them sad eyes." Ravenel grinned. "Man, you're deadly."

McClain was very tired.

"I'll just stay here tonight," McClain said.

"No hurry."

"But then I think I'll move on."

"You just take it easy. The war's over."

"No it ain't, Charley."

"Sure it is. Take off your shoes."

"I wish to God it was," McClain said.

"It'll pass," Ravenel said soothingly. He smiled. "You always were a gloomy drunk."

"I'll give it a try," McClain said. He was beginning to feel stubborn, mean.

"Nobody can ask more," Ravenel said. "Now take off your shoes."

"I'm a bad-tempered son of a bitch," McClain said.

"I know. I've seen you. You got a right to bad temper. But the war's over."

A little while after that Ravenel decided he needed another drink, but when he came back McClain was asleep.

FOUR

MCCLAIN stayed with Ravenel for three days, then moved to a room of his own. He had no plans; he found that it was impossible for him to think ahead. The room was clean and quiet, a good place to rest. It was panelled in dark wood, hung with pictures of clipper ships. McClain was the only roomer in the house, which was owned by a very old, very tiny woman named Mrs. Bezant, who lived below in a steamy jungle of African violets. She stayed out of his way and he rarely saw her. Later he learned that he was the first roomer she had ever had and that she had a vast respect for people who went to college. He never heard a sound from downstairs, not even from the huge cathedral radio she kept in the living room.

McClain slept late every day for a long time. At the front of the room was a wide window and a window seat. During the Indian summer of that year McClain sat there often, watching the sky and the girls walking through the blowing leaves, and the smoky autumn air. The window looked out on a street lined with tall elms, and when the leaves fell McClain could see all the way across town to the white spire of the university chapel. He knew he would not be there long, but still, even in the dark of the night and even after the nightmares that still came, and after the long walks alone in the cold rain of October, still there was something about that time and that place that was permanent.

All the stone buildings were rounded and old, like the hills to the north, and the river was flat and slow, the air was soft and ripe with the smell of burning leaves. And McClain had survived.

He stayed for a week, and then another week, and then finally he registered for classes. He did it because of Ravenel. There was no point in not taking advantage of the GI Bill. McClain knew he would not finish out the year, but Ravenel was right: he was lucky to have this place. And he was lucky to have Ravenel.

McClain never quite understood what made Ravenel his friend. After two years away McClain had not expected anything, would not have been surprised had Ravenel forgotten him completely. But there was a warmth in Ravenel, a genuine concern. And so McClain stayed.

Charles Emmet O'Neill Ravenel was at that time thirty years old. He had passed most of his life either in school or in the Army. He had been born with an almost appalling idealism—traces of which still remained fragmented around in his character like the debris of a flag that has been badly shot up. He had volunteered early for that other war, the Big War, and had gone on volunteering right into the paratroops and into action in North Africa, then to the mess on Sicily, and the even worse mess at Anzio. At Anzio he lost part of a lung, and most of his idealism, but by then the loss did not matter. He was healed in England in time to make the jump on D-Day, across the Channel and into Sainte-Mere-Eglise, where he not only took a bullet through the thigh but realized for the first time truly that there was no possibility of ever getting out of this alive. He passed through several very long, very bad days in a hospital in France, but after that went back to the outfit in a state of resigned doomed peace. He made the jump at Nijmegen, was promoted to lieutenant during the Battle of the Bulge, made the last jump across the Rhine into Germany. He was one of eight people in his company to survive the war. It was some time before he could believe his luck. He had adjusted himself to death—really adjusted to it and accepted it—and now that there was suddenly a future, it was still only a provisional future, and whatever time he had coming now was all somehow a bonus. One day in Berlin he realized that it was all truly done, that he had lived through it, and in that moment he knew also that nothing that happened to him from now on could ever be quite as bad as what had already passed. He was wrong about that, but he was not to find out about it for many years, and he lived in a sort of permanent capsule of hungry joy. He still had moments even now, eight years after the last shellburst, when he awoke with a huge, inarticulate love of living, of the sun, of the next breath. But even more than that, Ravenel needed to be useful. Although he had no describable faith in any explainable religion, he privately acknowledged a debt. When he analyzed it —a thing he rarely did, because analysis was seldom accurate and never practical—he knew that he lived as if he owed the world his life, that he was most happy when he was of use.

He had almost nothing in common with McClain. They had both come from the same hill country in Vermont, had both entered medicine. Beyond that there was, in Ravenel's mind, a vast blank. He had sensed in McClain, from the very beginning, something of value. He did not know what it was and he did not analyze that either. McClain was big and strong and had a good mind and was serious, but there was a darkness there, something black behind the brow, that drew from Ravenel not only an instinctive fascination, but an instinctive pity. McClain was, for all the muscle, somehow appallingly vulnerable. Once in the war Ravenel had seen a friend hit badly in the chest, and the friend had tried to hide the wound. He had pulled the jacket up tight around his throat and sat there not admitting, even to himself, that what had happened to him was fatal and that he would presently die, and the man had sat there not talking and silently waiting, and there had been something in his eyes that reminded Ravenel of McClain. But it was not something to talk about. Ravenel knew that the words were long in forming, just as the deep wounds take time to close, and Ravenel waited with curiosity, and pity, and a certain apprehension.

Ravenel wanted McClain to stay. He felt that if McClain left this time, if he got off the natural path—college and a degree and a woman and a job—that he would never come back and something bad would happen. As long as McClain was here it implied a certain faith. Although Ravenel was very busy all that fall, he watched after McClain as well as he could. They double-dated together and got drunk together at Harry's, and Jack Clawson joined them, beginning to fall in love deeply and desperately with a freshman girl, a virgin, and for a while it was like the days before the war. October passed. There were parties and football games. Sometimes McClain got very drunk, and Ravenel waited for him to talk, but he never did. He sat silently, dreamily staring up at the sky, into the smoky air, out at the legs of all those lovely lovely girls. . . .

ONE DAY in November Clawson asked to use McClain's room. The room had an outside entrance and was away from the campus and Clawson had to be very careful about being seen with one of his students. McClain passed most of that afternoon wandering down by the river and then he went up to the library. There was an exam due the next day and he tried to study. He got out all the right books and began making notes. The words moved through his head like clouds in a quiet sky. He sat for a long while without thinking anything at all, then suddenly looked down at his notes. Wandering paths of black ink, like the track of a demented ant. He had a moment of clear vision: the absurdity of all these words, himself in a classroom reciting, making noises in the air. He thought: you're not even neat, not even the Army could teach you neatness, you could never bounce the quarter on the blanket. He put a finger down on the paper and moved through the wet ink, finger painting. A boy across the table looked up at him dully, slack-mouthed, watched the finger move. Expressionless, the boy bent his head back to his own book. He was reading history. Beyond the boy there was a girl, a clean chubby girl in a red wool sweater and a red and blue plaid skirt. She was sitting carefully trying to keep her attention on the book in front of her, but she was sitting with her face to the door so that she could see everyone coming in and she watched them all over the edge of the book, her eyes shining up periodically like small blue lighthouses. She had lovely legs. He could see the edge of a pink slip under the heavy skirt, frail cloth snug against thick wool. The library was rustling, whispering. He listened to pages turning, rubbing like dry leaves. Feet clicked in the stone hall. He thought of yelling a dirty word. It seemed a natural thing in the silence. He remembered one lesson: nature abhors a vacuum. Into the emptiness: brute force.

He picked up the book and left.

It was a cold day, gray, windy. He walked on out to the bluff and stood looking out over the river. He was thinking about the vacuum. He looked up into the sky. A true vacuum there, beyond the clouds. Nine million miles of nothing. End in the sun.

He walked up to the gym, stood on the wooden floor watching the basketball team. He had tried to play once, since he'd come back. He had come out one afternoon and dressed and moved, bouncing the ball, tried to get the blood moving. The timing wasn't bad but the leg hurt, the leg wasn't ready. He'd dressed after that, and when he came out again the gym was dark and he knew he would never do it again, never dress for any game, hear any crowd roar, no girl would be waiting. A small door had closed.

He was increasingly tired; he went back finally to the room. There was perfume in the air, perfume and soap and sweat. McClain lay down and could smell them in the bed and got up and opened the window to the cold clear air, but when he lay down again he could still smell them and dreamed of them, and closing doors, and a fire a long way off. . . .

NOISE. The voice of Ravenel.

McClain looked at the clock, could not focus. Damn. He pushed back the covers, felt the room's cold floor, grunted, staggered to the door over the cold hard floor. Saw the pinched face of Ravenel, sadistic, grinning. Behind him someone round and dark. McClain focused.

Sam Gerdy.

"Hey man," Ravenel said, "look who's here."

Sam Gerdy had been McClain's fight manager before the war. McClain had not seen him in two years. He was a big man, hairy, soft, with pudgy hands. He stood in the dark of the hall staring grimly, cautiously at McClain.

"I found him wanderin' around lookin' for you," Ravenel said happily, "so I brung him by." He looked from one to the other with happy curiosity. McClain put out his hand.

"Hey Sam. Glad to see you."

Gerdy grunted, nodded, took the hand. He came into the room, looking warily around. His face was fat but pale, something sickly in it. He wore a thick gray overcoat, a stained fedora. His nose was running. He did not look McClain in the face.

"Whataya say, boy? How you doin'?" Gerdy looked around the room, estimating.

"Jesus, it's cold in here." Ravenel hopped across to the window, slammed it down, opened the heating vent.

"Well I'll be damned, Sam," McClain said. He grinned. "How's everything been?" McClain went back to the bed, got under the covers, shivering.

"I come out on the mornin' train," Gerdy said. "Ony train I could get. So how you ben, ha? You lookin' good, boy. You lookin' A number one. I heard you got shot. Where'd they gitcha?"

"It wasn't bad."

"Well that's what I heard. I'm glad to hear that. I mean, you got no problems for the commission?"

McClain looked at Ravenel. Ravenel grinned.

"So where'd they gitcha? Can I see?"

McClain thought: what the hell. He stuck the right leg out into the cold of the room. Gerdy knelt, squinted, probed. McClain looked down on the gray fedora, saw grease stains along the brim.

"Jeez," Gerdy said, "that don't look so good." He cupped the ankle, moved the knee. "But you can move around all right, ha? I mean, you still move pretty good, what the hell, you don't have to run."

"It's okay," McClain said.

Gerdy grunted, standing up. He looked worried. "First thing I heard, when you was shot up, I figured, well, there he goes. No good for nothin' no more. Another good one down the drain. Then when I didn't hear from you . . . how come you didn't send no word?"

McClain shrugged, embarrassed. He had never liked the man, he had never talked to the man about anything except fighting. But now McClain was glad to see him.

"So," Gerdy said. "When you want to get back inta action?" Gerdy regarded him belligerently, accusingly. "There's a gang a money waitin' around now, boy, what with this TV and all."

"Let me get some clothes on," McClain said. He got up and started to dress.

"Take you a while to get inta shape. Month a two. But I can get you some action first a February, if you want. Not much money, but you got to come back. You ben away a while, got to work up again. So you got govmint money anyways now, so that's no problem."

As McClain dressed, Gerdy was watching him, calculating, weighing, noting the movements, the muscle tone. But now abruptly he began to relax. He had never been a man to smile, but he looked around at Ravenel and the corners of his mouth twitched upward. Then he turned guardedly back to McClain.

"So whataya say?"

McClain thought: the vacuum. "I don't know, Sam."

"Whataya mean, you don't know?" Gerdy was wounded, angered, instantly ready to argue.

"Not just yet," McClain said. But he was thinking: why not? Answer to the vacuum. He sensed his body react, instinctively. He made a quick loosening movement with his shoulders. But then he thought of Wilson, and Singapore. There was a letter on his desk. He looked toward the letter and saw Ravenel watching him, dismay in his face.

"You want a little time to take it easy. Okay, fine, relax. But don't make no mistake, boy, don't wait too long. I could get you TV, in the Garden. I swear on my mother. TV. In the *Garden*. Where the hell else you get that kind a money?"

McClain dressed slowly. His mouth was dry, sleep-coated. He badly needed a cup of coffee. With Gerdy in the room he could begin to sense something of the old days coming back like a distant odor, the remembered taste of blood in the mouth, motion, get him, get him. Into the vacuum.

Gerdy made his pitch. He wanted to make one thing clear. His time was valuable and he had a lot of things to do and he wouldn't have got on that crummy train and come all the way the hell out here into the sticks, takin' his valuable goddam time, if he dint think McClain had the stuff. No doubt on it. He would stake his professional reputation. Here he was tryin' to do McClain a favor, sure, put him in line to really make a buck, but he wouldn't be doin' that if he for one wasn't certain that McClain could do it all. Jesus. He *believed* in McClain. He could make a bundle. He could make light heavy again easy and who the hell was there in light heavy now, nothin' but tumbleweeds, Christ, he could go all the way. Swear to God. All the way.

Gerdy paused, carried away with the wonder of it. There was nobody around nowadays who couldn't be had. And McClain with the goddam medal and the wounded leg and all, my God, a natural. A goddam natural if ever he saw one. And for Christ's sake, if he wanted more proof, wasn't Sam Gerdy *here?* Come all this way, takin' his valuable time? No sir, it's a cinch. That ought to show you what he thought of ole Mac. By Christ. Because he dint have to run around after no fighters, Sam Gerdy dint, they run around after *him.* What with TV and all. But he came out after McClain because listen, this boy was a scrapper, oh, he was a mixer. None of that fancy goddam toe dancin' these kids did now, nobody dint give a crap for that jazz no more. McClain liked to throw leather and he dint mind gettin' nailed and they paid to see that kind of stuff, a real fighter, because there sure wasn't much of it any more, and I tell ya, he's a natural. You ever see him fight?

Ravenel was watching, smoking. He was looking at Gerdy with that resentful respect the man of intellect bestows instinctively, unwillingly on the man of muscle. McClain noted that, smiled to himself. Ravenel nodded. "I saw him fight," Ravenel said.

Gerdy said nothing. He sat in the chair by the foot of the bed, looking out the window. He wiped his dripping nose silently, with a bare hand, and paused, frozen in the act of wiping, and his face was fat and old, but softer, dreamier. He looked out the window, holding his nose. He looked very silly and McClain started to grin, and then Gerdy said wistfully: "Oh Jesus he was good. He was a sweetheart."

McClain watched him. The fat man went on wiping his nose. He took a deep breath, slumped a little in the chair, then looked at Ravenel and shrugged.

"He was a regular sugar baby."

"He was pretty good," Ravenel said.

"What you know about fightin'?" Gerdy was instantly belligerent.

Ravenel shook his head. "Not a hell of a lot."

"Well," Gerdy relaxed, mollified. He seemed tired; the face still had the dreamy set, there was a softness around the mouth. "You have to know somethin' about it to know how good he really was. Punch. Jesus. Never figured a punch like that in such a skinny arm. All in the timin'. The way the muscles hang loose at the neck. Oh but he could hit. I tell you the truth. Hit like a fuckin' mule. And take a punch too, and come back an' kill you. He was better when he was hurt. That's the way with all the good ones. You hurt him and you made him dangerous. And he liked to hit, too. Dint you?" He looked to McClain, entreating. "Dint you liked to hit?"

McClain nodded.

"Like a fuckin' mule." Gerdy shook his head slowly. "Ah. Remember that boy in Albany? That colored boy? Remember that?"

"Yep," McClain said.

"Like to killed him. Christ, I thought maybe you did. You had me all shook up. But that, now that was a real fight. You don't get 'em like that any more. They still remember, you know? They really do. Ever' now and then somebody comes up and he says hey, whatever happen to that kid you had that night in Albany, that white boy light heavy? They still ask for you."

"That's fine," McClain said.

"So what you gonna do?"

The dreaminess was gone. Gerdy was staring up at him with an open hungry look. McClain thought: he needs me. He needs a fighter.

"I'll be in touch, Sam," McClain said.

"Okay. All right. You take your time." Gerdy closed his eyes, slumped down in the chair.

"Let's go get some coffee. Or a beer. Would you like a beer, Sam?"

Gerdy got up slowly, looked around the room.

"Them are nice pitchers," he said. "They yours?"

"They come with the room."

"Nice," Gerdy said. He looked at McClain seriously. "I wonder what the hell would have happen, if I ever went to college."

They walked back to the campus and down toward a coffee shop. McClain wanted Gerdy to come in for coffee, but he had no time.

"Got to get back to town. But listen, you keep in touch, all right?"

"Sure, Sam."

"Sooner or later you got to need a buck. Everybody needs a buck." A crafty joy, resurrected, shone briefly in his face. "You take plenty time. But you get to needin' a buck, you let me know."

They were standing in the door of the place and had to back away as three girls sidled past and went on into the shop. Gerdy watched them go with open hunger.

"Jesus. It figures why you want to stay here. But you watch that young gash. They get you for that, they hang you by the balls." He went on gazing meditatively inwards. "You watch all that jazz, boy. Too much of this jazz, no good for a fighter. Ruined more fighters than drinkin' ever did. All your fight goes out the end of your pecker. Well. See you, kid." He stuck out his hand clumsily, the same hand with which he'd wiped his nose. McClain shook it. Gerdy went away, hands in his pockets, round shouldered, grease-stained. McClain watched him go, felt a touch of pity. Back to the small room, the huge city. Back to plead and sweat and survive on little deals. Had never in his life owned a truly decent fighter. Now in the days of the long twilight of his profession he must know at last that he never would. McClain thought: poor bastard.

They went into the coffee shop.

"You know why he wears bow ties?"

"Why?" Ravenel said.

"Because a long time ago, when he was stout but not fat, he wore a bow tie once and a girl in a moment of sexual weakness told him that he looked like Roosevelt."

"Is that a fact?" Ravenel was looking around the room. The place was crowded with couples, thick with cigarette smoke. "Look," Ravenel said, "there's Clawson."

He was sitting far across the room, half hidden behind a tiled pillar. A tall blond boy, handsome, needing a haircut. The girl next to him was fair, wore no makeup, very young. She was gazing into has face.

"That the one?" McClain said. In my apartment. Last night. Her.

"Yep. But why the hell he brought her here. Everybody'll see him. You know, by God, I wouldn't be surprised. But I bet you he's hooked."

In my bed, McClain was thinking. She. In the nude. Imagination did not work. He was glad Clawson was not looking his way.

"Better not join 'em," Ravenel said. "Let's leave them the hell alone. But he's a damn fool." Ravenel found a table, squeezed down. McClain kept looking toward the girl. When he turned back to Ravenel, the small tight face was grinning.

"Gets a bit rough, I bet," Ravenel said.

McClain looked around the room. Faces. Bodies. He saw the boy from the library that afternoon, the boy who'd been studying history. His mouth still hung open.

"So what about it. You going to fight again?"

"I don't know," McClain said.

"You thinking about it?"

"It's an honorable profession." McClain grinned.

"*Sure* it is," Ravenel said dryly. "Sure it is." He looked down at McClain's hands. "You don't have the hands for it, you know. You already broke 'em. Keep after it and you'll mess 'em up for good. And you don't have the eyes for it either. You cut too easy around the eyes. Remember me? I was there. So what in hell are you thinking of?"

"Nothing," McClain said. He was looking at Clawson's girl. At that moment Clawson forgot himself and reached out to clasp her hands, then recovered quickly, guiltily. The girl sat back, white with alarm.

"Ah me," Ravenel said. "I guess he'll be needing your room. You might as well move in with me."

"I hope they don't catch him."

"Me too. But you can't warn him. I think by God he's really hung up. Listen. What are you doing this weekend?"

"Nothing."

"You sit around too much. You brood. You ought to get out more."

McClain nodded.

"One thing I've learned, in my long youth," Ravenel said. "The world has two joys. The one is work. The other is broads. That's the long and the short of it."

Work. McClain thought of Sam Gerdy. Why not? But then there was Wilson. And Singapore. Wilson's face, pleading, in the hospital. Singapore. Jerusalem.

"There was a girl asking about you the other day," Ravenel said meditatively. "Hell of a nice kid." He paused, grinned faintly. "I was just thinking of Malone. Remember? 'There are two kinds of broads. One you go out with. The other you marry.' You know what? He was right."

"That's the whole trouble," McClain said.

"At any rate, there is this one kid. Give you something to do while ole Clawson's using your room."

McClain looked again at the slack-jawed boy. He had the same book open, history, over a stained cup of coffee. There was a kind of permanence in the way he sat, brain soaking up fact, acting as middleman between the book in one hand, the note pen in the other. McClain thought: The study of history implies a certain faith in the future.

"And one of these days," Ravenel said cheerfully, "we ought to have a party."

THE GIRLS all lived in little white houses on the bank overlooking the river. When you went calling for a girl you had to go down a long stone walk by the music building and then out across a wooden bridge over a deep rocky gorge. The country there was heavily wooded with pine and maple, and in the bottom of the gorge there was a clear stream flowing down into the river. The bridge in the winter was always windy and cold, and sometimes there was a sound of music from the music building. McClain went over there several times that fall, and usually stopped on the bridge to listen to the blended music, to look down into the gorge and out to the river. There were almost always couples on the bridge, walking or standing, hand in hand, and while the weather was warm there were couples everywhere in the shadows of the trees.

The day McClain went calling for Lise Hoffman was the day of the first snow. He was just passing the music building when the first flakes fell and it began to come down very fast. By the time he was out on the center of the bridge it was falling thickly, steadily into the gorge and he stopped and looked up into it. It was already dark, the lights on the bridge had been turned on, the snow swirled silently in pools of light like swarms of white flies. He turned his face up into the snow and let it come down, the white stars rushing down out of the black giving him the sensation of speed, that he himself was rising up, rushing through space. He was alone. The bridge ended in darkness. He had one of those moments: I'm tired. He felt an increasing paralysis. He waited on the bridge, the body went on functioning, ticking, pumping. He could hear music coming down through the snow. He heard again that same dark call, that slow deep silent throbbing, toward darkness, toward rest. It was the worst moment since the hospital. He waited. It passed.

He found the house at the circle at the end of the road. He went up the steps carefully, slowly, the snow already thickening and slick on the smooth wood. He was admitted by a plump girl, who smiled and went away. He stood dripping and cold in the perfumed warmth. It was all cozy and warm, unreal. He waited in the hall, not taking off his jacket, hatless, the snow melting on his hair and shoulders and dripping in cold pools on the bare floor. There was a couple in the living room, a studious couple reading side by side from a huge book propped on the girl's lap so that the tall spindly boy had to lean over her shoulder to see, and he had to place his leg tightly against the length of her thigh and his chin almost on her shoulder, and the girl wore thick glasses but was pretty.

McClain waited patiently in the hall. There was a full-length mirror on the wall beside him. He saw himself tall and wild-haired, snow already melted and running down his face. He thought: I'll be a shock. It didn't matter. He saw the girl coming down the stairs.

The first thing he saw was a gray dress, a smile. She was very pretty. Is this the one? Yes. She walked up to him, silvery fur on her arm. She said hello, she was Lise Hoffman.

He introduced himself. She had a natural, open smile. He saw pearls at her thoat, pearl earrings. Clean, neat. Expensive. She handed him the coat and he put it on her awkwardly, with wet fingers, scenting the perfume when she turned her back, perfume and soap. The sense of unreality was overwhelming. She was much too neat, much too pretty. He made motions, an actor, remarked about the weather. She said she liked snow. She turned to the mirror to give herself that one last critical adjusting look, flipped her hair outside the collar, said something to the girl inside on the couch. The face in the mirror was unlined, untouched. Wide blue eyes, the soapy smell of innocence. He had an odd, trapped feeling, like a bringer of bad news.

He took her arm going down the stairs but at the bottom took his hand away. They walked side by side in the falling snow. He had nothing to say. He wanted to be pleasant and entertaining; he tried to remember words. Nothing came. He thought: I'll take her back soon. She waited for him, then she said, dutifully: "I was hoping it would snow for Thanksgiving."

He nodded.

"I'm going home, all my friends will be there." She paused for a moment. "Are you going home?"

"No," McClain said.

"Oh that's a shame." She had a pleasant voice. She seemed natural, perfectly at ease. "It isn't any fun to stay here, when everyone's gone. I was around here last summer during the break, it was awful. Like a cemetery."

"It's not so bad," McClain said.

"I can't wait to get home. We'll all be going skiing that weekend, now that there's snow. It's nice to have everybody gather again, all the people I used to know."

They walked out onto the bridge. A couple came running toward them out of the white blowing dark, slipping on the smooth wood. A boy was chasing a girl with a handful of snow; she was shrieking with delight and holding her collar up tightly with both hands so he could not get the snow down her neck. McClain stepped aside, stood for a moment under a light. He looked down at Lise Hoffman: she was smiling after the couple. She had her face tucked down into the fur of her collar, and the snow was gathering on her hair. She was a beautiful girl. The happy couple running by made him feel awkward. She turned to him, smiling. Then she said:

"Aren't you cold?"

"No," he said.

"You really should wear something on your head."

He was wearing an army field jacket. He looked down at the silvery fur coat, the ash-blonde hair.

"Do you mind if we stop here a while?" she said. She leaned on the railing, looked down into the black gorge. When she looked up at him again, he sensed for the first time that she was embarrassed too.

"I'm sorry I don't have a car," he said.

"Oh, I don't mind. I like to walk in the snow."

"Is there anywhere you want to go?"

She shook her head. Then she looked at him and broke into a sudden chuckle.

"Is there anywhere *you* want to go?"

"Nope," he said. He smiled.

"Then let's stay right here."

"Fine."

"There's no place to go anyway."

"That's true."

"We could go into the music house. Do you like music?"

"Fine," he said.

"You'd be surprised how much I know about you."

"Me?"

"Oh, yes. Let's see." She held up her hands, began ticking off fingers in gray wool mittens. "You were a fighter, a professional fighter, and you were in the war, and you belonged to some fraternity, I forget which one, and you're in pre-med. And, oh yes, you won a medal. Now, isn't that true?"

"Partly," he said.

"I must say you sound interesting," she said. Still the pleasant, childlike smile.

"You have a hell of an intelligence system," McClain said.

"Well you know the way it is here. Everybody talks. Honestly. You should hear the stories about you. You were supposed to have done something fantastically brave and dangerous, and they say you drink a lot and are mean."

"They do? Really?"

"Uh huh."

"Well I'll be damned. I didn't think anybody noticed."

Lise Hoffman chuckled again. "You don't know girls," she said cynically, cheerfully. "I'm just as bad. But I'm awfully curious. Is all that true? Did you really fight in the ring?"

He nodded.

"I never knew anybody who did that," she said, shyly, impressed.

"I'm not in pre-med any more," McClain said.

"Why not?"

"Well. Long story."

She did not probe. "I planned on going into nursing," she said, "but my folks were against it."

"Why?"

She shrugged. "It wasn't *proper*." She peered down again into the gorge. "Look at the snow falling into the water. Looks just like sparks going out."

"Why wasn't it proper?"

Lise looked up at him gloomily. "My mother thinks women should be brood mares." McClain smiled. "Even if I wanted to be a doctor it wouldn't make any difference. Of course, I'm not bright enough. I really have no talent at all. Do you have talent? I mean, do you play the piano or something like that?"

McClain shook his head.

"They *made* me play. I was awful." She held up her hands. "All thumbs. They shouldn't have done that. When I have a baby, I'll never make him play anything. But I'd like him to play."

"Did you really want to be a nurse?" McClain said.

The girl looked up and out into the snow. "I don't really know. I don't think I ever had time to find out. But . . . I would like to have tried."

He tugged a pack of cigarettes from his pocket, lighted one; she cupped her fingers in the gray mittens to shield the flame. He offered her one, she shook her head. Her face in the snow, the firelight, jarred him. She was lovely and close and clean. She looked at his eyes.

"I can't imagine you as a fighter," she said.

He thought: not in her world. He thought of her home: quiet, stable, pillar of the community. A piano, fine china. Mother waiting up.

"Did you like to fight?" she said.

"In a way."

"Of course . . . that's a hard thing for a girl to imagine, I guess."

"It's not bad," McClain said. "It's a different thing than most people think. People do worse to each other, every day. There's a lot worse things that can happen to a man than a punch."

She was watching him with an odd look on her face that he did not understand.

"You're not at all what I thought you'd be," she said.

"What did you think I'd be?"

"Well. Sort of . . . rough." She smiled an awkward smile.

"Is that why you came out with me?" he said.

"Yes. I guess so," she nodded.

"Why?"

After a moment she said: "I hope that doesn't bother you." She sounded genuinely concerned.

"No," he said.

"I'd heard so much. I was awfully curious." She paused, hesitated. "But you're not like that. There's something . . . you make me wonder what you're thinking."

McClain remembered Ravenel's remark: those sad, sad eyes.

"Don't put your trust in quiet people," McClain said.

She smiled. "You sound so fatherly."

"Don't trust that either."

"All right," she nodded. "I won't." But she was smiling, not taking him seriously. McClain looked down at her with a sudden violent hunger. He wanted to hold her, he wanted to talk. He did nothing. She leaned once more over the railing, then held her bright face up to the snow.

"Isn't it a lovely night?" she said.

ON HIS WAY HOME he stopped in at Harry's. His shoes were soaked through, his feet burned with cold. He had two quick Scotches but he did not thaw; he sat shuddering at the bar feeling the cold go all the way through him now that he had stopped moving. He thought of the girl as of a fire a long way off. She would be going up to bed now. Undressing. Sitting cross-legged talking to a roommate. "And how was your date?" And what would she say? He had not touched her. They had listened to music. He sat thinking of the long walk home in the silence, the snow, and couples standing everywhere under trees pressing against each other. When he brought her back to the porch there were two couples kissing, and so he stood there awkwardly saying good night, from a safe distance, and the couples did not even break the rhythm—one girl idly opened one eye and investigated him curiously over a round shoulder—and McClain stood back formally and said good night. She said thank you very much, I hope I see you again, and he walked away past all the kissing couples, who stood everywhere like twin trees.

"Hey!"

A thump on his shoulder. He turned to look into the red-eyed face of Charley Ravenel.

"Thomas, me lad." Ravenel sat heavily on a stool. His eyes were bleary, his face ran with melted snow. He peered cautiously down the empty bar, looked both ways, saw no one, bawled down to Harry:

"I'm buyin' for the house. Everybody drinks!" He peered happily at McClain. "How'd it go, laddie?"

"Fine," McClain said.

"She's a doll, isn't she? Is she not?"

"She is indeed."

Ravenel nodded several times gleefully. "Not much action, but what the hell. A man needs variety every now and then. Harry! Goddamit, I'm colder'n a well digger's ass."

Harry arrived with a bourbon. Ravenel sighed, surrounded it, lifted it tenderly to his cold-blue lips. "Well, anyway, you liked the little broad, ha?"

McClain nodded.

"I thought she'd bring out the ole homing instink. She does in everybody else. Most guys I know look at her and come all over gulpy and protective."

"What're you doing out?"

"Christ," Ravenel gloomed. "Who has a better right? I ben workin' my eyeballs to the bone all night. Goddam history of medicine. Jesus. A big one tomorrow. Dirty bastard. Loading us up before Thanksgiving. Hey, what you doing Thanksgiving?"

"Staying here."

"Good. So'm I. We'll have a blast. What you say? Clawson's staying too."

"Righto."

"He'll be here in a little while. Said to meet him here. He's got trouble."

"What kind of trouble?"

Ravenel grinned. "The same old trouble. Nobody around here ever gets in trouble over anything else. Throw a stone, you hit a broken heart. It'll happen to you, sonny boy."

McClain thought: no, not yet. I'm not ready yet. Not for that. Not even for fighting. Keep an even keel. Let the wound harden. Singapore.

At that moment the door opened and clouds of powdery snow blew in, and Clawson entered, pushed by the wind. He clumped forward shedding soft clods of snow, hunched down inside his collar.

"My God," he said gravely, bewildered. "It's snowing."

FIVE

THE PARTY at Ravenel's could be seen from a long way off, like summer lightning. McClain was early, but there was already wreckage on the icy ground below the wooden stairs: broken bottles, a table cloth, a black overcoat. McClain took the girl's arm; she gave him a frozen smile. She was a tall girl, a redhead. He'd met her in the coffee shop, sitting with Ravenel. Her name was Claire. She took her arm away and went up the steps in front of him. At the top of the stairs two couples were necking, glasses in hands, coatless. One boy waved a drunken hello, the other gazed seriously at Claire, eyes heavy-lidded.

"Wassa password?" the serious one said.

"Shit," Claire said. Easily, happily. The boy's eyes slowly widened, the awful impact of the word taking a long time to get into him. Claire turned, grinned cheerily at McClain, took his hand.

"That oughta hold him a while." She pulled the door open and a cloud of hot dry smoke poured out of the room, screams and laughter, the thin plucking of guitars. There was a crowd by the door; heads turned to see them enter. The serious boy said, "Jeez Crise," as they passed. Claire pulled McClain with her into the room.

The room was so thickly crowded there was nowhere to go. He stood holding Claire's hand, pressed tightly against her buttock. He looked around for somebody he knew, saw faces that were only vaguely familiar. Claire said hello to several people. Faces looked at McClain. They worked their way through the crowd, and McClain saw two boys sitting on the floor in one corner of the room, playing guitars, surrounded by a set of passionate, silent faces. One boy was singing something McClain could not hear. The boy's eyes were closed, dreamy. The other boy next to him was playing along with a grim look, nodding his head. Folk music. McClain came closer. Claire was talking with animation, using her head, her hands, to a well-dressed boy with smooth cheeks. McClain cocked an ear to the music, did not recognize it. It was the year of the guitar. You could not have a party any more without a sprinkling of guitars. Even this was new. Before the war they would sit around singing songs from the Spanish Civil War. McClain remembered Malone: "The Four Insurgent Generals." With a bottle of Irish whiskey in one hand, cigarette butt in the other. "Freiheit." "Hans Beimmler."

All now very old hat. He felt almost like an alumnus.

They made it finally into the kitchen, where Ravenel sat perched on the wooden icebox, leading a drunken chorus in a filthy song. He had a glass of whiskey raised high, to keep it out of reach; he was directing the music with a long, slightly bent pipe cleaner, a look of blissful drunken glee on his face. He was surrounded by people of varying descriptions and colors. Ravenel knew everybody, everybody knew Ravenel. There was a doctor from town, and his wife. The doctor was singing and grinning, the wife seemed acutely embarrassed. Next to the doctor was a short fat girl in a black sweater and black pants, accompanied by a frail boy in a beard. After that there were three couples, obviously fraternity types, well dressed, calm, drunk, and after that some medical students: dirty, bleary-eyed, obscene. It was Ravenel's usual crowd.

He looked down, saw McClain, waved hello, spilling whiskey on the doctor, who went right on singing, eyes closed.

"Hey, by God, there's the Big M!" Ravenel roared. He yelled something about where the whiskey was, but Claire was already leading McClain by the hand toward the sink. Eyes followed without interest. A drunken med student, eyes closed, took up the next verse of the song, the one which begins: "high above the stinkin' creek," but the rest of it was drowned in a general roar. McClain made it to the sink, which was filled with ice, picked one of the bottles out of the wild litter on the counter, began making a drink for himself and one for Claire. There was no point in trying to talk. He looked down and saw Clawson sitting in the corner behind the sink, back against a pipe, the freshman girl behind him, hidden by his shoulder. McClain wanted to say hello, see a friendly face, but Clawson was busy talking. McClain mixed his drink with water; suddenly, on an impulse, drank the whole glass. Claire was talking to somebody in the crowd. McClain stood waiting patiently, drinks in his hands, looking again at Clawson, saw the face of the girl. She wore makeup now. Eyes dark and wide. That same wide adoring smile. McClain was touched. He wanted to introduce himself, but he thought that might be a mistake. The man with the apartment. The man in whose bed. . . .

Claire was there, asking for the drink. She looked down past him at Clawson and the girl. Wheels whirred in her brain, she looked back at McClain, smiling.

"I made it with water," McClain said. "Too stiff?"

She tried it, shivered. "No. It's all right." She was shoved in close against him by the crowd behind her. She brought the glass up with both hands and held it against her chest, between them. She said something he couldn't hear. There was a roar of laughter behind her. Ravenel was giving a short dissertation on the value of the pipe cleaner. One of its main ancillary uses, he said, one as yet undreamed of by this peasant local society, was that of a cleaner of belly button lint, for which the thing was perfectly, and you might almost say providentially, formed.

"God," Claire said, "let's get out of here."

They moved back into the main room. The guitar boys had stopped playing and were arguing earnestly in a corner of the room, but now the record player was on and several couples were dancing. Claire turned to him with a bored look and put her arms around him, still holding the glass, sipping from it over his shoulder. They tried to dance: they could only stand pressed together, swaying. She was tall and lean in his arms, kept her pelvis tucked studiously, scientifically distant, her breath in his ear. She talked to people over his shoulder: bright, brittle, clever things. She seemed to like to swear. He didn't mind. All that was an act. He began to sense something vulnerable. She leaned back from him abruptly, cocked her head to one side, looked him full in the face.

"Hey," she said.

"Hey."

"You're pretty damn quiet."

"Can't make myself heard."

She nodded. She was looking at him with calm appraisal.

"Let's really get blasted," she said.

"Great," he said. She took her drink from his shoulder, drank it down. He joined her. This seemed to make them buddies. She came in closer when she danced.

"I like Charley Ravenel," she said in his ear. "He's such an . . . an *honest* person."

"True," McClain said.

"Don't you like him?"

"He's my buddy."

"That's good. Too many people around here . . . finks. Especially the music school. Oh God, the music school. Half of them are fruits, did you know that?"

"I've heard rumors."

"The things I could tell you." She told him.

"Well," McClain said. "To each his own." After a moment it occurred to him that that was pretty funny, but she didn't notice. She went on telling him about two queer pianists. She moved in closer against him; he locked both hands behind her back. He could feel her against him all the way down. She talked about the music school.

"You know, you're pretty strange yourself," she said. She backed off again to look at his face. "As a matter of fact, you're a mean-looking bastard."

"My nose has been busted," McClain apologized.

She rested an elbow on his shoulder, propped her jaw on her hand, gazed at him dramatically.

"I think I'll play some games with you," she said.

"All right," McClain said. "I'll be the bad guys."

She grinned. There was something lively and dark in her eyes. Possible? Yes.

"Let's *really* get stoned," she said.

THE PARTY reached its peak. Somebody goosed a girl named Frances; she turned and slapped the wrong boy. Ravenel, royally drunk, wandered gleefully through the house kissing all the girls, including the doctor's outraged wife. A large medical student named Cranford heaved a tall fraternity boy named Partridge clear off Ravenel's high porch and down into the snow. The boy sprained an ankle and sat there actually weeping while a girl sprinkled Scotch on him from above and kissed the medical student, who took the Scotch away from her. Several other medical students, impressed by Ravenel's talk on the virtues of the pipe cleaner, shaped the thing lovingly— it was by this time pretty dirty—and descended on a lovely brunette named Ida Wilkinson. They lifted her blouse slightly and opened her skirt slightly and cleaned her navel thoroughly with the pipe cleaner. This infuriated her date, a varsity basketball star named Sims, who started a genuine brawl which resulted in minor injury to five people, including one girl, who began punching away at the world in general for no apparent reason, and was punched back, and so lay upon the floor in spread-eagled and indecent stupefaction. The party was a success.

By the time people began drifting away—to long walks in the cold, to the back seats of cars—McClain himself was feeling no pain, and Claire was sloppy. She moved away from him to dance with other people; he sat alone listening to slow blues music and guitars. He went back inside for another drink. It occurred to him that Clawson might want to use the room, and he went looking to give him the key, but Clawson was already gone. Ravenel was sitting on the kitchen floor in earnest discussion with two beards and a pale red-head. The first beard was saying something about this country and intellectuals.

"Of course now," the other beard said, "you ought to define what you mean by the word intellectual." Ravenel winked at McClain. The redhead stared at him fixedly, mouth open, leaden braces on her teeth.

"The French gather on street corners to gawk at their poets," the first beard gloomed. "We gawk at the boobies of movie stars."

"True. Oh how true." Ravenel grinned. "One moment, lads."

"Where's Clawson?"

Ravenel took him by the arm, led him aside. Behind them the two beards continued to argue morosely. The girl still stared vacantly at McClain.

"Where the hell do you find them?" McClain said.

"Gently, lad." Ravenel smiled. "A touch of tolerance. Anyway, look at it this way: they're all future patients. Now, what's on your mind?"

"What happened to Clawson?"

"He took off."

"Damn. I wanted him to know it was all right if he used the room. I saw that. I tell you." McClain shook his head, moved. "She seems like a very nice girl."

"Oh, she's a jewel," Ravenel said.

"That wasn't so bright, bringing her here."

"True. The poor bastard. He was being rebellious. Didn't want to hide any longer. It's happened, you know?"

"What happened?"

"She's knocked up."

"Oh boy."

At that moment there was a hand grabbing his shoulder; he turned and saw Claire, face flushed, hair out of place—and beyond her shoulder and across the room, coming through the door, the face of Lise Hoffman.

"Wass all this plotting?" Claire said. "You schemin' somethin', Charley? You leave this boy 'lone."

Ravenel came in close to Claire, put his arm around her, kissed her noisily on the cheek, grunted.

"Just tryin' to get rid of him. Meet you in five minutes. Behind the icebox. It's cool there. I'll give you a nip."

Lise Hoffman saw McClain. She smiled, waved. She was with a tall, very good-looking boy in a black overcoat.

"I'm not as drunk as I look," Claire said stiffly. Then she giggled. "I'm drunker." She insisted that they were plotting something, and then Charley saw Lise Hoffman, and bawled hi, and went over.

"But don't you see, you've missed the point entirely," somebody said. McClain looked down, saw an earnest beard.

"Come on and dance," Claire said. She had a pouty look on her face. McClain held her, saw Ravenel go to Lise, help her with her coat. The blonde hair, flash of pearl earrings. Dress of black velvet. Ravenel said something; she laughed aloud. A truly beautiful girl.

"You've really got that one snowed, haven't you?" Claire said gloomily in his ear.

"What?"

"The Hoffman. What's the fatal attraction?"

Baffled, McClain pushed back to look at her.

"Don't give me that jazz," Claire said. "I couldn't care less. But I don't get it."

"What are you talking about?"

"Don't tell me you don't know about the jolt you gave Hoffman. She's mooned about you all week."

McClain was stunned.

"Telling everybody what an extraordinary person you are." Claire looked at him carefully. "She really did. I heard her."

"I was out with her once," McClain said.

"Well, that once seems to have been enough. What's your secret?"

McClain looked down at her. She wasn't as drunk as she'd seemed to be. He felt a mild disgust. "Let it drop," he said.

She watched him. He was not looking at Lise Hoffman.

"You're really steamed, aren't you?"

"Yes."

"Sorry." She came in against him. "Girls are finks," she said. "Jabber jabber jabber."

He saw Lise Hoffman beginning to dance with the tall boy, who bent over her and folded her in with a dark smile. McClain began to feel the need for another drink: the glow was fading.

"She's really a nice kid," Claire was saying.

"Who?"

"Oh, never mind."

"Want another drink?"

"I doody doody do."

They went back into the kitchen. He had one good long one, no ice. But the glow was truly gone. The record player stopped. More people left; the guitar players came back with some slow sad music. Lise came into the kitchen with Ravenel and the tall boy, and McClain turned from the sink to find her standing behind him.

"Hi." She gave him that extraordinary smile. She looked fresh, immaculate. She hadn't been drinking. She seemed nervous.

"Hey," McClain said. The tall boy came up behind her, looked at him without interest, looped an arm around Lise's waist.

"I guess we got here a little late," Lise said. "Charley tells me you've really had a time."

McClain nodded. He could think of nothing to say. But she was extraordinarily beautiful, all neat and fair. It must be the whiskey.

Claire giggled. Ravenel bustled by, mixing drinks.

"What you say, Liz," the tall boy said restlessly, "we've done the bit. Let's move on, ha?"

"Not just yet. Charley's making us a drink."

"There's nothin' left but my private stock," Ravenel said with vast disgust. "Them goddam boozhounds drunk it all. But wait just half a mo." He darted off into the bedroom, came back with a black bottle held aloft. "Gotcha! A Ravenel never runs dry!"

Ravenel chattered, mixing the drinks. McClain looked at his drink, at the wall, at Lise Hoffman. The world was narrowing down. He sensed a gathering darkness, that dreamy dangerous time when you let go of the world and begin to float. Lise had her hands clasped in front of her. Claire was talking to the tall boy. McClain said suddenly, to Lise: "Would you like to dance?"

Lise said: "I'd love to." She started to lift her arms. But the tall boy caught her shoulder. McClain was beginning to move.

The tall boy said: "The girl's with me, sport."

The next moment seemed very long.

McClain looked at the boy, then he looked at Lise.

He said again, softly: "Would you like to dance?"

"I don't guess you heard me," the tall boy said. He started to step around Lise. "Get lost, son," he was saying, and then Ravenel was suddenly there, saying something fast and bright at McClain's elbow, and McClain was thinking slowly, very slowly, a balloon blowing up in his head and a wind beginning to blow, something huge and black sitting up in his mind and beginning to roll over like an earthquake: sonny boy, sonny boy, and he hit the tall boy once before anyone had a chance to move, and hit him without warning as hard as he could, as hard as it was humanly possible for him to hit anybody, and even then in that moment still clear enough in the brain not to use the right hand and go for the head, remembering enough of the old days instinctively to use the left to the stomach first, because the gut was not a moving target and was easier to hit, and softer, and so used the left first, and then the right, both of them hitting exactly where they were supposed to hit, and the tall boy went down.

Ravenel had McClain by the shoulder, but McClain didn't move. He stood there looking down, the wind whistling in his mind, watching the tall boy's face and the blood starting to come out of the nose.

"Jesus, Mac, Jesus!" Ravenel was saying. McClain stood there.

The tall boy rolled over and put his face on the floor. He wasn't going to get up. McClain stood there. Ravenel bent down over the boy. McClain felt hands pulling him away. He let go, but he backed away still looking down. He was having trouble seeing: he blinked. He looked away finally and saw Lise Hoffman. He could not see her clearly, could not see the expression on her face. He became aware of people talking. Claire was by his side. He leaned back against the sink and watched Ravenel work on the boy.

Ravenel got help, moved the tall boy out into the other room. McClain stood alone. When he looked up again, Lise Hoffman was gone. Claire had his hand. He looked down and saw her running water in the sink, holding his hand. There was blood along the knuckle. The hand was numb. He hoped nothing had happened to it. He heard Claire, as she washed his hand.

"Oh, wasn't that lovely. Oh, the son of a bitch. He had it comin'. I never saw anything so beautiful. Oh God. Are you fast! God! I'll never get mad at *you*."

Claire stood on her toes impulsively and kissed him on the cheek. McClain felt the first reaction, the same sickness. In the other room the tall boy was saying something hysterical. McClain looked down at Claire and smiled.

"You tell Charley," McClain said, "that he better not let that one back in here."

Claire looked at him. McClain could feel himself smiling. Claire backed away. McClain stood waiting, mindless and free, no rules, no law, nothing to stop him. Let something happen now. Let someone come now. He waited alone. There was nothing to hit.

After a while he saw Ravenel's head staring at him from behind the door.

"Have a drink, Mac," Ravenel said. "I'll have this guy out in a minute."

McClain stood in a gathering silence. He looked at his hand, moved the fingers. It seemed all right. In his mind he could see the punches going in, the boy going down. He felt nothing. He leaned back against the sink. When he looked up he saw Lise Hoffman.

She was standing by the door, staring at him. She was a long way away; the look on her face meant nothing. He wanted to say something, but he was still far back in the dark. He lifted his hands toward her, palms up. There was nothing he could do. He could not even be sorry. He saw her lips move, but he could not hear what she said. She went away.

Everyone left. Claire came back into the room, silent, watchful, but in a few moments she cheered up. And then there was Ravenel standing leaning against the door.

"Well. Now *that's* over, let's all get down to some serious drinking."

SIX

AFTER THE PARTY came the Thanksgiving holidays, and when classes began again at the University, McClain did not go back. It was time to be moving on. He looked forward to spending Christmas in London with Wilson. But all that week there was heavy snow, and it was pleasant to lie in the room in the gray afternoon listening to music, watching the snow. And then at the end of the week he made love to the red-haired girl, Claire.

She came to see him in a borrowed car, and let him drive. She slumped down in the seat next to him and put her knees against the dash, and he could see the skirt ride up, the pink foam of her slip. They drove around slowly, silently. She smoked one cigarette after another; the heater fluttered her skirt. He did not know it was going to happen until she told him to drive out into the country, and then he was not sure, but he began to feel it in his stomach like a hot wet weight. She told him to find a place, but he didn't know the road. She directed him through a break in the fence along the road; he bumped over frozen snow down a rutted road and stopped under a grove of trees, and she came against him. He moved his hands over her, under her dress. He saw the white legs in the moonlight, white legs opening. She broke away from him and climbed over the seat into the back, and he followed her, touching her, his face all puffed and thick, the heat inside him like a mortal sickness. He had her once quickly, awkwardly, and finished too soon. Immediately after it was over she started to cry. He sat numbly, exhaustedly, trying to comfort her, but she pushed him away. After a while he had her again. This time he was slow and tender, careful, loving. She held him desperately, clamped him with her legs, grunting, heaving. He finished along with her in a long slow massive flood.

She was first to disengage. The windows were steamed. He lay watching her put herself slowly, drunkenly back together, reached out and patted her thigh. He felt gentle, kind; his mind was filled with an exhausted peace. She had a cigarette, said nothing, looked at her watch in the light of the match, swore. It was late. He kissed her once more and then they crawled together into the front seat, and he sat grinning foolishly in the dark and wanted to kiss her again, but she reminded him of how late it was. They drove back over the ruts and onto the highway.

Eventually she said slowly, breathing it out, "God, but that was good."

"True," McClain said. He put his arm around the thin shoulders. She came toward him reluctantly.

"I hope you haven't got any ideas," she said.

"Ideas?"

"You know. About doing this . . . all the time."

"Ideas? Have I got ideas? Let's see." He grinned.

"Well, you take it easy now. This was very nice and . . . and all. But don't get any whacky ideas."

"Okay. Fine."

"Well, this is all," she insisted, weakly. "I mean that. There'll be no more of this. You'd never fall for me anyway. Nor me for you. Never. So, you just wouldn't . . . so this sort of thing. . . ."

He waited, not really listening, still at peace. It did not occur to him that he was expected to say anything.

"You'd never fall for me," she repeated. "And this was very nice and I needed it, I'm human, but. . . ."

She began to cry. He held her gently to him, did not try to talk her out of it. She had a right to cry. All girls had a right, and a need, and perhaps good reason to cry. And so he held her consolingly, regretfully, but all the way home he felt the same sweet tender peace.

By the time they were back she had composed herself. She spent the last minute in fixing her face, would not let him kiss her outside the door. She stood for a moment with the door open chattering glibly, profanely about how much damn studying she had to do, and he sensed the warm musk of perfume behind her, soap, steaming showers.

"See you tomorrow?" McClain said.

She stared at him, at his tie. She was making twitching motions with her mouth. She stood on tiptoe and gave him a quick peck on the cheek.

"A real fun time," she said, and closed the door.

He wandered on over to Harry's. One need, at least, was at rest. He remembered all of her, everything, but it was already becoming unreal, drifting away from him, taking the warmth with it. He remembered Gerdy's warning: stay away from the young broads; and smiled. It was too precious a gift. He would have to tell her, tomorrow, how precious it was.

In Harry's he found Ravenel, consulting a beer.

"Hey there, Black Avenger." Ravenel grinned.

McClain wore a silly smile. He had an impulse to tell Ravenel about Claire, to share it. He knew it would make Ravenel happy.

"Where the hell have you ben? I ben lookin' all over for you."

"I took a ride in the country." McClain grinned.

Ravenel studied him.

"Well you look chipper, I must say."

"How's Clawson?"

"Oh, dint you hear? That turned out to be a mistake. She was just a little bit overdue. Came on all right after all. Good thing too. He was all set to marry her."

"Well, I'm glad it turned out all right."

"Hey. Lemme see that hand."

McClain pushed out the right. It was still slightly swollen, but most of the pain was gone. He flexed the fingers. Ravenel probed. That hurt.

"I think I may have broke it," McClain said.

"Well, you damn sure didn't do it any good. Did you get it X-rayed?"

"No. You think it's broken?"

"Hairline fracture, probably. Well." Ravenel gave a grin of satisfaction. "Well, you won't be beating on the troops with that hand. At least not for a while. Damn shame. Against that knucklehead. Hey—I ran into him a little while back. Guess what he said." Ravenel grinned widely.

"What?"

"He said to tell you he was sorry he lost his temper."

McClain digested that.

"Story is going all over. The way I hear it now, it was one hell of a brawl, lasting hours. Hee."

"Well," McClain said. He shrugged.

"Anyways, as long as you had to bomb somebody, you certainly picked the right man."

"Who was he?"

"Name of Lester Bateman. Real snake. Too much money. I never did like his lower lip. A pouter, you know?" Ravenel stuck out his own lower lip, demonstrating. "I've felt like giving him a rap many a time. But you know me, a man of peace. Have a beer."

McClain was remembering the face of Lise Hoffman as she stood in the door.

"I'll say this," Ravenel went on. "You've still got the old right hand. Fast? Jesus! I tell you, for a minute there, you scared hell out of me."

"Her too."

"Claire?"

"Lise."

"Yep." Ravenel grimaced.

"I guess she never saw anything like that."

"I guess not."

"What do you suppose she thinks?"

"Oh, don't you worry about that. There's iron in that little broad." Ravenel eyed him thoughtfully. "There's iron in most broads. More than you think."

"She seems like a nice kid."

"You haven't seen her?"

"No."

"Why not?"

McClain shook his head.

"Funny," Ravenel said. "I would have thought *that* one . . . well, what the hell. Listen, I've got to push off. Burn the bloody candle. Don't hang around too long, that slob is rich enough already." He waved at Harry, wandered to the door. When he opened it, a fresh wave of new snow swirled in around him. Annoyed, Ravenel stared up at the sky. "All right, you guys, let's knock it off."

Harry came down the bar, hesitantly, bashfully, a beer in his hand.

"That's all right, Mac," Harry said shyly. "You stay here as long as you want."

Harry retreated. McClain sat at the bar. He had nowhere to go in the morning, and he had slept late that afternoon. It had the makings of a long night. He thought about Claire again: the vision came back with a physical shock. The girl opening her arms, folding him in. He wondered how many others there had been. For there had been others. But he did not want to think about that now. It was still a gift. A very important gift. It had been such a long time, he had forgotten how precious it was. He was glad he had not told Ravenel. That would not have been the gentlemanly thing to do. He smiled to himself. You sir, a gentleman. With a bloody broken right hand. But that's one rule at least that seems to be sound. When a girl does that, you ought not talk about it.

Harry had to close, by law, at two o'clock. McClain walked home in the silent snow, which reminded him of Lise Hoffman, and he paused under a streetlight to watch the snow come down like stars.

HE AROSE in the late afternoon, wandered out in search of coffee. He was passing by a statue somewhere when a voice spoke in his ear.

"Mr. McClain?"

McClain focused, blinked. A tall thin man was speaking at him through the folds of a blue wool muffler.

"Ah, how are you, Mr. McClain?"

"Oh. I'm fine, sir." McClain recognized the distant eye, the bleak, vacant face of—what was his name?—the sad one, the philosophy prof? The name, the name.

"I haven't seen much of you, of late." The voice was dry, weak, softened by the muffler, but there was no sarcasm in it. There was no expression at all.

"I thought you might have been taken ill. Or that you might have left school."

"No, sir."

"But I checked and found no record of either."

"Yes, sir."

The thin man gazed at him with vacant eyes, not looking right at him, but at something right next to him, as if McClain had a companion. He coughed into the muffler, lifting a gray glove to his mouth. McClain was suddenly aware of something shy in his manner. Phelps. That was the name. Dr. Something Something Phelps. A noted authority in his field.

"I haven't been sick, sir," McClain said.

The thin man moved his head awkwardly, looking everywhere but at McClain.

"Yes. Well, no doubt you have, ah, well, it is December, you know. Late, but I think, really, there is still time. For one of your capacity. I took the liberty of, ah, going into your reason . . . that is, I mean, your *record*." The eyes blinked in confusion, he coughed again. McClain was touched. "I shouldn't want you to be discouraged. I really think that, with a little effort. . . ."

"Well. Thank you, sir."

"Of course, that's entirely your affair. I did think that, ah. . . ." Now he seemed acutely uncomfortable, his face was taking on a strangled look. He looked around in a feeble search for escape. "Well, it would be unfortunate if you began to work too late, and, ah, I didn't want you to be discouraged."

"That's very nice of you."

"No trouble. We all have these, ah, times of, ah, well. Good-bye." He gestured stiffly and raised his head and walked off. McClain stared after him. He had not known that the man even knew his name. It had not occurred to McClain that anyone would even notice his leaving. It was a good feeling: to leave a vacancy. McClain felt a twinge of guilt. He remembered the classroom, the patient permanent silence. He had sat by the door looking out into the hall while Phelps lectured on the nature of reason. McClain remembered thinking: the more you study reason, the less you believe in it. Reason answers nothing. Because there are no answers. But the class faced out onto a hall, and a bulletin board which belonged to the Sociology Department, and at the top of the board was a sign: REERS IN SOCIAL WORK. McClain smiled. There's reason enough in that. And Ravenel's remark: two things of value—work, broads. Claire.

McClain watched the retreating figure. That was damned nice of him, he thought.

He went down the stone steps of the walk and out across the Common. He was dressed too warmly, he began to perspire. He opened his collar and took several deep breaths. The air was heavy and wet, very warm for December. The sky was clear except to the east, over the river, where brown and yellow smoke boiled north from the factories. McClain walked on soggy, sucking ground, past rounded mounds of melting snow. There were colored lights on some of the trees, stars and tinfoil on the streetlamps. The campus was already decorated for Christmas. He thought of Wilson, a long way away. He thought: not yet. But if I don't leave soon I can't be there for Christmas.

He had coffee by himself. At the next table three grave girls were earnestly discussing the difference the H-Bomb had brought to war: was it qualitative, or merely quantitative? On the other side of the room a very young couple were Indian-wrestling on the table. He saw no one he knew. He wondered where she'd be. Practicing, probably. She studied voice. He had not heard her sing. He had no idea of how she would sound. Memories of the night in the car revolved in his mind, in his stomach, like a hot primordial globe. He stared at the very young couple. Her face without makeup, scrubbed, bright with hot blood, like Lise Hoffman. Did *she?* He pictured it. Doubted it. Noticed finally that there was only one other person in the room sitting alone: a grim, bearded man in a white turban.

McClain left, walking toward the music building. He breathed the clean wet air. He was thinking: luck. It's a fine day. What I need now is a bit of luck. He looked ahead and saw a girl coming across the bridge, and there was something familiar in the walk: Lise Hoffman. He slowed. She didn't see him. She was walking slowly, with purpose, arms filled with books, brooding. She started to turn in toward the music building, saw him, paused, stopped. She stood waiting, smiling.

"Hi," she said. She looked like the co-eds in expensive advertisements: poised on stone steps, sunlight in her hair, wide blue eyes, perfect smile, books in the round arms, just slightly breathless. He felt wary, awkward, vaguely confused. He waved a hand foolishly.

"Well how *are* you?" she said, just the one faint note of lovely accusation. He said he was fine. He found himself grinning. He stood looking at her, and she said nothing for one long second and it occurred to him finally that she was nervous too.

"Charley said you hurt your hand," she said.

"Yep," he nodded. He had his hands in his pockets.

"Well, I hope you didn't break it."

"Don't think so," he lied.

She grimaced. "That awful Bateman. Honestly."

"And how is he?" McClain said.

Lise smiled. "I haven't seen him." Abruptly she chuckled. "It isn't ladylike to feel so . . . *satisfied*, is it? But I can't help it."

"I've been thinking," McClain said. "I was a little worried."

"Why?"

"I'm sorry you had to see that."

"Oh." She dropped her eyes, then looked up at him wryly, gloomily. "You really shouldn't worry about that."

"Well."

"I'm really not all that delicate," she said wistfully.

He nodded. But she looked so very young.

"Where are you going?" he said.

"In here. To sing." She gestured toward the music building. "We're practicing *The Messiah*. For Christmas."

"I didn't know you sang."

"Oh no, just in the chorus. I'm not very good." She smiled that extraordinary smile. "They give you one hour's credit, you know, for singing in the chorus. But I do like it. It's a tradition, you know, it's sung every Christmas, just before we all go home. Have you ever heard it?"

"Yes. Do you have to go in right now?"

She shook her head. He sat next to her on the stone wall beside the steps. He thought: if Claire should be here. But he wanted to talk. He was wary, but he wanted to talk. Thinking of Claire made him feel an unnatural guilt. He wondered what Lise would think if she knew. Not that delicate. Thinking of Claire made him aware of this lovelier body on the stone wall beside him. Hair in the sunlight: perfume and soap. He looked away from her toward the bridge.

"Will you be going to *The Messiah*?"

"I don't know."

"Please come. Or don't you like that kind of music?"

"I like it," he said.

"We do a pretty fair job. If I do say so myself."

"I used to sing it, when I was a kid," McClain said. The wooden church in Vermont. Thunder of the organ. Voice of a reedy God.

"Did you really?"

He nodded. "At least I practiced it. Boy soprano. Practice every Tuesday and Thursday. Only trouble was, on Sunday mornings I was always too sleepy and I couldn't sing, I could barely talk. So I went to all the practices but I never sang on Sunday, I just moved my lips. But I liked it."

She waited, encouraging him.

"I'll try to come," he said.

"It's one of the best things about Christmas," she said. "*The Messiah* and candlelight service."

He nodded politely.

"Do you go to church?" she said.

"No," he said. He looked at the blue crystal eyes. "Does that bother you?"

"Oh no," she said, startled. She looked at him with that same sad wistful expression. "Of course it doesn't bother me. You must really think I'm . . . I wish people would stop that. People are always protecting me. Even the girls—do you know they won't even tell dirty jokes when I'm around? Honestly."

"There is that about you." McClain smiled.

"It's a terrible feeling," she said earnestly. "I feel that I'm . . . shut out. Except every now and then you have some disgusting boy who *paws*, but of course I don't mean that. I mean, I get fearfully weary of this darned *amused* look people get, as if I were three and my diapers were showing and I was all chubby and cute. Honestly, you have no idea how disgusting that is."

"I'm sorry," McClain said.

"I just meant, about the church, that candlelight service is nice, even if you don't pay attention to the rest. You don't have to listen to the rest. But it bothers you, doesn't it?"

"What?"

"Religion."

"Yes."

"It bothers you very much," she said.

"Sometimes."

She waited again, but he said nothing. He did not want to start talking about that.

"Are you Catholic?" she said.

"No."

She seemed pleased.

"Don't you like Catholics?" he said.

"Oh, it's not that. It's just the more practical aspects, like birth control and the papal infallibility and all that; I admit it bothers me some. But I just got over a mess with my parents about a Catholic."

He waited. A mess with my parents. He had a vision of a stout bald man with a pipe, a frantic weeping mother. The little girl, tear-stained, sent to her room.

"This boy I went with was a Catholic. My parents couldn't stand the idea. I do believe my mother honestly thinks the Pope lurks, viciously waiting to kill all the Protestants. They never said anything as long as we were going together, but then he wanted to give me his pin. And then they made me give it back. Oh, it was some row." She smiled thoughtfully. She looked up at McClain and gestured with her palms. "So now," she said dramatically, "I'm free."

"Do you still see him?"

"No."

"Do you want to?"

She looked out toward the bridge. He thought she would be tender and tragic about the affair but when she turned back to him her face was happy, almost mischievous. "No," she said. "As a matter of fact, I must confess that it was about over anyway, and if my folks hadn't of made such a fuss it would have died of natural causes. We'd gone together all through high school, but we were both about ready for new horizons. But when my parents came in like that, it gave me a chance to be wounded and noble, you know, to be all dramatic and to suffer." She chuckled. "Isn't that awful? But you know, really, it was wonderful to suffer like that. Knowing that all along, in the end, it doesn't really matter. And to part so dramatically, alas"—she put a hand to her brow—"farewell." She giggled.

McClain shook his head, smiling.

"And so we both went our lonely and imponderable ways. And now I'm a-kicking away at the shell. And one of these days I'll break out." She looked back toward the bridge. Her face softened. "But on the other hand, I was very lucky. If I'd really loved him. . . ."

"What would you have done?"

She glanced at McClain. "I'd have married him." She said it with a pleasant smile. McClain remembered: iron in that little girl.

He heard the music begin inside, an organ playing. She heard it too, but she didn't move. The chorus began: "For unto us a child is born. . . ." They sat side by side, silently.

"One thing I wanted to ask you," she said.

"What?"

"I've never seen anyone get that mad. As you did. Does that happen often?"

"On alternate Tuesdays," McClain said.

"I don't mean to pry."

"I'm sorry. I don't mean to be flip."

"Charley Ravenel says you're leaving."

"Yes."

"Where will you go?"

"I'll just wander."

"Will you be coming back?"

"I don't know."

"Well." She smiled, stood up. "I wish you luck."

He stood up with her, not wanting her to leave.

"Are you coming to *The Messiah?*"

"I'll be there."

"I hope you like it. Good-bye." She stood looking at him without smiling; he felt awkward, strained. She hunched the books up in her arms and he let her go. She walked up the stone steps and stopped in the door, smiled at him, went inside.

He walked out onto the bridge, stopped. His mind had always been slow, instinctive; it took him a while to realize how much the girl had shaken him. She was there, lovely and innocent, waiting for him, singing inside the building. If he called her, and went to her. . . . Such a lovely girl. It's the innocence, he thought, the blessed innocence. I want to be with something warm and clean. Because I myself am not warm and I am not clean. Well, that's absurd.

But as he stood on the bridge a flock of girls passed him, moving like bright birds, chattering, hair flying. They were talking of a party, of Martha's new car—he listened from outside. But that was not his world. There would be no bachelor's degree, no American dream. No slow steady progress in the economy of rising expectations. No slowly unfolding home, no burning of the mortgage, no raises, no promotions. His future was blood, his own life led toward a vast and implacable silence. He knew it as certainly as he knew the day was ending. He looked down at his hand, his still swollen fist. He treated it tenderly, old injured friend, and walked home, away from the music.

TWO DAYS later he had Claire in the apartment in the afternoon. She called first and told him to wait there, and he watched from the window as she came slowly up the street, head down against the wind, looking fragile and cold and scared. He felt nothing except his own eagerness, the warm liquid draining of his belly. She was wearing a thin gray coat and a soft gray scarf, looked like any other solemn college girl on her way to the library. She stopped for a moment in front of the house and looked up and saw him watching. Then she looked up and down the street, alert, head flicking like a watchful squirrel, then bounded up the steps and let herself in.

Once in the room she asked him to make it as dark as possible. He pulled down the shades, and when he turned she was undressing. She did not take off her slip. She got under the covers and he came in after her, restraining, trying to be tender. He told her how lovely she was, the words coming strained and awkward; her arms came up coldly, uncertainly, not like the other time at all. With fear. He put his face down in the pillow and made love to her in darkness, his eyes closed. She joined in with him, but there was something mechanical in the movement. She helped him. He tried to hold back, listening to her breathing. When she began to breathe deeply, he could not hold back any longer, he let go. The force of it exploded him, exhausted him. He dreamed, drifted, lay for a while in numb blind hot soft silence.

After a while she got up on an elbow, holding the blanket over her breasts, began stroking his hair. Her face was calm, thoughtful, wore a slight quiet smile. Gradually the blanket slipped down and he looked into the marble skin of her throat, her shoulders, where the white slip straps cut deeply. He felt a spasm of fondness. Her face was not pretty; there were pimples on her forehead. But he felt a wave of sudden, appalling tenderness. He took her closely in his arms.

They made love once again. He leaned back, supporting himself on his arms, watched the pain come over her face. This time it was better for her. He guided her to the finish, helped her. When it was over he felt completed, very fine. Now it was good for both of them. She lay next to him with the slip up high above her waist and his hand on her. She was his. He did not think about the future. There had been too many days away from this: the warmth there in his arms. Even the name did not matter.

He got up, a gentleman, and found her a cigarette. They lay smoking with exhausted joy. The room was much warmer; he pulled down the blanket and they lay under the sheet. He wanted her to pull that down and take off the slip, but he said nothing yet. That would come. It occurred to him that this time last month he had not even known her. And this time next month? Christmas. She'll go home for Christmas. Two weeks. Two weeks at home. He did not want to think about Christmas. He looked down at her and she was lying with one arm curled under her head, blowing slow blue rings of smoke in the air. He thought suddenly: how many others?

"What are you thinking?" she said.

"Truth?"

"Please."

"Well. I was just wondering how long it would be before I got you to take that slip off."

She smiled, pulled the sheet up primly. "That's not much to hold back."

"It's got to go," he said decisively.

"Not yet."

"All right."

"I bet you think that's foolish."

"No."

"I don't want you to see me. I . . . have an awful body."

He grinned. He reached down and cupped her small breast and looked at his fingers, dark against the white satin slip.

"No. I really do. If I had to stand up and have you look at me, I'd die."

"Don't do that."

"What?"

"Die."

"Hee. I can see you trying to explain that to your landlady."

"I wouldn't explain anything. I'd wait till dead of night and drag you out and dump you somewhere in the cold snow. One of the great mysteries of our time. The Girl With The Awful Body."

"That's mean and cruel."

"And then on the other hand I would probably keep you here for a while. Although you'd be a little chilly. But even that way you'd be warmer than many a woman."

"What a horrible thought."

"It's a fine old southern custom," McClain grinned. "Anyway, I tell you one thing. I'd finally get that slip off."

"That bothers you, doesn't it?"

"Oh hell," he said.

"Is it so awful for me to want to hold something back?"

He shook his head, but now it was running away with her, there was an edge in her voice.

"Hold something back," she said. "Just how much do you want, anyhow?"

He tried to kiss her but she ducked away.

"All you want anyway is to lay me," she said. "You can do that with clothes on."

"Don't spoil it," he said.

"Well, what the hell do I care." She was suddenly deeply upset. "I come all the way up here and throw pride the hell out the window and come up here to do this for you and all you can do is want more."

He waited silently. She was sitting with her back to him, and he sat looking at the thin pale shoulders, the frail bones. So there was to be just this one moment, after all. And already over. He put out a hand and touched her back, just above the hip. She said nothing. Then she turned slowly and looked at him over her shoulder. Her eyes were wide and soft, not angry any more.

"I'm sorry," she said.

"What can I do?"

"Nothing." She turned and kissed him, moved back in under the covers.

"I want you to be happy," he said.

"I'm happy."

"I'm so damn glad you're here."

"Yes."

He held her. It was not a time to make love. They both needed the warmth. Later he asked her: "Why me?"

"I was a bit obvious, wasn't I."

"But why?"

"Who the hell knows?" She turned away from him. "These things happen."

"Not like this. Not very often."

She looked at him oddly. Then she smiled. "It doesn't happen often. If you're worried—"

"I didn't mean that."

"As a matter of fact, it was like a damned drug, if you really want to know. It had something to do with when you hit that guy. You made me feel. . . ." She turned her face away.

He thought: an animal. He remembered Ravenel: with sad eyes.

"Let's not talk about it," Claire said.

He reached for another cigarette.

"We have to go," she said.

"Not yet."

"Yes." She stood up. "It's getting dark. If you want to go out tonight I'll have to go home and get dressed."

"The hell with going out tonight."

"No. I feel like a blast."

"You really do?"

She was picking up her panties. She put them on easily, without embarrassment.

"I wish you'd brought your clothes," he said.

"Now how could I do that? My roommate would have seen."

"Sometime I'd like you to bring a nightgown."

He knew instantly it was the wrong thing to say.

She paused just slightly pulling on her dress and then pulled it the rest of the way down with a jerk. "You want quite a bit, don't you, lover?"

He could feel himself withdraw, disengage. He was tired. He sat up in bed, swung his feet over the side.

"I'm sorry," he said. He dressed in silence. He turned on the light and saw her standing next to his bed, ready to go, her face edged with the soft gray scarf, strain in her eyes.

"Let's have a cup of coffee somewhere before we go back," she said.

"All right." He looked at her, tried to smile. She came to him and kissed him on the cheek. He knew she wouldn't be back to this room. But maybe it would work out. It still might work out.

Nobody saw them leave the building. When they walked together down the street no one looked at them. She had his arm tightly: he could tell when she began to relax.

"I really am sorry," she said.

"Let's forget it."

"The thing is . . . I'm not playing any games."

"Of course not," he lied.

"I'm . . . honestly. Everybody here plays games. Everybody I know. But I just wanted you, and I knew what I was doing. I'm old enough and wise enough. I thought it would be. . . ."

He looked down at her face, but it was too dark to see anything but the sharp line of her jaw.

"It doesn't seem to work," she said. "I keep trying to be all light-hearted and gay. But it doesn't work."

They passed under a streetlight. He turned and stopped and took both her arms. He saw that she was crying.

"I thought I could just do this," she said. She was looking straight into his chest. "What the hell, you know. Lighthearted me. I needed you. It didn't matter what you thought. Who gives a damn? But . . . oh God, I can't say it. It's no good this way, do you see? I just can't do it this way."

She pulled him in and held him. His arms went slowly around her. He felt that same appalling tenderness.

"There, there," he said.

"You could never love me," she said.

So it wasn't too late. All he had to do was say the words.

"And apparently," she said, "I seem to need that."

When he looked down at her he felt awkward, cold. He could not say the words. For a moment he saw the world around him go absurd, ridiculous, like a lens thrown out of focus. What are we talking about? Why are we fighting? It's cold and dark. He felt incredibly foolish: my nose is broken, my hair's too long, I'm nothing. He put his arms around her and looked over her shoulder down the long dark street.

"You're not mad at me?"

"No," he said.

"It was . . . it's been very nice."

"Yes."

"I think I'd better go."

"All right." He put his arms down.

She backed away. She seemed glad to be away from him, but she hesitated. Then she went by him, touching him on the arm. He thought she would turn and wave but she kept on walking all the way to the corner, and it was dark between the lights—if she turned he didn't see it.

He stood for a while leaning against the lamp post. The street was quiet and very cold. Well, he thought, that didn't take long, now did it? Two days. One night, one afternoon. In and out of your life she comes, dangles from strings, is plucked away. He stood aimlessly by the light, reluctant to leave, like a man on a pier after a ship has gone. But a car came around the corner sweeping headlights brightly toward him; he started up automatically and began to walk, trying to look like a man with a purpose, a place to go.

SEVEN

CHRISTMAS EVE. He took a long walk along the river, thinking about the war. At night he couldn't sleep.

Christmas Day. He went out early. He was beginning to feel that something else had to be wrong, this couldn't all be mental. His body lost coordination; he was having trouble breathing. He went downtown and looked into store windows. He went to a movie but couldn't sit still, had to get out. He wandered along wishing it would snow. It was too late for London now. He went back to the room and started a letter to Wilson, but couldn't finish it. Harry's was closed. He went back to the river and thought again about the war. He began to hold conversations with an absent God. He knew there was nobody there but he was rehearsing it, the way you plan a speech in advance in the hope of meeting somebody someday in the right place at the right time. Well here I am, Absent Friend, back from the dead. Assuming You're there, for the sake of argument, it seems You wouldn't let me die. So here I am. In rather a bad way. No doubt You had Your reasons. But I'm getting tired of reasons.

He was interrupted by a curious policeman who wanted to know if he was all right. He said he was fine, the man wished him a merry Christmas. McClain wandered along, but the conversation didn't resume. There was nobody there. All the same, when he thought about the war he couldn't help feeling that he had been brutally resurrected. And yet nobody comes back from the dead. Not even Christ ever truly came back. He dropped in on a few friends, after the stone was rolled away, but shortly after that, even Christ went home to heaven.

The day after Christmas. The luck which had begun on the last day of that last spring held good again. He was alone in the room in darkness, had not eaten or slept, had just passed through the worst day and night of his life. And then he had a visitor. Lise Hoffman came back into town to exchange some presents, and decided to drop in on him.

She stood smiling radiantly in the doorway, like a child come to get a present. He started gathering himself together, tucking the loose ends of his mind forcibly back out of sight, afraid that she might see and run away. She thought he was sick. She said he looked like he was coming down with something. She felt his forehead, and there she was standing close to him, face down there inches away below his chin, the blue eyes in shadow. Then she went past him into the room and started straightening things up, fixing the bed, emptying ashtrays. She opened a window and let cold bright air into the room, and he went on assembling himself, putting his hands into his pockets to hide the shiver, afraid that he must look like something terrible. She asked him if he wanted to come out for a ride; she had her father's car. She waited on the bed, chattering happily about presents and all her relatives, while he shaved. She explained that she had come back into town to exchange a few presents, and thought she'd drop in, just to see how he was getting on. He went with her out to the car, letting her lead him, letting her drive.

They drove out to a place overlooking the river and she had a banana split, to celebrate Christmas, and he tried to eat something, but he was not hungry. She was extraordinarily beautiful. He had nothing to say, but she did not seem to mind. She radiated an incredible reviving warmth. He sat watching her. He was awake now, back in the world, alert, alive. But something was missing. The control was gone and he knew it, could feel it. There was nothing holding him any more, he was drifting on the swell of the bright afternoon. He did not think; he watched her and felt the young clean warmth break through him as through an opening in his chest. He did not know if she knew it. She was looking at him with an increasing shyness.

They sat for a long while silently. He could see her begin to be nervous. He tried to think of something light and bright to say. She said suddenly: "I wish you wouldn't look at me like that."

He didn't understand.

She smiled apologetically. She was not looking at him. "You look so awfully sad," she said.

"But I'm not sad," he said.

"Your face," she said, still not looking at him. "You have an extraordinary face."

"I'm not sad," he said.

"What were you thinking?"

"Just then? A minute ago?"

"Yes."

"I was thinking. No, I wasn't thinking. I was just feeling. I wasn't thinking anything. I was just sitting watching you and feeling very good."

"But your face looked. . . ." She stared at him with the huge round eyes, shook her head.

"I guess my face is just naturally sad," McClain said. He smiled, but she looked away.

"Will you be leaving soon?" she said.

"Yes."

"I wish I could do something like that."

"Yes." He thought of her at his side, riding in a far country. Sleeping in a tent at night, sitting up to watch the stars.

"Well," she said, "I've got to go exchange those presents."

"Let's not go," he said.

She looked at him, searching his eyes. Then she smiled and nodded.

"I really do have presents to exchange," she said. "That wasn't just an excuse."

"I know," he said.

"But I wanted to see you. I kept thinking of you all alone. You must—" she broke off, blushed suddenly.

"It's not so bad," McClain said.

"Yes it is," she said. "It's all in your face. Do you have any idea? Do you know what shows in your face?"

Now he could feel himself giving way, beginning to loosen and slide like the breakup of a mountain top.

"It will pass," he said. "It always passes. You mustn't worry. It's no good to be alone too much. I should have known that. You sit alone and you think too much and of course you get tired, and when you get tired you can't think clearly and everything looks worse than it really is, but mostly it's because you're tired."

She sat waiting for him to go on. He felt himself moving toward her.

"It doesn't matter about Christmas," he said. "That isn't what matters. What matters is that a man has to be of use, a man has to be trying to do something. A man is built for use, his hands, his brain, his feeling, and you can feel the pressure all the time. I should be somewhere doing something that matters and that I was made to do. Only the thing is, you see, that all I can do well is fight. I was a good fighter. I was a good soldier. Only there aren't any more wars. At least not right now. And anyway that's not right, it's too bloody. I don't want to kill anybody any more. I want to. . . ." he paused. He did not know what he wanted. He wanted peace. He wanted a sign from Heaven.

"I want to believe," he said.

They left in darkness and drove slowly along the river. She was supposed to be home, but neither of them mentioned it. He let her drive, not touching her, not even then, although it was already almost time and he knew it, could feel himself dropping toward her with increasing speed as from a great height, and could feel now also for the first time the beginning of a weak desperation, a trace of fear. But she was looking at him with those vast blue eyes and her glance was eroding him in successive waves, because there was something different here, even if she was so very young and so tenderly innocent, and even if all it was was sympathy, the natural concern of a good clean child for an ailing stranger, still it was warm, still it was genuine, and even if it wouldn't last but a moment and even if she should look behind the sad face and see the appalling sick blackness that lay just inside the bone vault, just under the white brow, and even if she should see the reality for what it was, a mindless man in a godless world, a killer, a suicide, and even if then she should run away it would all make no difference, it would all have been worth it. And so, when they parked along the river bank to watch the moon rise in a cold but immaculate sky, he did not reach for her even then, although by then she was waiting, and it was time, past time. He sat looking at her in the dark, in silence, never having felt this before in his life and so treasuring it for the moment, the long moment, holding back that one last second before giving what could never be returned.

He put his arms out and held her, held her before kissing her. He was the meteor. She was the earth.

SHE WOULD DRIVE into town every day just before noon. He would be waiting for her on the steps of his house. First he would kiss her good morning and then they would drive somewhere and have breakfast together and after that they would drive out along the river or walk hand in hand through the campus, which was utterly empty, suspended in silence, their own quiet world of statues and snow. There were some mornings when he did not believe she was coming, but she always came. She was always breathless and smiling, running up the steps toward him. She wore schoolgirl clothes: a pearl-gray sweater, skirt of green velvet, a green ribbon to hold back her long blonde hair. Once she came late and they went to dinner, and she was wearing a black dress with pearls at the throat, and he backed off from her to look at her, and she stood before him awkwardly, embarrassed, so beautiful he could not speak. She was not graceful; there was comfort, patience in the way she walked. He discovered that her vision was poor, she wore glasses, but she would not wear them with him. She liked to touch him with her hands, touch his hair, his face. He could make her laugh. When he kissed her he held her face in both his hands. He touched her carefully, awkwardly: she filled him with a great need to be gentle.

One day she could not come: she was duty-bound to stay home with relatives. When she was not there he could no longer believe what was happening. When she was with him he was a strange man, rested and warm. He passed that day up at Harry's, talking about old-time fighters. He went to two movies. When she came the next day, he tried to ask her why it had happened.

She smiled. He realized that he'd asked an impossible question, but he did not understand any of it, he had to ask questions.

"Did you know any of this would happen?" he said.

"Oh yes."

"When did you know?"

"The first night."

"No."

She went on smiling, staring past him into the broad blue air. "That first night I went upstairs in a daze. I just sat there and dreamed. And then after that, you know what I did? I knew you would be at Ravenel's party and so I went out with Les Bateman and talked him into going there just so I could see you."

He was amazed.

She kissed him on the cheek, chuckling, watching him.

"Oh I'm crafty," she said, "crafty and shrewd. You had no chance at all. I used to walk along that bridge hoping you'd come along."

He shook his head. "Why?" he said.

She gave him that extraordinary smile.

"I don't understand," he said.

Now there was something else in her face, a touch of sadness. "Why do you find it so hard to believe someone could love you?"

"But I'm not even in your world," he said.

She stopped smiling, looked at him with calm tender eyes.

"That's what you don't understand. I didn't have a world."

During the days they talked, and during the nights they would park above the river and he would hold her. He would kiss her, but he would not touch her breasts or her legs. It was too soon, but it was more than that. When he held her he became very still inside, quiet and cold, as if a wind was coming up. He had never really valued any woman before, and she was altogether too perfect; what would happen would be more than sex, it would be grave and permanent. As time went on he could feel the hunger begin to burn in his stomach; he became steadily more silent. He kissed the color off of her lips and watched her when she moved, the small soft swelling of the young bosom, the long clean tender legs. He said nothing about it. It was coming. But not here, not now. Not in this way. Too soon.

It was all too much like magic. It could vanish in a moment. He decided to tell her what he was, what had happened. He told her all about Vermont and the war and the hospital, not knowing how she would react, what she would understand. While he was telling her about that last day, she started to cry. He did not understand that either, but in some way, from then on, they seemed to be closer.

SHE HAD A DATE for New Year's Eve. She'd made it a long time before, long before the holidays. She could not break the date; it was a matter of honor. They both agreed that it would be very bad form for her to break the date. They agreed that one night apart could not hurt them, after all, even if it was New Year's Eve and even if they wouldn't be together in the last seconds of this year in which they'd met. It was all a matter of honor. She asked what he would do, and he said he would go up to Harry's and drink himself numb. She said wistfully, "You know, I've never been drunk. I've been high, but never drunk."

He remarked that this was not actually a flaw in her character.

She said: "I want to be with you."

"Yes."

"I'll break the date."

"Yes."

"Oh but I can't."

"No."

"I've never done a thing like that. I can't stand people who break their word."

"Yes."

"But I want to be here with you."

"Yes."

In the end they agreed that she would go with the boy to the party, but would leave early as possible and drive over to see him at Harry's. So that was the second day she did not come to see him, New Year's Eve, and he walked around the empty campus by himself. It was all ending: the Christmas holidays, the year, the long sweet afternoons along the river. He could feel time moving on, the world rolling on under him, mindless, inexorable; he could feel the people come pouring back like a flood wave in the distance. He sat on the river bank and watched the sun go down, early in the day, because it was the darkest time of the year, and he thought again about the war, and then went up to Harry's and began drinking early, slowly, wanting to be sober enough when she came but at the same time needing the darkness of the bar, the warmth, somebody to talk to.

Harry's was deserted, except for Harry, and they sat talking about the old days and Charley Ravenel and fighters and the war. They turned on the television, and there was a movie on, a love story, all filled with scenes shot lovingly through the flower-laden branches of dogwood trees in the spring. The girl wore flowing white robes and was dying. Lise was lovelier. Lise was warm and healthy and it wasn't even spring now, but the dead of winter, so none of the props were right, McClain thought, and the movie was touching and sickening at the same time.

It was a long wait. Harry came out with a special bottle of brandy he was saving for such a moment as this and McClain wondered: Who is he? When he closes down for the night, where does he go? What has he done on other eves?

"I used to be married," Harry said. He smiled foolishly.

"What happened?"

"She died."

"Oh," McClain said. Harry leaned back, his head off to one side.

"Didn't you ever want to get married again?" McClain said.

"I'm a Catholic," Harry explained. That seemed to end the discussion. They sat watching the new year come in on television, in Times Square. McClain got progressively drunker. He remembered last New Year's Eve and Lieutenant Hubble with a bottle of Courvoisier. Hubble with the bottle and a round of drinks in canteen cups in the dark. Happy days. Hubble sitting looking young and skinny, talking happily into the night about infantry tactics and the new inventions which would make all infantry obsolete, but not soon enough, and showing a picture of his wife, which McClain saw by the light of a flare, and lapsing into silence afterwards, never to see another year and certainly unaware of it, no grim foreboding there, no signs in the sky, and right now lying empty bones in the ground, already plucked clean, perhaps beginning to rot.

"Happy New Year, kid," Harry said. He poured a stiff one. "All on the house, kid. Lots of luck, ha?" Harry was weeping. He sat in the corner by the big front glass, uncorked another bottle, and sat staring out at the night.

A new year.

What will I do?

I can bring her nothing.

In a few days they'll all be back and nothing will be the same.

He was getting much too drunk. He drank to her. My lovely Lise.

New Year's in Chicago. He saw it on television. It wasn't until after one o'clock that she came. By then he knew that he would be leaving there soon, leaving all of it behind, going on to Jerusalem. She came hurrying in the door with snow on her hair, ran to him, ran right into him, hugged him, held him.

"I'm so sorry. They wouldn't let me go. I kept trying to come, but they wouldn't let me go."

One kiss now that he had his arms around her, his eyes closed, standing there holding her, the hair fragrant and wet against his face, warm body against him, holding him, smell of snow and warmth and perfume, her.

He introduced her to Harry. Harry with tears rolling down his face, pounding them both wordlessly, shoving bottles at them. They drank together, gazing into each other's eyes.

"I love you," she said.

He said it too.

THE DAY AFTER Ravenel came back and found what had happened and was so overjoyed he almost kissed McClain, McClain went downtown and bought a railroad ticket. He left a note at Ravenel's place and went home to pack. He had nothing much to take, it would all fit into a duffle bag, but he wanted Ravenel to have his books. He really didn't want to go. He went on downstairs and told the landlady he was leaving, and she was very sorry. He was paid up until the end of the month, and she tried to give him back some of his money but he wouldn't take it. He went back up to the room and sat trying to write a note to Lise. He sat by the window looking out. The day was cold and gray, January, the endless winter. He worried about Lise, thinking: This is a bad thing to do to her right now, with exams coming on. He knew she had a lot of work to do. But maybe it would be better for her with him gone.

Ravenel didn't come until after noon. McClain was already packed, was sitting on the bed surrounded by empty drawers, empty closets, the fat duffle bag on the floor. Ravenel was stunned.

"What the hell are you doing?"

McClain tried to explain.

Ravenel didn't understand. "For Christ's sake. Are you serious?"

"Charley, this is no place for me."

"But why? My God, now that you've got Lise. . . ."

"Listen, that's one of the reasons. Charley, a school like this is no place for me."

"But for Christ's sake. . . ."

"What can I do for her? Charley, you know me. There are things wrong with me. Me and Malone. So I can't do that girl any good. And I can't lean on her either. I can't do any of that. She deserves . . . I'm not up to it yet."

Ravenel listened for a long time, and then he said: "You love the girl?"

McClain paused. He was standing by the bed tying the strings on the duffle bag. He took a deep breath. "Yes," he said.

Ravenel nodded. "Well. It'll all work out. I hope. One of these days. Christ." He rose and stalked around the room. McClain offered him the little pile of books. Ravenel began absently tucking them into his pockets.

"You going to call her before you go?"

"Sure," McClain lied.

"That's going to be rough. The poor kid."

"You'll look in on her every now and then?"

"Hell yes. So will everybody else. She won't be alone long, you know that."

"Yes."

"But then—" Ravenel shook his head. "She just might. You never know. I think the girl's really in love with you."

"Could you give me a lift down to the station?"

Ravenel nodded vaguely, then started. "Hell, I've got a class. I can't cut it. I can take you down now, and leave you, okay?"

McClain heaved the duffle bag to the shoulder, took a long last look around the room. It had been a good room, except for some of the nights. He had always liked the pictures of the clipper ships.

They went on down the stairs. The landlady rushed out and was sorry he was leaving; she wanted to make him one more cup of tea. He thanked her and told her how good it had been to be with her. She said: "If you ever come back, Mr. McClain, please come here." Her face was trembling. McClain was touched. As they went out to the car she was standing in the doorway, waving, unmindful of the cold air rushing in on the African violets.

"Seems like a hell of a nice old lady," Ravenel said. He started the car and let it warm up for a minute. He sat looking out the window and then said: "I wonder where the hell we'll all wind up."

McClain was thinking of calling Lise. He had to either call her or write her. He didn't want to call. They drove past the familiar streets, the bundled crowds rushing to the last classes. Nobody would cut today.

"You'll be back, laddie, won't you?" Ravenel said.

"I'll try," McClain said.

They went down to the station. McClain dragged the duffle bag into the baggage room. Ravenel, who was no good at this sort of thing, stood self-consciously shifting back and forth from one scrawny leg to the other.

"I hope to God I see you again," he said.

"Right," McClain said.

Ravenel pushed out his hand. "Write a letter once in a while, damn it."

"I will," McClain said.

"You always know where I am, if you need me."

"So long, Charley."

Ravenel squeezed his hand, turned, got in the car, waved through the window, drove off toward the chapel spire. McClain watched him go, then went into the waiting room out of the cold. There was almost an hour to go. He had a cup of coffee in the waiting room, then he went to one of the phone booths and dialed her number. He was very nervous. He didn't think she'd be there, she must be in class. But there was her voice.

She knew immediately something was wrong. He told her he was going, he would write a letter. She was bewildered. She said in a plaintive, small girl's voice, "Why?"

He said, "Because I have things to do now."

"Well, when will you be back?"

"I don't know."

"Will it be a long time?"

"I'll come back when I can."

She wanted him to come over. He said he couldn't, the train was going now.

"Was it anything I did?"

He couldn't answer that. "I love you," he said.

"I'll wait for you," she said. He could tell she was crying.

"It may be a very long time," he said.

"I'll wait for as long as it takes."

"I have to go now."

"Please come back," she said.

He hung up and walked out onto the platform. He had never been as sure of her as he was at that moment. But it was the right thing to do. He looked down across the black iron railing at the chapel, the bare trees, the cold and endless sky. The train came in and he boarded and sat by the window, still looking at the chapel. He felt a new tension, a readiness. The train began to move. He watched the chapel recede, and then he was out over the river, and he could see forward across rolling hills all the way to the edge of the world.

THE JOURNEY: SUMMER, 1954

ONE

THE ROAD TO JERUSALEM ran south from Damascus along the edge of the desert. The land there was brown dirt ribbed with rock, there was no sand; the air had a clean burned smell and the sky in summer was a soft whitish blue. Along one side of the road there was one thin power line strung on frail dusty poles; on the other side was the desert. There were a few small villages along the road: huts of brown clay burned gray-white by the sun. The heat raised small winds in the stillness, whirlpools of dust drifting across the hot rock like willowy dancers. At night the stars were very beautiful. Much of that land, for one reason or another, was holy: to the Jews, to the Christians, to the Moslems. The road ran south into Jordan, then west across the Jordan River to Jerusalem.

McClain and Wilson passed that way in August. They left Damascus early in the morning, to avoid as much as possible that brutal August sun. They had to leave their own car in Damascus: there was another crisis and no private car was permitted on the road. They came in a rented government car, driven by an Arab. There were two other passengers in the car: a man and his daughter. The driver drove with that fine high Arabic abandon that knows that Allah wills all and knows all and what will be is already written, and repeatedly terrified his passengers. But the land was flat and there were very few cars on the road and they reached the Jordanian border just at sunrise.

They were stopped by a squad of soldiers at a black iron crossbar across the road. A Syrian officer, a handsome young man with a very serious face and a black mustache, took their papers into a long low building. The border was a rise of gray dirt, topped by rolling barbed wire. Several hundred soldiers in sandy mustard uniforms lounged near the wire, around the building. There was a row of small tanks and oil drums along the road, and in a field to the east there was a battery of artillery, six black guns pointing south into Jordan. On the other side of the battery a company of men was drilling, marching silently, sloppily in the cool early morning. The road ran down under the black gate and through a sharp cut in the ground, between barbed wire, out onto a flat, barren plain.

"That's a minefield down there," Wilson said happily, pointing down the road.

"Where?"

"Both sides of the road. You'll see the signs in a bit. It pays to stay on the road in these parts."

McClain looked carefully across the empty plain. The road was a thin black path fading out into the morning haze. It was a dead land. He could sense the mines, resting like metal seeds in the dead earth.

The two other passengers had gotten out of the car, had not heard the remark about the minefield. The man was a Baptist minister from Sarasota, Florida. He was a stocky, cherubic little man named Kellogg. The drive down from Damascus had been hard on his nerves; now among all the soldiers and guns he was obviously jittery. The girl, his daughter, was pretty but thin, slack-jawed, no more than seventeen. She slouched for a moment against the fender of the car, getting the back of her skirt dusty, looking thoughtfully around at all the soldiers. Then she began to wander slowly away from the car, along the barbed wire. She walked aimlessly, in a bony attempt at a languid stroll, swinging one thin leg after another, her hands clasped behind her back, knowing the soldiers were watching.

"Barbara!" The minister called her name twice faintly. She did not notice. The ground by the wire was rocky; she had to stop the graceful stroll and pick her way delicately, arms extended for balance, among the rocks. The minister stared after her, began rubbing his wristwatch.

"What do you suppose is taking so long?" he said to no one.

Wilson shrugged. He was leaning contentedly against the car, watching the girl. All the soldiers were looking at her.

"I hope there's not going to be any trouble. I don't see why there should be," Kellogg said. He saw the girl go up to the wire, put out a finger, and touch a sharp point. An Arab soldier standing near said something to her, she turned and gave him a girlish smile.

The minister called her name again in a sharper tone. The girl looked at him, said something to the Arab, began to walk slowly back. Some of the soldiers were grinning, nudging each other, talking about the father's worry. The minister was becoming increasingly nervous.

"All these soldiers." He turned to Wilson. "You don't think there's been fighting anywhere? I mean, they have real tanks here."

"Fear not," Wilson said. He was sounding increasingly British again. "If there was genuine trouble they'd be scurrying every which way. Relax. These things always take a bit of time."

"Well," Kellogg waited anxiously for the girl, "well, I wonder, really, if it's a good idea for my little girl . . . I mean, in this country. . . ."

Wilson shrugged again, losing interest. He asked McClain if the tanks over there were American. McClain said no, but the artillery was: 155s. Wilson chuckled. "The wily Arab," he said. He turned reassuringly to Kellogg. "Don't worry. The Arabs are very polite people. You must have noticed that by now. Far more polite than we are. Interesting thing, but people get more polite the further east you go. Now you take the heathen Chinee, for example. Most polite people on earth. So, rest easy. Oh, by the way. Has anyone warned you about the left hand?"

"The what?" Kellogg said. The girl came up, gazing airily at the sky.

"The left hand. It's a very touchy thing. You really ought to be careful."

Kellogg was mystified.

"Well, you see," Wilson said gravely, "the Arab lives in a land without trees. And no trees: no paper. No paper at all. You may have noticed an absence of paper in strategic places. Embarrassing.

You will also notice that no Arab touches his food with his *left* hand."

"Why not?" Kellogg said.

"Well now." Wilson grinned. He glanced happily at McClain. "The Arab uses his left hand for, ah, private matters."

The girl giggled. It was a moment before Kellogg flushed.

"So never touch one of these lads with your left hand," Wilson concluded profoundly. "Monstrous breach of manners. Horrible." He shook his head.

The Arab driver came down out of the white building. He was a fat little man in a black coat and a white shirt open at the neck. He was obviously happy to be away from the military. Kellogg asked him if everything was all right, but he shrugged with wide-eyed innocence: it was all in the hands of Allah. He walked off to talk to the soldiers. The girl leaned back against the car.

"I'd like to get moving," McClain said. He did not like the military smell, the guns, the tanks. He wanted to get on to Jerusalem. He looked down across the empty plain and thought of being caught out there, held out there, in the dead land between two countries, where nothing grew.

Wilson squinted to the east, where the sun was a pale hot furnace low in a pastel sky.

"Going to be a fearful hot day," Wilson said.

THE GIRL sat in the back seat next to McClain. Heat poured in the open window. She tried to roll the window up but that made it worse. The air had an odd dry odor, the taste of something burned but clean. For a while they were able to talk, but the heat sucked the energy out of them. The girl told him about high school in Sarasota and wanted to know if he played football and was impressed because he'd gone to college. She didn't want to go to Jerusalem. McClain gathered that her father had dragged her unwillingly all this way, away from *something*. There was a hint of rebellion, a suggestion of something recent and sordid. It may have been that the father was making one last desperate effort to instill a little piety in the girl, who obviously had none. While it was cool she was cute and coy, batting her eyelashes at him. But then it got too hot and she wilted, exhausted, sat back to stare with glazed vacant eyes at the hot flat land.

There was no sand: it was not what he had expected. The land was fine brown dirt, ridges of gray shale. Once they passed a Bedouin camp, a sprinkling of black tents on gray rock, and in among the tents a tiny yellow sandstorm was moving, twisting, like a small waterspout. He wondered why they used black tents, and not white, to reflect the heat. He wondered how hot it really got out there. But it was wide and still; in spite of the heat there was something deeply restful about it. East of the road there was nothing, nothing at all for a thousand miles: rocks, brown dust, the long heat.

The girl lay a bare arm against him. He felt the heat of her flesh, the tickle of fine hairs. Where she touched him he began to sweat; she pulled away, then gave it up. They lay slickly side by side soaking each other, slipping against each other. She reached down, gasping, fanned her skirt up high above the white knees. The father in the front seat was collapsed, wasn't looking. McClain looked down at the knees, the white edge of a slip stuck to the thigh, saw the stain of sweat at her waist, the stain down her throat where the blouse was melting against small breasts. And here, even here, boiled in the roasting air, he felt a spasm of desire.

He looked at Wilson. He was asleep, his mouth open, head hanging down loosely, bumping with the car. In sleep he seemed exhausted. Sick too much. He caught dysentery too often. Must keep him well. He has no great natural strength. McClain lay back, trying to rest. He looked down at the wet young knee lying against him and was reminded suddenly of the whore in Athens, the dirty bar, the girl sitting there in the dark lifting her skirt and complaining of the heat, flicking the skirt with practiced businesslike glee, so that he could see the tiny white G-string she wore underneath, across the hard belly. Afterward a long walk arm-in-arm down a rocky street, clutchings in a dark room, fake moans, strange smells, gasps —oh Yank, Yank, you do it—no more of that. But Wilson got a kick out of it. Wilson came back rejuvenated. Surgical purposes. But McClain remembered Claire, hard pelvis in a cold room, slip strap cutting the shoulder, perfumed animal slowly opening. Ah. No more whores, no more of that. Athens. Up the hill toward the Acropolis, the Parthenon in the late red sun. Lucky to see it just like that, in the afternoon, the setting sun on the broken columns.

The girl stirred, moved her head against his shoulder, woke, grumbled, tried to move away. She moved her knees wider apart and fluttered the skirt, trying to unstick the wet slip, flush air in underneath. He studied her critically. She lay with her head back against the seat. Mouth open, like a fish. Very young. But older in many ways than Lise. Has been around, this one. Football players. Remember high school and how that was? Just after practice, still sweaty. A girl then too. In the bushes in back of the field. Who? While the rest of them were still running. That was good, that was exciting. Her name? Elaine.

He stretched in the seat, felt his shirt suck away from the back of the seat. He would need a drink soon. The River Jordan. He looked at his watch. Not far now. He was fumbling in his pocket, absently extracting the picture Lise had sent him in her last letter. He stared at it now. It was soggy in his hand, the sweat had gotten to it. Lise. Such a lovely girl. She was perched on a ladder by a tree, reaching dramatically for a peach, face alive with that marvelous smile. She was dressed in tight, light-colored shorts and a loose peasant blouse. He looked at the smooth legs, stretching, felt another spasm. There were two girls holding the ladder, grinning, one dumpy, the other pug-nosed and cute. There was nothing written on the picture. He wondered who took it. Lise was working that summer at the experimental station on the university Ag farm. It was more a joke than a job. He looked out at the burned land gliding by, tried to think of all that green land, the river, but he could not remember. His brain was fogging. He kept thinking of the body of a woman.

They came to the Jordan in a burst of green. McClain sat up. The driver prodded Kellogg, who sat up and fumbled for his camera. But there were crowds of soldiers, more rows of iron tanks. An officer stopped them, peered in the window, waved them on. They crossed in a hurry, there was no time to see. Kellogg was not allowed to take pictures; the bridge there was heavily guarded. One swift glimpse of thick mud, a startling band of flat brown water no more than a few yards wide. No more than a creek. They passed over to the other side, through gaunt pines, were out again in open land, the burned earth.

"That's *all?*" the girl said, shocked. "I didn't see *anything.*" She looked accusingly at her father. But the Reverend Kellogg was awed. He gazed back emotionally the way they had come.

"Gah," the girl said with vast disgust. "Back home we got *drainage* canals bigger'n that."

"Well," Wilson said quietly in McClain's ear, "you done crossed over Jordan."

"Too damn fast."

"You were expecting maybe the Amazon?"

"No. But I would like to have time to get a real look."

Wilson settled back. "Bridge is too important. We aren't too far from Israel now."

"Deep River," the girl was saying with gleeful sarcasm. She chuckled.

"It's low now, of course," Wilson said. He sounded apologetic. "Midsummer and all. Won't fill up again until the fall rains. And then, they use the river so much, you know. They practically drain it dry before it gets to the Dead Sea."

"I'd like to have stopped," McClain said.

"Impressed?"

"Some."

"It's impressive country. The names have halos around them. Jericho is up ahead just a bit. Then the Dead Sea."

"Let's get him to stop in Jericho."

"Nothing much to see. Just a rather large Arab village. Has a gas station, I think. Jerusalem more impressive."

"When do you figure we'll be there?"

"Nightfall. Or thereabouts. Hey."

The car slowed, swerved dangerously. Fine clouds of dust were blowing in the windows, over the windshield. McClain looked forward, saw a gray tank, another, coming toward him out of the dust in ominous blurred shapes. They jarred him. The car pulled off the road and stopped. The tanks went on by, and then more tanks, and then trucks filled with dusty soldiers. The dust was so thick they were all dark murderous shapes. It was an armored column moving back up the road toward the river. When it had passed, the driver started up again and got back onto the road, but the dust rose in a dry fog all around them. McClain felt dust on his lips, in his eyes.

"I wonder if anything's really afoot?" Wilson said.

McClain was spitting dust.

"There were a hell of a lot of soldiers by the bridge," Wilson said.

McClain looked at the driver. The man had his nose pushed up against the dusty windshield, trying to see.

"Wouldn't that be an adventure," Wilson said cheerily. "Plopped down in the middle of a bloody uprising."

"What'd you say?" The girl leaned across McClain to listen.

"That was the Arab Legion," Wilson said proudly. "Very good boys. British-trained."

"Gah. All the dust."

"Aren't there U.N. troops at the border?" McClain asked.

"Sure. But you never can tell. I just wonder why all the armor."

"Dramatic bastard." McClain grinned.

Wilson chortled. There was dust all over him. He had been growing a beard ever since Yugoslavia and though for a long while he had looked simply hairy, now in the dust and heat he was shaggy and impressive. The edges of the thing were beginning to curl and thicken and it was becoming a real beard.

"I think she's hot for your body," he whispered.

The girl was shaking herself, whipping her skirt. "Some river," she mumbled. "You could *walk* across that river."

"So that's how he did it," Wilson said. "I've often wondered."

"I think I need a drink," McClain said.

"Minister's daughter. Always solid gold. The promised land. In The Promised Land. Hey?"

"What country is this now?" McClain asked.

"Which? Who?"

"I mean, from the Bible."

"Oh. Well. Wait. I think, yes, south of here you go along the Dead Sea. Clear to the Gulf of Aqaba. Nothing. What the hell was the name. Oh. The Wilderness. Down there. *Edom*, that was it. The land of Edom. You remember, Christ wandering in the Wilderness."

McClain looked south. Rock and dust. Christ wandering. He could sense the presence in the desert, a figure in a hot cloak, empty air, ragged, bearded, a staff, silence and heat.

"I'd like to go down that way," McClain said.

"They'll never let you. There's something big going on."

Tanks blocked the road. They had to stop again. When they came into Jerusalem, it was very late at night and the girl was asleep on

McClain's shoulder. They entered the Holy City behind a convoy of troops.

THE HOTEL was located just outside the walls of the Old City. Across the street from the hotel was a high brick wall with barbed wire along the top, and beyond that was Israel. McClain had a room on the third floor; he could look across the wall at more plowed ground and barbed wire and some small low buildings far away on a ridge. The wall ran right into Jerusalem and through it and out the other side. The street was patrolled by U.N. soldiers: tall Swedes in blue and white helmets. The walk along the wall was broken dirty concrete, but the front yard of the hotel was lush with flowers.

The first morning they drove out to Bethlehem. Wilson hired a car and a guide, a small listless Arab in a white shirt without a tie. They drove east around the old walls and up over the Mount of Olives, with Wilson chattering happily all the way. The sky over Jerusalem was still the same pastel blue; the road was still crowded with army trucks. The long wall around the city was impressive, edged with battlements. Wilson explained that it had been built by Turks, this present wall, and then went on to talk about General Allenby and Lawrence and the Turkish occupation and the fighting of 1918, and the Arab guide couldn't get a word in and became increasingly annoyed. But Wilson ignored him. They drove the few miles to Bethlehem, with Wilson giving a rambling account of the history of Jerusalem since the Roman occupation, and the guide didn't break in until they passed the Shepherd's Field, and he pointed it out in a voice that was very loud and undeniably annoyed.

"This was the field in which the shepherds were tending their flocks when an angel of the Lord appeared unto them." He gave it as a dramatic reading. Wilson stared.

"You don't say. Well, I missed that last time. You mean that cement over there?"

The field was a flat place a few yards wide on the side of a hill, ridged with a wall. On top of the hill was the cluster of buildings that was Bethlehem. The guide swerved to miss an old man on a donkey, went on reciting in grim bored nasal tones the words from the Good Book. Wilson stared earnestly at the hill, photographing it with his eyes, then turned back to McClain, ignoring the guide.

"Of course, they don't really know. Nobody knows anything.

They tell you all this but it was so long ago, they stake out some convenient plot and build a church there, and worship heavily. But, it might very well be. I mean, the place where the angel came down. It's possible, after all."

The guide gave a long wounded angry glare, then stomped the accelerator. The car lurched and swerved.

"I say, old friend, try to take it with a bit more care, will you? That's a good boy." Wilson gawked at a young girl walking by the side of the road. Blonde hair flowed in vagrant wisps from under a dusty shawl. Wilson leered his appreciation. McClain turned to catch the face as it went by, was startled by the sight of blue tattooing around the young mouth, a lacy pattern etched all over her cheeks. The guide started to expound on Bethlehem. Wilson sat musing on the tattoo.

"Spastic," he said. "But, one doesn't tinker with the local customs. Try to stop that sort of thing, have a damned uprising on your hands. But a genuine shame, mar a lovely little trump like that."

"You'd better watch those leers, friend," McClain said.

"Oh. Did I leer?"

"You leered."

"Hm. Yes. Have to be careful of that. But she was blonde. Hell of a lot of blonde Arabs, you know. Did you know that many of these people were Aryan? Name of the country—Iran—came from the word Aryan. Arabs admit anybody, none of this color nonsense. Mohammed himself married one of his daughters to a Negro."

The guide said something under his breath, braked to a skidding stop in front of a large white church. McClain stepped out into a cloud of hot dust, the dry heat of the morning sun.

"Right here is the jolly old manger," Wilson said with joy. He had the superior, disenchanted ease of the tourist who has seen all this before. He was interested more in McClain's reaction than he was in the land around him.

"Where?"

"Down under that church." He began to explain, but the guide came stubbornly forward and tried to break in, and so they walked to the entrance with both of them talking, Wilson and the guide, and McClain understood nothing. At the door of the church a tiny priest waited in a dusty black robe, his hand out. Wilson paid, the priest grunted. He had a black beard streaked with dust and what appeared to be dried spit.

"Greek," Wilson suggested.

"You'd think they'd get somebody else to take the money," Mc-Clain said. "They could at least hire somebody."

"Oh well, this keeps it in the family. Besides, he probably has nothing else to do anyway. They've got more priests in this town than people. All kinds. Moslems and Christians and Jews."

The guide was explaining, with an edge of desperation in his voice, how the church had been built over the very spot. They went down into cool darkness, into a tunnel, a dank cave. The sudden descent was startling to McClain, who was not expecting it. Candles sunken in red glass cups lighted the way through a passage of black stone, then there was an opening, a cut in the wall, a square ringed with red lights. McClain stood in a puddle of water, gaping.

"This was it."

"The jolly manger," Wilson said. "Or so they say. Nobody knows for sure. But it *could* have been here. Certainly must have been somewhere around here."

"Funny. I always thought it was outside. All that business about no room at the inn."

The guide was watching them both with a sick strangled look on his face. He turned abruptly and went away, and when they came out of the place, he was sitting in the car smoking a cigarette.

When they were alone Wilson said: "Well?"

"Well?"

"Well, what do you think?"

McClain shrugged. "I don't know. It's . . . not what I expected."

"Are you impressed?"

"It's interesting."

"But you're not impressed."

"Well, as you say, we don't even know if this is the place."

"But if it were. Can you picture it? The whole bloody thing began right here. Right here."

Woman in childbirth. Lying there. McClain looked into the red lights, felt nothing, saw nothing.

"If this was the place, if this were the beginning," Wilson said dramatically.

McClain stood in the dark wet air, expecting to feel something. He felt nothing but a kind of eerie foolishness. His feet were wet, he was aware of sweat in his clothes.

"Let's go on back up," he said.

They found the guide sitting in the car, the door open, a moody look on his sunburned cheeks. He drove them silently back to Jerusalem.

"He didn't have far to go," McClain said.

"Who?"

"Christ. You can almost see Jerusalem from here. I thought it was farther away than that."

"The trouble with America," Wilson said grandly, "is that it's too damn spacy. You get so used to everything being five hundred miles away you can't be impressed by these short foreign distances. In those days, laddie, from here to there was a hell of a trip. Any way you look at it."

"Oh, hell yes," McClain said. "It was undeniably that. A hell of a trip."

"With a cross at the end."

McClain said: "How do you feel about that?"

"Oh well, you know." Wilson gaped again at two girls in red dresses.

"Were you raised Anglican?"

"Yep. Haven't been in years."

"You don't believe in it?"

"Well, now." Wilson squinted cautiously up to Heaven. "I wouldn't want to rub it in."

McClain grinned. They were driving down again toward the wall; he saw sunlight gleam from the Golden Dome.

"How about you?" Wilson said.

"No," McClain said.

Wilson looked at him, then suddenly smiled.

"Still, there's a bit left, isn't there? The old conditioning."

"Like a bloodstain," McClain said.

They stopped at the Dome of the Rock, where it was believed that Mohammed had ascended to Heaven. It was a white church, with another dirty priest standing by, his hand out. They stepped out onto a flat roof and looked back toward Jerusalem, and the guide started to talk again. Then they went down into the Garden of Gethsemane. The Garden was a small plot about thirty yards long, enclosed within a church, guarded by an iron fence. Within the garden there were flowers, geraniums, a few brutally twisted olive trees.

"This is where Judas turned Him in," Wilson said.

It was very quiet, there were no other tourists. But it was very hot. McClain touched the blistering iron rail and jerked his hand away.

"I've often wondered about that," Wilson said. "A problem in psychology. Now, if *you* knew a fella like that, would you turn him in? I mean, here's the point. We know there was a Christ, and there was a Judas, and this Judas followed him around and knew him pretty well, and then turned him in. That's about all we know for sure. Raising an interesting question. If this man was doing all that preaching, and performing all those miracles, Judas undoubtedly must have seen him. And if you ever saw a man work a miracle, would *you* turn him in?"

"Damn railing's hot. About how old do you suppose those olive trees are?"

"Oh, they're old enough. They live forever anyway. Well. Maybe a few hundred years. Not original. Although they try to say so, these buggers. But—would you turn him in?"

"Can't say. I guess it depends on the miracle."

"But don't you think it's a good point?"

"It's a point."

"Hm." Wilson was annoyed. "I think it's a damn good point."

"We don't even know if this was the Garden."

"Well, it was bound to be around here somewhere."

They drove down into Jerusalem, left the car parked outside the great Damascus Gate. Going in under the gate, the Turkish stones, they made two sharp turns, passed out into a narrow street lined with small stores and stalls. The guide explained that the gate had been built in the old Turkish system allowing no direct entrance, so that attackers breaking through the first gate would find themselves trapped between the walls. McClain was shaken by the smell: heat and garbage, urine, rotting food. But he looked around with intense interest.

To his left was an Arab paper stand, a book stall filled with gaudy leaflets, bright magazines. Down the street in front of him crowds of people moved on smooth rounded cobblestones, barelegged hawkers sat in front of small stalls. Down the right side of the street water was running, a slimy stinking trickle. He saw a small boy in rags sitting watchfully in the gutter.

Wilson was quiet. They walked along behind the guide. Close among small people McClain felt very big, conspicuous. They stopped for a drink in a narrow, cavernous store, were served a damp bottle of a winy orange liquid. He drank it, feeling a sickening lurch of his stomach, bathed in the stink of urine, rotting vegetables.

"Hard on the nose," Wilson said quietly. "But then, you should smell Calcutta."

"This probably hasn't changed much since those days."

"Not a whole hell of a lot. Pretty much this way since the Romans. Smaller then, at the time of Christ. There were other walls here. Nobody quite knows."

The guide had stopped to chat with an old man. The old man was grinning, glancing at them with glee. McClain watched the small boy across the street playing with his toes in the water of the gutter. There were sores on his legs like the punctures of bullet holes.

They moved on down the street. He passed a table set out into the street where four bearded men, young and strong, bigger than average, silently watched him come, judging him as to muscle. He knew the look. He stared into empty eyes.

"This is it," Wilson said. McClain walked into his back, bumping him. "The Via Dolorosa," Wilson said. "The Way of the Cross. See?" He pointed to a stone plaque set in the wall, the Roman numeral V engraved upon it, some lettering in Latin underneath. "This is the fifth station of the Cross. Do you know all that, about the stations?"

Wilson was obviously impressed. McClain looked up a very narrow street, only a few feet wide, branching to the right. There were smooth stone steps leading up and turning to the right so he could not see the end of the street. The walk was overhung by round arches of stones. Two monks in black led two donkeys past him, going up the path. A flock of small boys, giggling through ragged teeth, ran down, away from something. He looked up at the plaque, the numeral V, tried to recall. But he felt a peculiar vacancy.

"They're not sure of this either," Wilson said. The guide was standing off to the side with a look of dignity, of disgust. "But up there, theoretically, is Golgotha, where He was crucified."

"Can we go up?"

"No. This ends at the wall. What was probably the place of crucifixion is in Israel. But nobody knows for sure. Anyway this path goes up, and there's a knob at the end, so this was probably it."

McClain looked up the road. He had no desire to go up, but he wanted to look. There was another plaque a short way ahead. He walked that far and looked. He remembered a joke from a long time ago: I don't care *who* that cat thinks he is, he'll never get that cross up that hill. Thinking of that made him feel foolish.

"The Arab Legion held all this," Wilson said.

"What?"

"During the war. The Israelis were winning and the Arabs couldn't get together. Hussein withdrew the Arab Legion in a huff. But when Jerusalem was threatened, the Legion was sent back in and held most of the Old City. South of here the Israelis went all the way to the Dead Sea. North they made it to the Sea of Galilee. But the Legion held Jerusalem. British-trained, you know."

McClain was standing still looking up the path. He moved into the shadow of a stone arch, looked up suddenly at the blue sky. He could not picture anything. He had expected some sensation, but there was nothing. An uneasy vacancy. He looked down at Wilson, and there beyond him was the Reverend Kellogg and the daughter, Barbara, coming this way in the midst of a group of elderly people. The Reverend was open-mouthed, fascinated. The girl was obviously disgusted, stepping daintily through the filth, the smell. She looked up and saw McClain and made a move of disgust. McClain nodded.

"Want to go on?" Wilson said. Then he followed McClain's look. "Ho. The skinny one." The group in which the two Kelloggs moved paused at the first plaque, the letter V. An ancient, well-dressed guide began to lecture in subdued tones. The girl looked at McClain and gave him a languid smile, a wink. Wilson caught it and grinned. The guide suggested they go on.

"No," McClain said.

"But, but—" The guide was astounded, almost outraged. "But you have not seen Jerusalem."

"It's too hot," McClain said. "I'll see it some other time."

AT THE HOTEL two letters were waiting: one from Lise, one from Ravenel. He took them both into his hands with physical joy. Wilson saw the look on his face.

"From the girl? Amazing." He started to say something else, then stopped. He was perpetually warning McClain about the inconstancy of women. They didn't wait, any of them. Fires burned in all the smooth young bellies. But he watched McClain, as he had been watching him all the way back from the Way of the Cross, and he said nothing.

There was no mail for Wilson. There was never mail for Wilson.

"Think I'll pop into the bar. You going up?"

McClain nodded, unseeing. Wilson went away. The hotel lobby was a wide stone floor covered with faded rugs and ancient wicker chairs. All the people were gray-haired, gentle. McClain started to open Lise's letter but waited until he was upstairs in the room, the cool room, refraining. Then he opened it and read it while taking a bath and then read it again. Schoolgirl handwriting, round and jumbled, watery blue ink on paper of eggshell blue. She said that Ravenel was in love. A girl named Dawn, red-haired, quite young. A bit wild. Lise had seen Ravenel, wished him well, he'd asked for McClain. Then:

I thought sure you'd be home this spring. But then when you didn't come I was certain it would be this summer. But now I don't think you'll be back for a long time. Charley said he thought you might not come home at all. It's been such a long time. School is almost ready to begin again. My last year.

But I don't mean to complain, really. Actually I'm having a good time this summer. I've been dating a lot and eating a lot of peaches. Ugh. I don't think I'll ever again eat another peach.

I liked your last letter. Please tell me more about the things you see. You describe things so well. This Tony Wilson sounds nice. He's lucky to have you to keep him out of trouble.

I wish there was something exciting to tell you about from here but nothing much happens. All I ever do is just dance and then talk about silly things that wouldn't interest you. It must be very interesting where you are. I've always wanted to go to Jerusalem. Do you think you might be home by Christmas?

She signed it: Love, Lise. After he read it the second time he lay back in the tub staring at the rounded letters, some of the first warm grateful glow still in him. He lay thinking of her, of that one week after Christmas. Then he thought: she's tiring.

Her last year.

A long way off. I am a long way off. Seven thousand miles. More. He wondered how much time difference there was. Eight hours? She would be just getting up, early in the morning. Now she would be . . . it would be cool there, she in her bedroom in the huge house on the stately permanent street, white lace curtains blowing in the morning breeze: on the wall behind her, a pennant. First touch of autumn already in the air, the nights would be cool around Labor Day. This was . . . Friday. She would be dating tonight. She was twenty years old. Almost twenty-one. Her last year.

Come home.

Is it home?

He put the letter down. I'm a long way from home. He thought suddenly of the Way of the Cross, the Via Dolorosa. The heat there, the donkeys. Nothing. Odd. But what were you expecting?

I don't know.

He read Ravenel's letter:

I'm marrying the lass come spring. No jokes. Nobody around here is yet over the shock. Least of all me. But she's a marvelous girl. I wish you knew her. Also wish you were here. Must admit I'm getting nervous. There are wheels within wheels. Tell you more when you're here. . . .

There was an attempt at humor, a forced lightness. He loves her, McClain thought. Ravenel in love. He read:

Saw little Lise the other day. Blonde and bushy-tailed. You ought to write more often. I feel sorry for the poor kid. If you don't plan on coming back you ought to tell her. But excuse me for sticking the red nose in. I just thought you ought to know she's still Queen of the Torchbearers. Never could understand it. Girl like that hung on the likes of you. But I digress. The wedding will be a blast. . . .

He read it again, then put it down. He thought: she's getting tired.

He got out of the tub and dried himself, stood staring at the little sign over the mirror which begged guests to conserve water until the autumn rains. The autumn rains. He went to the window, looked out across the stone wall into the gray hills of Israel. It must be something to be here when the rain begins. Smell of water on baked ground. Raw smell of revived earth. I'd love to feel rain again. I'm a long way from home.

He sat in a chair and had a cigarette. He felt a gathering weight of depression. Two very good letters. But he had prepared himself for her to forget him and not to write, and now she was still writing after all this time and he could sense her growing weariness and he was not quite prepared for that.

He stared out the window, felt the strangeness of the country come at him with a new shock. The land was alien, Martian. He was alone. He looked down and saw a line of tanks come around the bend, gray tanks moving along the wall. They came up the street, hatches open, guns pointed straight ahead. They didn't look like U.N. tanks. There were no markings. Something was happening. The tanks rolled by the flowers in front of the hotel. He looked back down the street, but he saw no soldiers. The tanks passed.

McClain stared down at the blue letter in his hand. Women. War. Blood and sex. That was what it was all about. You screwed when you could, and you fought for everything you got, and sometimes there were flowers. Even in the desert. He had a sudden desire to get back out into the desert, into clean flat silence. The Via Dolorosa. The way of pain. Means nothing at all. He was all alone. Long way from home.

He went down into the lobby just at sunset. He sensed the strain immediately. The old people were moving about with tight, scared faces. He couldn't find Wilson. By the tobacco counter he bumped into Barbara Kellogg. She was breathless, delighted. It was a pleasure to see a clean girlish face.

"Did you hear? We're confined to the hotel! We're not even allowed out in the street!"

She stared hungrily at his face, feeding on the excitement.

"What happened?"

"There's been some shooting up there somewhere." She waved vaguely with her right hand. "Isn't that something? We're not even allowed out in the garden. This big Swede came in here just a while back and said we had to stay here. They've even blocked the roads!"

"Did he explain anything?"

"No. But did you see those tanks? Golly. We're right in the middle of it. Poor Papa. He's scared right out of his skull." She giggled with rapture. "Oh, there he is now. Look at him, isn't he a gas? See you later, alligator." She winked lewdly and moved off toward her father, who was standing in the lobby, beckoning to her urgently. He'll scream to the consulate, McClain thought.

He wondered what was going on. He asked the clerk, but the man said nothing new, was obviously worried, was the kind of man who automatically makes people more worried just in trying to calm them down. McClain felt himself growing a familiar calm. It was good to feel trouble coming, action in the air. He grinned at himself: good old neurotic. He hunted down Wilson, found him in the bar. He was talking with a rather attractive woman in a pink candy-striped dress that was much too long. A schoolteacher, Mc-Clain thought. She was.

No one knew anything. There was a rumor that the King of Jordan had been assassinated by Israeli agents. They had dinner in a room filled with tense people who were rapidly—as nothing happened—beginning to enjoy the tension. Wilson was working heavily on the schoolteacher, whose name was Miss Sales. She was in her late thirties, rather frail-boned, soft dreams flickering in vague blue eyes. She didn't seem to mind that Wilson was obviously no older than twenty-five. She leaned on his words, spoke in a voice that was fragrant, hesitant. Her eyes were too close together, she had spaces between her teeth. McClain waited, saying very little. After a while he realized he was listening for the sound of guns. He excused himself and went out into the garden.

As he stepped toward the front walk, two soldiers moved out in front of him. He couldn't tell what uniforms they wore. They stopped in front of him and said something in a language he could neither understand nor identify, and shook their heads. He tried to explain that he only wanted to wait in the garden. But they wanted him to go in. He went on up to the balcony on the third floor. There were lights in Israel, faint white sparks far off in the dark hills.

He stayed on the balcony for a long time. The night was clear, without a moon. The dark of the moon was a good time for an attack. He remembered the feel of the cold gunstock, smell of gun oil, footsteps coming in the snow. Blood and sex. He began to understand that he had made a remarkable discovery. We fought all the time, and all we ever talked about was women. We have to fight, but we want to love. Not love, he amended, not love. We want to screw.

He looked up into the black sky of Jerusalem. There was too much light from below; he couldn't see the stars. Over there Christ walked. Here. Upon this ground. But nobody knows anything any more. He went up that hill, and died. McClain wanted to see it. Poor struggling body, ragged clothes, filthy crowds. Three of them crucified on that hill over there. But they crucified thousands in those days. All those crosses all over Italy, all the way to the sea. A highway of crosses. And all so long ago. Just another day in the life of the world.

He was startled by a giggle. Barbara Kellogg came out of the dark.

"Whatchu doin' up heah?" she said, very very southern. "Can you see anythin'?"

"Nope." He smelled the raw perfume, saw the bright dress swirl in the faint light from the hall.

"Ah saw yo frayund with that school teachuh," she accused. "That's scandalous. She's old enough to be his mothuh."

"Everybody needs mothering," McClain said.

She giggled again. The chuckle was low, throaty. In the dark he couldn't quite remember her face; she seemed somebody new.

"Isn't it excitin'?" she breathed.

"Not yet it isn't. It could be."

"What you think could happen?"

"Well, somebody could start shelling this place."

"They could what?"

"There must be guns up on that hill across the way. If the truce has been broken, it could get messy."

"You don't think they *would?*"

She was shocked almost out of the accent.

"Hell—" He started to say that they wouldn't, of course, that this was just another minor border scare, probably caused by a rumor. Then he shrugged dramatically. The sweet mist of perfume sucked at him.

"Oh my." She backed away from the railing.

"Hell with it," he said, bravely. "Would you like to dance?"

"Oh. Oh, ah *couldn't.*" In the midst of fear the coyness survived.

He could not see it, but he knew she was fluttering her eyes. "If we went down and Daddy saw me. . . ."

"I don't mean down there. Right here."

He stepped forward, reaching for her. She didn't move away. When he put his arms around her she came weakly against him, suddenly very fragile.

"But, we haven't any music."

"Hum," he said. "Like in the movies." He held her closer. She was thin but surprisingly soft. "I haven't danced with anybody in a long time."

She put her arm behind him, found his hand. She giggled again. "If Daddy was to see me."

"Hell with Daddy."

She chuckled into his throat. He felt the trembling of her body, the gathering heat.

"What would you like me to hum?"

"You name it."

"I know one they're all singin' back home. Everything's fast now, but this is nice and slow." She hummed in a nasal whisper something he did not recognize. They began to dance slowly, hardly moving from where they stood, pressing in together.

She pulled her head back. He could not see her face, but there was a point of bright light in each of her eyes.

"You know, you're kind of nice," she said.

Later he said: "Let's head for my room."

She was scandalized. She came. Inside the room he didn't turn on the light. He kissed her by the window. She was afraid, began losing her poise. He went on kissing her. Now it was time. She said she couldn't. Not here. She kissed him back. "You got a bottle?" she said. He gave her a long drink of warm brandy. They made love in the bed in quick hungry movements. Blood and sex, women and war. He knew she was thinking of her father, downstairs. He knew also that part of why she did it was because they were in Jerusalem. And she would never see him again. He thought: and I also, Jerusalem? Remembering the whores of Athens, but this was much better. She sat up on the edge of the bed.

"Let me 'nother drink."

He gave it to her, took one long one himself. Blood and sex. Good old blood and good old sex.

"Oh my. I don't know how I'll face you tumorruh. I don't know what came over me."

"I'll tell you what came over you," McClain said. "Me."

She giggled again. It was really a rather charming giggle, when you were used to it. "You. Hey now. How long you goin' to be heah?"

"Who knows? They have the roads blocked."

"Oh. I forgot. Well, now listen. We have to be careful. When we go downstairs, don't let on like you even *know* me."

"Hell, your father knows I know you."

"Well you be careful."

"Right. And you." He reached for her.

"You be careful. Now."

She slipped out into the dark hall. He bathed again, feeling at rest. And thought of Lise. Who would be doing now, at this moment, what? This same thing? A pang of something, not guilt, not even pain, went through him. Where she lived it was only . . . about two in the afternoon. She would be picking peaches. He smiled into the dark. I love her.

The words flared, silent firecrackers in a quiet mind. He had not thought those words in a long time. But he was beginning to feel strange. Something had happened today, he did not know what it was. He lay back in the bathtub and thought: it's a rare thing to be hopping out of bed with one, and suddenly realizing you love another one.

But in the silence of the mind he felt no guilt. He went back out onto the balcony, smoking a cigarette. It was a long night. Toward midnight there was a breeze from the west, the wind bathed him with the soft desert smell. He was still sitting there when Wilson found him much later. Wilson told him a colorful tale about the schoolteacher, who had promised herself for the next night. McClain did not mention Barbara Kellogg.

"Hum. I sure hope all the borders stay closed. Makes a lovely shrouded little moment. Love under the guns and all that."

"What have you heard?"

"Oh, everything's closed. Although that may still be a rumor. They say Syria and Turkey closed up. Also Iraq and Lebanon. May be a few days before we move on."

"Have you any idea what's really going on?"

"No way to tell. There was some sort of raid up around Galilee. God knows which side started it. But it seems to be big stuff. Rumors everywhere."

"I hope we don't have to stay here long."

"Well now, why not? Couldn't be more comfortable."

"I liked the desert."

Wilson was silent. He meditated. "Does grow on you. Has a sort of roasted charm. Can't quite explain. The bloody Arabs love it. Some white men too. Ever read Lawrence?"

"No."

"You should. Damn strange duck."

"The city stinks. God awful smell."

"Welcome to the Holy Land."

"I didn't think it would smell like that."

"The odor of putrefied saints."

Wilson rose, walked to the railing. He stood for a moment looking down across the quiet courtyard, then out across the night buried wall toward the tiny lights of Israel.

"God. We're really getting on."

"That we are," McClain said.

"Did you think we'd make it this far?"

"Hell yes."

"No you didn't." Wilson eyed him. "I don't think you did."

McClain shrugged.

"I tell you one thing," Wilson said. "I'm damn glad you came. I'd never have made it far without you."

"Would you have gone on alone?"

"Sure."

"Dysentery and all?"

"Yep."

"That would have been dumb."

"True."

"Why?"

Wilson took a long pull from his cigarette. The red light glowed briefly on the flat dusty face, the curling beard. An excitable man: proud, shy, arrogant, uncertain. Somewhere tucked deep in the back of their gear was a fragment of a novel he'd been writing when McClain arrived in London, but he had not shown it or talked about it. They did not ask each other probing questions. McClain, looking at him, remembered him suddenly as he had been in the war: an actor moving through the right lines in the wrong play. The British accent didn't fit the American infantry. He had no coordination and had never learned to drill and was hopeless with a rifle, terrified but stubborn. And so here we are in Asia. He and I. Friends.

"I never did think you'd come," Wilson said. "I was always sure something would come up. And then even after you got here I knew for certain something would happen and you'd bug out. You'd get sick or turn blue or something. . . ."

"Blue?"

"The blues. I mean,"—he glanced at McClain, went on hastily— "like that morning when I found you in that damned gulley. They were digging you out, you know, and the first I saw you, nobody had cleaned your face and you looked thoroughly dead. There was dirt in your eyes. Two pools of dirt. I thought sure you'd had it."

He was beginning to sound very British.

"Well the first thing I thought was, well, he'll never make it now, he'll never get to see it."

"See what?"

"Oh Christ, you know. See the whole thing. Just wander. 'Round the next bend. You know jolly well what I'm talking about. Or else why did you come? You have to wander around and see as much of it as you can, to see it as it really is, to make up your mind about it. A few years now and there'll be supermarkets in the desert and a four-lane highway with goddam neon signs running right through Samarkand. But now it's still there."

McClain smiled.

"Don't you feel," Wilson said, "when you get to the end of it, that a man owes it to himself to see as much of it as he can, just to get out and look at it, just to wander and watch?"

"Yep," McClain said.

"Simply because," Wilson struggled with the inexpressible thing, "just because"—he waved his hands vaguely, then stopped, slipped, his voice took a sudden light shift like a fighter sidestepping—"why because, as the fella said on the way to the mountain, because it's there."

He paused. "You know," he said thoughtfully, "in the cold clear light of the evening, that *does* sound rather profound."

"What will you do when you get there?"

"Oh I don't know. May settle down with some Eurasian beauty. No more lovely lasses in the world, you know. Wait on you hip and thigh, wash your feet like jolly old Christ, or was that Judas? I've thought of teaching, out of my travels. Then again, I might just possibly roam the barrier reef, or the Aussie desert. Might even go on to Bali, but that doesn't really appeal. I've never been much for that jungle rot—oh, I say!" He chuckled at his own pun. "Jungle rot."

"I can see you in Singapore," McClain said. "Genghis Wilson."

"Hee. Wouldn't I make a lovely despot?"

"Not if you have to keep hopping off to the bushes."

"Ugh." Then Wilson grinned craftily. "Say, by the way, how do you feel?"

McClain stood up. "Sleepy."

"You feel no approaching need to defecate? No slow turning of the bowel?"

"Not a turn."

"No sensation of impending crap? No sense that somewhere in the old gut, bacilli romp?"

McClain laughed. Wilson turned back toward Israel, the desert night. "Ah," he said softly, deep in his throat, " 'tis a lovely night." Then he said: "Jerusalem."

McClain recalled a hymn from long ago, a small boy singing with a strained throat, in a cold church: Jerusalem, Jerusalem, oh turn thee to the Lord thy God.

Wilson said: "I wonder what really happened, do you know? To the bones of Christ?"

TWO

THROUGHOUT SEPTEMBER AND OCTOBER they moved slowly eastward. They stopped at all the places Wilson wanted to see: Petra, Palmyra, Baalbek. The border into Iraq was closed; they had to take the northern route, back up through Turkey almost to the Black Sea, east along the Russian border through Iran to Afghanistan. The

Russian border was also closed. There was no other passage east to India but that one narrow black road that ran just south of Mount Ararat. The weight of all Russia always to the north was a pressure on both of them. They drove every day in the shadow of that wall: wire and mines and ploughed guarded earth. One of the places Wilson had always wanted to see was Samarkand, the tomb of Tamerlane, but no one was allowed into Russia from the south. There was only one other place they could not see: the battlefield of Gaugamela, where Alexander fought; that was in Iraq just east of Nineveh.

They went on being sick; there was no help for it. They no longer tried to avoid it, except that they used chlorine tablets in their water. They ate whatever was available along the road: rice, lamb, tea. Occasionally they broke out a tin of something from home, and the best of all turned out to be half a dozen cans of thick beef stew, most of which they ate in the desert in Iran. They were steadily weakening. They looked on themselves as lean and hard, and for a while were proud of it. They had lost weight, their muscles were hard and their skins beaten tough by the weather. McClain let his beard grow, finally, going north through Turkey, and so they were both scrawny and hairy and liked the look of each other: explorers, adventurers, men who'd been back up country to the edge of the world.

But they were weakening. When they moved abruptly out of the desert and into the mountains, when there was frost one morning and a wind blew from the north, the cold was a shock that was stunning. They could not get used to it. They shivered all night, wrapped in the sleeping bags, and when they crossed Iran, they moved south, through Shiraz and Isfahan. It took them a long while to get used to the cold, and McClain, who was born in New England and had never before minded cold weather, dreamed of the beach and a burning sun.

· They passed through Meshed and crossed the border into Afghanistan sometime late in October. They did not know exactly what day it was. They had been on the road for almost five months and had traveled, according to the odometer in the Rover, almost eleven thousand miles. What they remembered was not so much the ruins, Roman or Persian, but the barren miles, the rock and the dust, the small mud villages that were everywhere, perched in the earth, clinging to rock, the small people in the wind, flakes of green

ground, all those miles and the flatness of the desert and the people
living somehow on the earth, and snow in the mountains, and a hot
cup of tea in the morning, and the frost. Afghanistan was the top
of the world. Winter was coming down off the Himalayas; you
could feel it in the air in the mornings and sometimes even at noon,
a black raw odor of a cold so vast it made the hackles crawl. They
moved east through the mountains toward Kabul, the Khyber Pass.
The land there was the most rugged of all; the road ran straight
through streams already glazed with ice. They had to cross sagging
wooden bridges over terrifying gorges, and the road was a wagon
track filling with snow. They began to hurry, for the first time since
Europe. It was necessary to get through the Khyber Pass and down
into India before the winter came down.

They reached Kabul in the last week of October. They checked
at the embassy but there was no mail. They relaxed with some
Americans who taught at the University there, and were entertained
at the embassy, and McClain felt that they had come a long long
way and was ready to rest. The winter was holding off. Kabul was
a city out of the past, at the edge of the world. He could lie in his
bed in the morning, a real bed with a feather mattress, and look
north to the mountains of the Hindu Kush. Beyond the mountains
were Russia and China. McClain looked and did not hunger. He
began to understand how tired he really was.

They had been in Kabul only two days when Wilson decided to
make a quick run north to the border. The road was still passable;
Mazar-i-Sherif was only a day or so away. It was the road to
Samarkand.

The embassy warned him, officially, that the trip was dangerous.
It was a brutal road and there was no way of knowing how long the
weather would hold off, and the tribesmen in that country were the
least "controllable" of all. Wilson happily readied the car, which he
had come to admire and trust. He said to McClain: "We've got to
go, man. It's the top of the world. From here on in, it's all down-
hill. Once you get down through the Khyber it's open and flat all
the way to Calcutta. This is the last chance. You'll never see country
any more remote than this, and we've come all this way, and I want
to see this one thing. The road to Samarkand. Listen, you don't
have to come if you don't want. It won't take me long. I want to
drive over that same damn route through the Hindu Kush as far as

the border and at least *look* across. After this, dammit, it's all down-hill."

So McClain went. He did not go because he thought Wilson would need protection or because the embassy was right and that if he didn't go he'd have to admit to himself that he was afraid. He did not worry too much about either the weather or the embassy. The embassy did not want to have to go looking for lost Americans or be responsible in any way and so was taking no chances and you couldn't blame them. And as to weather, McClain also had faith in the car. He went more than anything else because Wilson was dead right: it was the wildest country left on earth. It was the top of the world.

THE ROCKS VANISHED like knives in a flat gray sky. There was no way to tell the direction of the sun. The road crawled up past the timberline and in and out of the mist, ten thousand feet high, and the mountains on each side rose up in black walls and ended in the sky. Rime ice formed on the windshield; they had to stop and scrape it off, and standing by the hood looking up into the mist, they could hear an odd roar like falling water, but it couldn't be that because everything was frozen.

Late that first morning Wilson said: "Christ, I've got a hell of a headache."

"Want me to drive?"

"Would you mind?"

"Hell no. I've been sitting here scared to death. I damn near put a hole in the floor stepping on the brake."

"I'm just as good as you are, by God."

"You have the reflexes"—McClain grinned, feeling his face cracking and drawing in the cold—"of a barrel of glue."

Wilson mumbled defensively, moved around to the back of the car, and hunted for the pillbox. When he sat back down in the cab, he looked at McClain with a frozen, disgusted face.

"Dammit. I must have gobbled every goddam pill known to man."

"Including ratpills," McClain said.

"Blah." Wilson stuck his tongue out. "Kee-rist, it's come up quite a chill. Have we got enough anti-freeze in that radiator?"

"Down to zero. I wasn't expecting this last little jaunt."

"Well dammit, why the hell didn't you check it? You're the goddam mechanic around here."

"Sorry," McClain said.

"This'd be a hell of a place to freeze up."

"That it would. But we're running most of the time, and when we're not running, the car's good to zero and a bit below. We're all right. We can cover it at night."

"You should have checked it. I can't think of every goddam thing."

McClain started to drive.

"Goddam nitwit move," Wilson said.

McClain said nothing. He looked over at Wilson from time to time and watched him slouch lower in the seat and knew he was getting sick again. He thought: we might as well go back. But in a little while Wilson was feeling better, and so they went on into the Bamian Valley and camped there for the night. They slept on mats in a post house of the Afghan mail, and when they came out in the morning it was bitterly cold, but the car started without trouble.

Wilson still had the headache. McClain watched him gulp down more codeine at breakfast—tea and bread—and said, "Listen, that stuff is addicting."

Wilson looked at him, just looked at him, and McClain knew he was sick.

"We stay here today," McClain said.

Wilson nodded. They went back in the post house, and Wilson sat on a bench and stared dully at the wall. They drank more tea and then noticed that there was sunlight outside. By eight o'clock Wilson had revived and looked much better and said, "Hell, let's get going. I'm chipper, laddie, I'm chipper." McClain went outside and the day was so clear and fine that it was a different world. Wilson wandered on out of the hut and stretched and grinned, and so automatically they agreed to go on. It was just a headache after all. Not anywhere near as bad as the dysentery. They would be at Mazar-i-Sherif by nightfall, and that was as far north as they would ever go.

North of Bamian the road followed a river into the mountains west of Kafiristan, where the peaks rose up past an altitude of sixteen thousand feet. The river was the Oxus. It rose in the Uzbek marshes a thousand miles to the north and flowed down from here into India and south into the great Indus and all the way down into the Arabian Sea at Karachi. The road followed the river along the steepest cliffs McClain had ever seen. For a while Wilson talked about Tamerlane and Genghis Khan, the code of the Mongols, how a Mongol army was organized. He was proud of the Mongols, and said they'd been underestimated. They were never hordes, they knew exactly what they were doing. There was never an army quite like them. He explained how the code worked, and how they fought their battles, and about the Mongol roads and the Mongol peace, and all the while he talked, McClain listened and drove with cold nerve and great care. They passed a donkey train moving south, then a string of camels. Then there were clouds to the north and east, and Wilson said, "Goddamit, that headache's back."

It was at about that same time that McClain began to feel a headache of his own. It began right behind his eyes and spread to the back of his neck. He was beginning to feel the tension of all that driving along the edge of the cliffs, and the clouds were beginning to worry him. Wilson slumped down in the seat and said. "Goddamit, we should have brought more pills." McClain's headache got worse; he stopped to take some codeine. It was good to stop the car, and he got out and walked around at just that moment when the sun was covered by a cloud, and he felt the cold float over him in a deadening wave, as if it had been waiting.

There was a thermos of hot tea in the back of the truck. He took it out and washed down two of the codeine tablets, and then, going around to the front seat, he got his first clear look at Wilson.

Wilson's mouth was open, he was breathing in sudden pants. His face had a peculiar, shiny look. McClain looked closer.

"Tony. You've got a fever."

"I have. I have definitely got a fever-o."

McClain swore.

"How do you feel?"

"Stupid question."

McClain handed him the codeine, the thermos of tea. He looked at the red plastic cup and thought that they'd both been drinking from it, and put up a hand and rubbed his eyes, thinking of his own headache. And beginning to get organized, he thought: it's hours yet to Khanabad. But that is better than anywhere else. That's closest. Unless the weather turns. In which case we'll find a post house. But there aren't any doctors in post houses. No doctors anywhere. Might be one in Khanabad. No. Not likely. Doctors in Kabul.

"No chance for Kabul."

"Well, it isn't bad yet."

"Lousy luck," Wilson said.

"Gobble the codeine. Might's well move on. Wait. I'll get some aspirin."

"What the hell good is aspirin?"

"Brings the fever down."

Wilson blinked, wiped his face. "I do have a fever. I definitely have one fever."

"Got to head for the next town."

"Righto."

"Do you feel anything else but the fever?"

"Stomach's a bit queasy."

"How long have you had it, dammit?"

"I don't quite know. Wait a minute." He pulled himself out of the car and walked over to the side of the road. "Just like to take a look around, long as we've stopped."

It was a magnificent view. They could see clouds breaking over the rocks above them like great white frozen waves. The silence had that same odd roar.

"Let's get moving."

They drove into a freezing, blowing mist. Wilson fell asleep. McClain drove on, trying to remember the symptoms, what they meant, any treatment he could give. Headache, fever, nausea. Headache followed by fever and nausea. But he did not know enough and he never had known. He could not think clearly because he had to concentrate on the road and not hurry. There was nothing he could do but get somewhere in out of the cold as quickly as he could. Headache and fever. His mind there was a blank. He didn't know anything. He couldn't do anything. Charley Ravenel was a doctor now. No doctor in Khanabad. But there would be drugs. Antibiotics. Antibiotics would do it. Or Wilson would do it himself. A bug from the food. Too cold now for most things. The climate much healthier. I'm very tired. I've got a headache.

He drove with intense concentration. There was the sound of the windshield wiper and the look of the instruments, and the steady grinding lovely roar of the blessed gutty engine. He had to get out to scrape the windshield, and when he got back into the cab, Wilson was in spasms. He was having a convulsion. McClain said aloud, "Oh my God." He got a blanket out of the back of the truck and wrapped Wilson in it and went on driving. Wilson fell against him; McClain pushed him back and drove with a hand on him. The blanket slipped down and McClain stopped and tucked it back on, tried to think of a way to tie it. Wilson's eyes were partly open, but he was unconscious. His breath had a bitter, dreadful smell. McClain touched his forehead and recoiled from the unnatural heat. Wilson had spit up yellow phlegm and chunks of something foamy and white; it ran into his beard and down the side of his face. McClain had nothing to wipe it with, did not want to touch it. That'll wait, he thought, and went on driving.

His own headache began to swell with a red bloating pressure just back of his eyes. But they were passing trees now, black trees and bushes. They were going down. It couldn't be very far. He passed through a small village, gray huts tucked under a huge white rock. There were no lights, but he saw two people standing by the road. Two small round shapeless forms. They waved at him. He went right on driving and thought: I should have stopped. But there was nothing there. There was nothing but a place to lie down. I can still drive.

The road ran down through wet ground; he was almost stuck. He shifted to low and the car pulled up through it and up onto the jolting rock. It was becoming very dark. The mist began to freeze again on the windshield and his headache took hold of his head like a fire smoldering through the dark coals of his brain. He was having trouble seeing. He drove down into a deep grove of trees; it was so dark he had to turn on the lights. He felt the first dull weakness in his arms, his own exhaustion. This was foolish, he thought, this was so goddam foolish.

Wilson had his second convulsion. His body jerked and twitched and struck out; his knees hit the dashboard. McClain stopped the car. He had trouble walking around to the other side; he was too dizzy. This won't do, he thought. We have to stop. Wilson grunted and shuddered. McClain stood by helpless.

When he drove on a little way, he knew that he had to stop. He was functioning within a very small space, one incorrupt cave in the center of the pain. He could feel a blackness coming and his own impending doom, and this thing in him that was cold and clear and impersonal said, all right, now you stop somewhere and get warm. Turn back and go back to that village. Go somewhere and get off your feet and get something in you. Sleep, rest. Both of you. Convulsions are bad. He'll more than likely die. When people have convulsions they usually die. And soon, the fever for you. Rest. You'll go off the road and wreck. Rest.

He drove looking for a place to turn around. After a long long time he found a flat clearing and when he swung the car, the lights flared slowly across the roadside and he saw a hut. A low gray building. He kept the lights on it, looking at it. He saw no people. He sat for a moment looking out of that one quiet cave, which was growing steadily smaller, steadily darker, and knew that he would never make it back to the village above. He drove off the road and up to the hut and killed the engine. The hut was empty and dark. There were no windows, but there was a wooden bench and a table. McClain no longer felt the cold. He dragged Wilson out of the car and into the hut, and noticed that he got the phlegm on him, but he did not think about it. He went back and forth to the car, dragging blankets and the Coleman lamp, and thought he'd make some tea, but he was too tired. He got Wilson on the floor, lying on blankets, covered, and got the lamp lighted, and saw the walls wriggling, the white stone flowing back and forth like liquid being stirred. He wrapped himself in a blanket and rested.

He came awake abruptly. For one long second his mind was clear, and then the pain clamped his skull with a savage joy. He saw Wilson lying directly in front of him, the blankets thrown back, one long arm pointing toward him. Wilson's mouth was open, and there was more scum on his beard and teeth. McClain looked clinically. He was breathing. His forehead did not seem really warm. He's better. McClain felt a weakening, softening sigh. He'll get better. He'll get over it. He's a good boy.

Now McClain could make tea. It took all his energy to pull out the stove and light it, get the water jug, fill a small pot. When he went outside, he staggered and rolled, bumping against the door, the car, and it was snowing outside. Very light fine flakes that were pleasant against the face, soft and sweet like a cool dusting. He was not cold. He knew he had a fever himself and his brain thought: which is better, to heap himself in blankets or let the cold fight the fever? Blankets. Must keep him warm. Why? I think the blankets are better. But why? Don't they sometimes use ice to bring down a fever?

He forgot all about that and went on in and made the tea. He drank some, but he could not get any into Wilson. Wilson was shuddering and moaning, and McClain comforted him and put the blanket over him and fell asleep.

When he awoke the next time, Wilson's eyes were open in a flickering, peculiar light. His face was smooth and calm, and McClain thought for a moment he was dead, and then Wilson looked at him and blinked. The peculiar light was only the lamp dying down. McClain pumped it up, grinning at Wilson. He talked to him, and Wilson just looked at him, his eyes soft and dreamy. Then Wilson talked but McClain couldn't make out what he was saying. He bent down very close, and Wilson said: Special. Very special.

"What's special?"

"Very far."

"I want you to drink some tea."

Wilson blinked and focused on him, and saw him. "Tom."

"Yes, sir."

"Is . . . very far?"

"It's too damn far," McClain said.

Wilson nodded. "Tom. You take good care."

"You drink some tea."

"I want. . . ."

McClain had the tea but Wilson wasn't looking at it. He was looking over his shoulder at the wall, and his eyes were closing.

"Write me a letter," said Wilson.

McClain tried to get him up to drink the tea.

"Promise write letter," Wilson said.

"Sure," McClain said.

"Want t'hear from you."

His voice faded away. He was asleep on McClain's shoulder. McClain held him there and was still holding him there sometime after that when he died.

McClain held him for a while after that. He felt the last shudder and knew what it was, the clicking in the throat, the spasm, the sigh. But he went on holding him, and the space in his mind closed down to one tiny hole, a pinprick of light. Then it widened again and he lowered Wilson to the ground and made the mechanical check, the pulling back of the eyelid, the touching of the wrist. Then slowly he disengaged himself and set Wilson properly with his arms by his sides, under the blanket, but did not cover his face, didn't think of it, but backed away and looked at the beard showing streams of red in the steady light of the hissing lamp.

McClain sat and looked at him, and felt something black and evil coming up out of his mind, some blackness so bitter and suffocating that it quenched the pain, it drove out sickness. Moving slowly, carefully, because he was infinitely tired and his arms felt not quite whole, not quite attached to him, and would function only under brutal command, he poured himself one more cup of the tea, the red tea with the flakes floating soggy and black, and drank it, and looked at Wilson, and was suddenly so immensely, unbearably sorry that he could not stand it; he pulled back and heaved the cup and the filthy leaves with all his strength, heaved it all away, and then put his face in his hands and said things and cried, and opened his eyes into a burning, blurry, terrible world, and in among the pain and the darkness, the rising black, the awful sadness, he felt the first coming of a monstrous rage.

The snow fell all that night and all the next day. McClain endured. He enjoyed it. He lay chuckling in the dark and fighting the thing off, knowing it couldn't get him. Nothing could get him. He fed on his hatred and his anger, and so endured. He could feel himself grow stronger as the thing got worse, as his vision went, as the enfolding arms came down. He remembered his mother telling him that once when she was sick, as a child, she had looked up at the bedposts and seen the angels there, two angels sitting and smiling, and had thought she was going to die. But McClain opened his eyes and saw no angels. There was something grinning in the dark, but it wasn't an angel, and he grinned back and hugged himself and chuckled with a ferocious impregnable glee, because nobody could get him. They would not take him if he would not go, and there was something in him so impossibly strong that he knew they could never get him, and he lay back and smiled with an angelic joy, a crafty and sadistic mirth.

The second night was very cold. The lamp went out and he couldn't light it. He slept where he lay. In the morning his vision was clear and he saw Wilson asleep under the blankets. He said good morning. He made tea. It tasted strange, he could not finish it. He looked at Wilson lying there, and he looked so much at peace. He asked Wilson: "What do you see now, Tony? Can you make anything out?"

He sat there and began to be aware that he was cold. His body came back on slowly: tremors in the muscles, twitchings in the nerves. He could feel pain in his bones and the bitter fur in his mouth.

"I'm better, Tony," he said. He lay trying to think of what to do. He tried to stand up but he couldn't make it. There was no feeling in his feet, it was like standing on a painful cloud. He fell down and tripped over the lamp and broke the glass.

He sat up again and said, "I've got to drink that tea." He used the last of the water and got the tea down. He slept.

When he awoke again it was still daylight, but the cold had gotten into him. He reached back into the reserve of anger, which was illimitable and inexhaustible but still very far away. He could use it, but he had to reach for it. That got him to his feet, and he grinned craftily, saying, "See? see?" and staggered around the hut. He went out to the car through heavy snow and tried to start it. Nothing happened. The key turned but there was no sound. He tried only once. He looked at the sky and grinned. "That's a hell of a trick," he said. He went around to the back of the car and got out a tin of hash. He opened it and ate the whole thing cold and made some more tea from melted snow and sat looking at Wilson. That was no good, because when he looked at Wilson he started to cry.

Then he noticed it was darker outside. He went out and balanced against the wall, staring up into the flat gray ceiling of the sky. There was a wind coming up the road, so cold that it hurt his lungs to breathe it. Now this was serious. He stepped back inside the hut and stood there. He was not afraid, but one had to take this seriously. Up to now they had been foolish, but another night like last night would be pushing it too much. He was too weak and too cold. He went out to the car again and found another can of something to eat. It was also hash. He ate it with a mechanical calm, putting it inside him just as exactly as he would fuel a car. Then he wrapped himself in the blanket, putting it up around the head to cover his ears, and sat for a moment out of the wind to get what warmth he could, to store it up. He looked at Tony Wilson with the gentle, compassionate look of a father looking down on a sleeping child.

"I better go, Tony. If I stay here it might get too cold, and there isn't any heat. I'm going to walk up to that village. I'll be back in a little while. I'll come back for you."

Then he went out the door and had to stop. It was cold back there, so cold, so dark. He looked back in on the form on the floor. Too far, he came too far. It was always there waiting. But then he was crying again.

And so he began the walk back up the road toward the village that was up there somewhere beyond the trees. He had enough strength to make it; he would be all right if there wasn't any more snow and if it didn't get too dark before he found it. But even that wouldn't make any difference because snow or not, cold or not, there was a village up there and it wasn't that far away and he would find it, because they couldn't get him if he didn't want to go, and he walked along grinning, knowing how serious it was, but grinning all the same, plodding through the deep snow up the long road that ran under the pines and over the marsh and up the steep rocky hills toward the village.

WILSON was buried in a field north of Khanabad. The service was given by a Buddhist priest, but Wilson's head was marked with a rough wooden cross. McClain stayed for a week in Khanabad and then went out to see the grave on the day he left, but the field was deep under new snow, and even the cross was covered.

McClain drove back to Kabul. He sold the car to the American couple at the University, and kept only a very few things: some of Wilson's clothes, his camera, the unfinished novel. He wrote a brief letter from Kabul to the uncle, the drama critic. He started letters to Lise and Ravenel, but never finished them. He left Kabul on the tenth of November, traveling by bus through the Khyber to Peshawar. From there he moved by train across India, by boat to Singapore. He remained in Singapore only one day, long enough to book passage on a freighter going home. He spent that last afternoon drinking good Scotch and water on the balcony of a bar which overlooked the seething street, the damp fragrance. At the American Express office there was a letter from the drama critic.

Dear Mr. McClain:

I am indebted to you for your account of Anthony's death. I agree with you that he should remain buried in that country, as I can see no useful purpose to be served in moving him. I am of course deeply grateful for your efforts in his behalf, and congratulate you on your own recovery.

As to the questions you raise concerning his effects: I have been in contact with Anthony's lawyers, and have been advised that there is a letter dated 4 June 1954, in his hand, in which he names you as sole beneficiary. I have been assured that this constitutes a legal will. I assume therefore that you may make whatever disposition you choose regarding the automobile and other appurtenances. For further information you should write Messrs. Doane and Farkow, New York City.

> Cordially,
> Alan Clarke Thorne

ONE OF THE things McClain had kept with him was Wilson's map of the Asian continent. There was a line drawn in red ink along the path of the journey; Wilson had filled it in carefully every night. The line ended in Kabul. McClain spread the map out on the table and ordered a tall Scotch. It was late in the day but the sky was clear and bright, tufted with small white clouds. McClain sat in a warm wet jungle wind and drew the last line north to Khanabad, and let it end there.

THE MOUNTAIN: SPRING, 1955

ONE

RAVENEL drove slowly upward in the fading light and came out into a clearing. The view was magnificent. He stopped the car and got out into the cold blue air; mountain silence. The house lay at the end of a narrow dirt road. Beyond the house there was a gray rail fence and beyond the fence the land fell away down into a vast dusky valley. Ravenel could see twenty miles into the setting sun to Burlington, and beyond the city and across the lake to the black mountains of New York. Ravenel stood breathing the wet air in the windy silence, smelling the earth warm and dark beneath the snow. It was Vermont spring, late April. The valley was green but there was snow on the mountain, snow on the ground among the pines. Ravenel, who was very tired, felt a moment of extraordinary peace. He walked to the door and knocked, but there was no answer. Mc-Clain was not there. Ravenel opened the door and went in.

The room was small, with a low beam ceiling. There were stone walls and a fireplace. There were no pictures on the walls, but there was a bookcase and a record player and a gunrack, and the gunrack held only one rifle. Across one end of the room there was a wide window which overlooked a small porch and the valley. Ravenel wandered out onto the porch and sat in a wooden chair and propped his feet against the railing. This was a fine place for a house. Away from people. You could rest here. Ravenel closed his eyes.

He heard the call of a crow, very far off, the call again, the blunt thump of a distant shotgun. He looked back up the mountain. There was a trail leading back into the woods, and darkness, then beyond the trees was the sudden rise of the mountain peak, still white with snow, beginning to burn and glisten in the sunset. McClain was up there somewhere. Ravenel glanced at his watch. Plenty of time. He closed his eyes again. There would be a fight tonight. He had not seen a fight in years. He thought of that vaguely and then of Mc-Clain as he was that time: a big round-shouldered kid with dark eyes. He had not seen McClain in a long time. He felt a pleasant exhaustion. He had been on duty in the emergency room for almost thirty hours. He put his feet up and closed his eyes and felt the cold wind and fell asleep.

He woke to a touch on his shoulder. The air had turned dark. A black head bent over him: he jumped.

"Charley?"

McClain. For a ridiculous moment Ravenel was afraid. He jerked upright, blinking. McClain backed away.

"Ho boy," Ravenel said. "Jesus."

"I should have let you sleep," McClain said.

" 'Sawright. 'Sawright." Ravenel blinked, trying to see. McClain's face was shadowed in the last red light from the west. "Listen. Hey." Ravenel focused on the familiar face, the open vulnerable smile. Ravenel was an emotional man: he felt a gust of affection. "Well how are you? How the hell are you?"

"Fine." McClain grinned.

"Well you look great. Be Jesus. You look great." Ravenel squinted. He sensed a difference. He started to rise.

"Let me get you something." McClain moved away. Ravenel realized suddenly that he was chilled to the bone. He moved numbly, stiffly, into the room after McClain, watching him move into the light, moving with that loose animal grace that Ravenel had forgotten and saw again with cheery sleepy joy, remembering that this had always been a big man, a dangerous man, and wondering where the hell he had been and what it was all about.

McClain opened a cabinet and extracted a bottle. Ravenel perched his frozen body on the edge of a couch, tucked his hands in his pockets, shuddered. Most of the people Ravenel saw he saw too damned often, or only when they were sick. McClain had bubbled up out of his youth and those other days; the days of poverty and hope and broads. Ravenel felt inordinately glad to see him.

"Christ, got a million things to talk about." Ravenel shivered. "But you look great. After I heard about your buddy, I'll tell you, I worried. What was that, do you know? That he died of?"

McClain shook his head, handed him a glass. Ravenel drank. He sensed again a difference in McClain, a silence in the face. The absence of youth.

"We haven't got much time," McClain said. "Got to get moving. I'll tell you, Charley, I'm glad you could come." He smiled. "I see you still got some hair. Amazin'."

"Sign of virility," Ravenel said. "Hey listen, I'm getting married next month."

"I heard. Did I ever meet her?"

"Don't think so," Ravenel said. "She's a good little broad. You'll have to come. Doing the thing right, you know, in June. Real formal deal. She wants it that way, what the hell. I'll be finishing up the intern bit then, and after we come back from the honeymoon I'll set up in private practice. Everything's all set." McClain was putting on a coat. Ravenel drained the glass. "Want you to meet her."

"Sure," McClain said.

Ravenel saw his face clearly. White lines of scars around the eyes. Ravenel remembered: the eyes cut too easily. And the hands. There was something about the hands.

"Got to go, Charley. Got to get there early in case somebody takes a rest."

"Right. Jesus, this is a nice place." He glanced admiringly around at the stone walls, the fireplace. "What a lovely spot to campaign in, ha? Well, them days is gone. Well what the hell. Say listen, what do you hear from Lise?"

"Not much," McClain said. "I keep meaning to get down there, but it's a long way off."

"Last I heard," Ravenel said watchfully, "she was engaged to some idiot with money."

"Oh." McClain had picked up a rifle and was wiping it with an oiled rag.

"Well, so it goes," Ravenel said. He remembered Lise's lovely face, the radiant hair. "We'll have to blast some time," Ravenel said.

"I know some people. There's this priest you ought to meet—no kidding, a real good egg, only he drinks too much—and there's this surgeon refugee from Hungary, and then of course you got to meet my little broad. She's a good little broad. She's a little young, and she will probably be scared to death of you, but that's all right."

"Got to go," McClain said.

"No sense taking two cars. I'll drive."

"I didn't think you'd want to come. To a fight."

"Hell. I go for this jazz. Professional jealousy. Ah," he sighed. The moon was huge in the night sky, lovely above the soft mountain peak. "Christ, I wish I had time for things like this. A place like this. But it must be bloody lonely. How come you to pick this place?"

"I was born near here," McClain said. He was looking at the moon.

"And now you've been all over the whole bloody world," Ravenel said. He was again intensely curious. "Why'd you come here?"

"It's home," McClain said.

Ravenel chatted all the way in to town, letting McClain relax. McClain slumped down in his seat with his head against the window and did not speak, and Ravenel felt a gathering tension. He talked about his girl, his plans, and McClain lay silently in the dark. They parked near the arena and McClain walked with a slow patient rolling walk, like a sailor just off a ship, and the policeman at the door gave him a respectful nod. They went down a long hall and into a tunnel of dirty gray brick walls and pipes. The hall was empty, but there was steady noise from above. Ravenel could hear feet thumping and scraping and one man's voice yelling something hoarse and bloody.

"It's too goddam cold in here," Ravenel said.

"It's all right."

"How you gonna warm up?"

"I don't need much."

"Well. All right. But goddam, I am now your personal physician. And all my goddam fighters, they do what I tell 'em."

They went into the dressing room. Ravenel saw two long tables covered with dirty towels. There was a row of damaged lockers along the far wall, and a shower room to the left, and the place was very cold.

Ravenel blew out experimentally, was surprised not to see his breath. "Like I told you, they should heat the joint." McClain yawned and lay back on a table, crossed his arms corpselike on his chest. He seemed composed, serene, almost sleepy. He yawned again. Ravenel watched, nodded. He was aware for the first time of Mc- Clain's tension. But one had to look really hard to see it. Ravenel sat on a rickety chair and brooded.

"Don't anybody ever clean anything in here?"

"Have you seen Lise lately?" McClain said, his eyes closed.

"No. Been too busy. Listen, they've got a permanent doctor around here, don't they? He ought to look into the way they keep this place."

"Relax, Charley. Nobody dies."

"The hell they don't."

McClain opened his eyes, cocked his head, gazed at Ravenel with a rueful smile.

"Well, goddamit," Ravenel said, flustered. "Well, anyway I should have brought a bag."

McClain chuckled.

"But I got my Christopher medal."

"That's for travelers," McClain said.

"Is that what that's for? I'll be damned. I thought that kept you from getting pregnant."

There was a sudden roar from the crowd, like a wave breaking on the roof above. Ravenel looked up. McClain did not move, had his eyes closed. Ravenel took the silence as long as he could, then got up to pace the room. The roars exploded, increasing, coming in like a barrage, rose to a steady scream. McClain opened his eyes, looked up, sat up, stretched slowly, thoroughly, yawned, rubbed the muscles of his chest. "Well," he said. He got down off the table and began to undress.

"Where's Gerdy?"

"He'll be along." McClain's tone indicated that Gerdy was un- necessary. "He'll be there to get the money."

"How much money do you get? For a thing like this?"

"I don't know yet. Couple of hundred, maybe." He glanced at Ravenel, smiled briefly. "Only a few minutes' work."

The room was chilly. Ravenel smelled liniment, sweat, something else thick and unclean. McClain finished dressing and got into an old black bathrobe. After a while the handler came in to tape McClain's hands. He was an old man with a fat face and delicate hands, the face overgrown with white stubble. He was very dirty. McClain introduced him as Brother Mary. Ravenel wondered how come the name, but McClain did not explain it. Brother Mary sat on a stool by the table, and McClain sat above him holding out his hands.

Brother Mary went to work on one hand. Ravenel watched with professional curiosity, a rising respect. The tape had to go on tightly and in just the right places but not too tight. Ravenel remembered how much trouble McClain had always had with his hands. There was something he, Ravenel, was missing.

"Brother?" McClain said. "You see this guy come in?"

The old man nodded.

"What's he look like?"

"Money." The old man's voice was feathery, inaudible.

"Nice clothes and all?"

"Yep."

"You know anything about him?"

The old man paused, stopped taping. He said slowly: "He moves real good."

"Any bets down?"

"No."

McClain grinned. "Odds too long?"

"They got respect for you. They figure to beat you, but they got respect. They a little worried. Not much money down." He paused again. His head never rose, never looked at McClain. "How you feel?"

"Pink." McClain said.

"You want a rubdown?"

McClain shook his head. The other hand was done, and he lay back again and yawned and put his arms under his head. There was another roar from above, but he did not open his eyes.

"Got to go now," Brother Mary said. "I see you in a minute."

"Peace," McClain said.

Ravenel came over to inspect the tape, the hands. It was a good job, good and tight. Ravenel wanted to ask questions, but he could begin to feel McClain thinking about the fight, the time was getting closer, he kept his mouth shut.

"This is the last small one," McClain said suddenly. "Once I take this one, the next one will be a big one. Next month. Gerdy said so."

"Does it really matter?" Ravenel said.

McClain looked at him. "It matters," McClain said.

Ravenel started to say: it's such a damn waste, but he stopped. It was no time to talk about it. He was beginning to sense that what was about to happen was a thing of enormous importance. That did not make any sense, because it was only one more fight and not for much money and certainly not for pride either, because it wouldn't prove much one way or the other, and dammit, you looked at the man you knew so well and didn't know him at all.

"Aren't you even going to loosen up?" Ravenel said.

Somebody knocked on the door, called McClain's name. Brother Mary came in. He stood by the door.

McClain took a deep breath. The two men stood silently watching him. He got down from the table slowly, almost wearily, yawned, stretched.

"You want a few more minutes? They can wait." Brother Mary was looking at him without expression, but there was a shade of kindness in his voice.

"No. Thanks. Might's well go." McClain stretched, bobbed, made a few quick thrusts. He looked at Ravenel. "What the hell, Charley. I haven't got so much energy I should use it up here." He grinned sleepily. As he went out the door Brother Mary tucked a towel around his neck.

Back down the white hall, through a crowd, past two huge policemen who grinned curiously, excitedly and patted McClain on the back. Ravenel followed. He felt something grand about this strange procession, some Roman memory stirred, gladiators and swords and a hairy thumb pointing downward. Out into the arena, the smoke-blue air, the hustle, the curious faces. McClain walking in front of him toward the ring, head down. Ravenel looked down and saw the other man already in the ring, a man in a bright silk bathrobe, crimson, with white piping, and Ravenel felt for the first time the flame of a primitive rage. Take him, Tom. Go take him. Win, Tom, *win*.

MCCLAIN fought them all the same way. It was a weakness and he knew it, but there was nothing he could do about it, the pattern was set. He had fought this way all his life. He never thought about the fight before it came. Later on when he was important enough there would be films to study, but now there was nothing to learn, nobody to trust, so he had trained himself not to think about it until he got to the dressing room, and sometimes not even then, sometimes he didn't think of it until he came down the aisle and climbed into the ring and saw the other man for the first time, and even then he didn't think, he just waited.

You didn't look into the eyes. You looked at the face vaguely, but not the eyes. When you touched gloves in the center of the ring you were nervous, but you never let it show. You didn't move, you were perfectly calm. Then when the bell rang you took a deep breath and went out very slowly, and covered, and watched. The first few rounds you did nothing. You watched, you waited. You saw what he did and how he moved and you adjusted, but you were never in a hurry. All that while you were getting stronger. It came naturally, like a quick bloody growth. Lately they knew about him before he came, and some of them tried to swarm him early, building up points in the early rounds before he got going, so that nowadays he was usually far behind after the first few rounds. That was not important. If they came in after him, he could see what they were doing and he learned quickly. What was bad was when he ran into one like himself, one who wanted to wait and watch, and then the fight got dull and he had to take chances. But none of the fights were ever dull for long. McClain knew exactly what he was doing. You began using your head and you ended in a rage. You saw his mistakes—and there were always mistakes—and somewhere in that red black jungle of the brain something else watched and saw it too, grinning, cataloguing, and then slowly you began to move in, going with brain and hands and instinct toward the weak places, probing, thrusting, always faster, always just a little bit faster, giving him a slow punch first and giving him time to adjust to that, and then coming in suddenly with a fast one, which he almost never was able to time and get out of the way of, and McClain had that naturally, the ability to punch at three or four different speeds. You hurt him but you didn't follow up. You never followed up the first time. You kept moving in and moving in until suddenly, finally there was the right time, which was always instinctive, and you never knew it was coming until it was there, it opened up right in front of you like a bright red tunnel leading down that way toward him, and you went in, and once you went after him that one last time, you never let up.

This was McClain's great virtue: he was a finisher. It was a rare talent, even among the very good fighters. He had the desire to kill. When he had a man hurt, he could sense it, and that one sensation turned him on, like the pressing of a button, and he went in after the hurt with all the barriers down, everything shattered and flying away and nothing but a red rage, a genuine raw red blindness, and nothing too evil to do, no rules, no law, nothing but an absolute, unbounded, indomitable urge to move in, down, destroy. If he could hurt a man, he could finish him. He had won every fight so far except the one in which he had broken the hand. After the first few rounds, he was always an exciting fighter to watch. He pleased the crowds, they remembered him. Except for the brittle hands and the eye that bled too easily, he would have been a very good fighter, even a great one. He alone knew that. He knew that he got better with every fight. He could hit, he could take a punch, he had no physical fear. The body meant nothing. He did not even have to treat it kindly, preserve it with care. It was always there when he needed it. He had watched most of the good ones, and he knew that given time and knowledge he could take them all. He knew also that if he went on fighting or if they let him go on fighting, the left eye would be damaged permanently and might even go blind and the hand would break again, but that was all in the distant future, the time ahead that was a fog and an ending and therefore did not matter. You didn't think about that any more than you thought about a particular fight. He did not fight for money, or for a future, or even, in the end, for the hate that was let out, let go, used up. He fought because he knew when his arms were moving that this was his natural life, he was a fighter. He knew also that it wouldn't last. But he would do it while he could.

The man across the ring was a colored boy named Baker. McClain had fought a lot of colored boys. There weren't many good white fighters around, and people paid to see a white boy tear up a colored boy. Even here, in the emancipated North. A white hope, that was what McClain was. Sam Gerdy's white hope. That at least was one sickness McClain didn't have. But more and more lately he had begun to want to fight more white men. It seemed that everybody was black, you were always punching a black face, blood looks different on a black face, less like blood than something else—thicker, stronger, more important. When a white man bled it was only blood, and he didn't think about it afterwards. He sat on the stool and looked across at the black man, and waited. Smooth black face, untouched, no marks. Be careful. If the face was so smooth, then this one would be hard to hit, others had not hit him. Round head, hair a dusting of black fuzz. Face young, expressionless. A thoughtful fighter. McClain glanced, saw without studying, noted, waited. This might be the thinking kind. Not good. Prefer the ones who came in swarming. Well. Wait.

Sam Gerdy was there, talking. McClain didn't listen. He took slow deep breaths, flexed his arms slowly. Smoke in the air around him, he wished for a cigarette. They met in the center of the ring. A mumbling of words. McClain looked down and saw the purple trunks, a glistening of light satin, the black legs thin, almost scrawny, hairless. He made himself stand there motionless. Never move until the time comes. Hold the machine motionless. Back to the corner and off with the robe. Cold over the back and arms, aware of the sweat on the body, a spattering of faces looking up at him like dirty flowers. A girl with her legs crossed high, blowing cigarette smoke at him. Gerdy talking, fat Sam Gerdy. McClain moved, bobbed. His body was all right. It seemed numb and much too slow, but he was used to that. It would be all right. He bobbed and moved, stretched; when he turned he saw the black boy on one knee, mumbling, crossing himself. McClain was irritated. Don't go calling on God. I have nobody to call. Well, we'll see if He helps you.

Then forward carefully, watching, absorbed. Eyes on the chest, the hands moving. This one is fast. Flick of bright leather, a touch on his face. McClain covered, moved, watched. The first moments were very slow, unreal, but then after that it all narrowed down and he heard nothing and felt nothing, just saw the man moving in front of him and noted the motions, and moved along with them, sensing, waiting, watching, moving. This one was very fast. McClain took one high on the side of the head and another on the forehead. Can't hit but can move. McClain did nothing. He probed with the left, the boy moved in under it and hooked a good right to the body. McClain felt the blow but no pain. He moved back, but the boy did not come on. He thinks, this one. McClain feinted, the boy moved back sharply. And is cautious, McClain thought. Not good. More pressure soon. McClain moved in close. The boy tried to get away. Does not like infighting. McClain hooked once in close, a right just

under the ribs, just off the heart. It landed well but was not a dangerous punch and the boy made no sound, no grunt, nothing. The
round ended and McClain went back and sat down, feeling peaceful,
patient.

In the second round the boy began to come in after him, throwing
more punches. He was using his left now, a very fast long left, beginning to aim for the eye, McClain's scarred eye. McClain backed
and covered and lost the round, but somewhere in there just before
the round ended he was aware that it was only a matter of time, he
was going to win it.

RAVENEL had a stool below the ring, in McClain's corner. He couldn't
sit. He had to stand, his arms resting on the apron, was fascinated,
intensely nervous. The fight moved back and forth above him; once
they clinched and fell into the ropes above him, and he had to back
off to keep from having them step on his hands. He could hear the
punches and the grunts and the crowd yelling and the referee's
words telling them to break it up, keep 'em up. After the first round
he was worried. The black boy looked sleek and smooth, beautifully
coordinated. McClain looked slow, clumsy, almost tired. The black
boy was younger than McClain and much thicker through the chest,
his arms were longer and he was definitely quicker with his hands.
In the second round Ravenel knew that he was going to have to
watch McClain be picked apart. When McClain came back to the
corner, Brother Mary bathed the face and looked at the eye, and
Gerdy talked about watching out for that left hand, for Christ's
sake, but McClain seemed to pay no attention. Gerdy talked and at
the same time couldn't help glancing out over the crowd, as a man
will do passing a mirror, unconsciously, proudly, here I am, Sam
Gerdy, everybody's looking. McClain sat in a world of his own.
Ravenel moved around to the side, trying to look but trying to
keep out of the way. McClain's left eye was already puffing. But he
was in a world of his own. He sat quietly waiting, his eyes dulled;
it was impossible to tell what he was thinking. He went out for the
third round, and Ravenel gripped the ring apron.

The black boy was moving in, his face beginning for the first time
to show his effort, his concentration. McClain was hit several times
on the eye; his head bobbed. Ravenel saw the spray of sweat jarred

loose from his head in repeated fine showers. McClain took a good one to the body, and another to the head, and one straight into the center of the face that brought a huge roar from the crowd and sent McClain back into the ropes. The black boy came in to crowd him, the black arms moving and sliding, ripping, but McClain moved out and was not hit; the crowd went on screaming but there was no solid punch, and then the next time the black boy moved in Mc-Clain caught him with a short right straight into the stomach, a punch that did not travel very far but must have hurt, Ravenel could hear it go in, and the black boy stopped and clinched, but the crowd didn't see the punch and thought McClain was taking a beating. McClain got butted in the clinch, and when he came back at the end of the round, the eye was beginning to bleed.

Brother Mary stopped the bleeding. McClain was breathing hard.

"You gotta cover that left hand," Gerdy insisted.

"It was his head that did it," McClain said.

"Move in low and hook him to the belly. That's where you hurt him. Hook him in the belly and slow him up."

McClain turned suddenly and searched for Ravenel, saw him, grinned, then turned back to the fight. Ravenel thought, dammit, he's got to take care of that eye. It's criminal what he's doing to that eye. Gerdy went on talking and McClain paid no attention. Across the ring the black boy got up early and danced nervously in his corner, anxious to get on with it. Ravenel looked around him at the crowd, saw two friends sitting in the haze, out of the lights, their faces smiling when they saw him, waving, enjoying it all very much. A good fight, a happy crowd. Everybody knew something was going to happen. The bell rang, McClain rose slowly and moved out, the black boy already waiting for him.

Brother Mary touched Ravenel's shoulder. "He ain't started yet. You watch. He'll begin to start pretty soon. He'll be all right."

"How's that eye?"

"Well, he better be careful. But he knows what he's doing. He's a smart fighter. You watch. This boy here is flashy but he can't hit. He can't really hurt you. You watch now."

But it went on the same way. The black boy threw a lot of punches and none of them were solid but they all counted. McClain wasn't hurt but he was bleeding again from the eye, and the crowd was screaming, and when they clinched in the corner over Ravenel, some of the blood came down on Ravenel's shoulder. The blood was seeping down McClain's cheek, coming into the eye, he was blinking, wiping at it; the black boy's glove was smeared. But the black boy could not seem to hit him. McClain moved, ducked, put up a glove; the black boy kept throwing punches and then toward the end of the round came in with his hands just a little too high, and McClain hit him twice in the stomach and again with a left on the side of the head, and Ravenel could feel them from where he stood, they were the best punches of the fight.

Brother Mary cleaned McClain's face. The commission doctor, a round little man with thick glasses, came up into the ring to inspect McClain's eye. He was a distant friend of Ravenel's, a GP named Hutchinson. He stared at the eye gloomily, shrugged, then looked down at Ravenel.

"Hey Charley, what do you say?" He climbed down, caught Ravenel's hand.

"Friend of yours?"

"Yep."

"You lookin' after him? Good. He needs it."

"Listen, how's that eye?"

"Well, I tell you, he ain't doin' it any *good*. But I'll give him a couple more rounds. It's only superficial. Bled a lot, but isn't hurt yet. How's everything?"

"Great."

"Haven't seen you around here much lately."

McClain was moving back to the fight, Ravenel's eyes followed him. Hutchinson remained in friendly conversation.

"This guy hasn't done much yet. Is he really a friend of yours?"

"What round is it?"

"I forget." Hutchinson looked around for the sign. McClain was moving forward. His head was down, his chin was tucked in behind his shoulder. There was something different in the look of him. Ravenel forgot Hutchinson. The black boy came in with the left, danced away. When he moved back this time, McClain followed him. The black boy danced, jigged back and forth, hitting with the left. McClain looked foolish. But he was moving in. He pawed out with a left, and left the eye unguarded, and the black boy came in over it with a good right, then another good right, then a fast flurry, and the blood began to flow again, and McClain backed up, backed away. But there was something different, something ready and watchful. The black boy came in after him, and McClain again pawed with the left, and then the black boy landed a long dramatic right to the head, thrown from a long way back, and in almost the same moment McClain hooked him to the stomach, and hooked again with both hands so fast that Ravenel didn't see it, but heard the punches land, and the black boy froze for a second and his hands wavered. Ravenel could see the pain cloud his eyes from all the way across the ring, and then McClain hit him in the jaw with the right hand, and the black boy went down.

The black boy was on hands and knees, facing Ravenel, shaking his head. The sound of the crowd was an enormous, beating, enveloping scream. The count went to five and the black boy stood up, then fell backward against the ropes as the referee came over to clean his gloves. He shook his head again violently, and Ravenel looked to see McClain standing across the ring, in the corner, his face transformed now into a look of stunning, incredible desire. The referee stared into the black boy's eyes, backed away slowly, McClain came on. The black boy tried to cover up, but McClain went in after him with a brutal, indomitable certainty. McClain seemed bigger, more powerful. He began punching. They were all short hooks, digging into the arms, the shoulders, the stomach, the chest. The black boy tried to break away, but McClain was suddenly all speed, all motion, beginning to envelop him. McClain's arms moved, his hands ripped the black boy's stomach and face. The boy fell back into the ropes, started to go down. McClain hooked his left arm under the boy's shoulder and held him and ripped away with the right and then let him fall. But he got up. Ravenel thought, my God, stay down, stay down. The boy's mouthpiece had come loose, and blood was coming out of his mouth. The referee let it go on, the round was almost over. McClain's face was something horrible. He went in after the boy and this time hit him in the head, and the last punch was a left hook that spun the boy around, dropped him where he stood, and the referee stopped the fight.

The handlers were out after the black boy, and the referee was lifting McClain's hand in a huge roar of sound. Everyone was standing, screaming. McClain came back to the corner, blood on his face, his chest, smeared on his gloves. His mouth was open, spitting out the mouthpiece. His eyes were cloudy and dull. Gerdy was yelling at him and hopping up and down, and Brother Mary was grinning a broad, toothless grin. When McClain came at him, Ravenel was momentarily afraid, repelled. McClain did not look at him. They wrapped his robe around him and a towel around his neck, and Brother Mary took the gloves off and began cleaning off his face, crooning to him lovingly. McClain stood dumbly, blinking, trying to breathe. Gerdy pulled his hand up again for the reporters, and flashbulbs exploded, froze his face in white light. McClain looked down dumbly, from a long way away. Then they took him out of the ring and back down through the massed people who tried to grab him, touch him, yelled at him as he went by. Ravenel followed the broad back, had to push his way through.

In the dressing room Sam Gerdy was talking to reporters.

"Well, now you seen him. *Now* whataya think, *ha?* Dint I tell ya? I tried to tell ya, but you guys. Ha! It was only a workout. My boy coulda taken him any time. Whad I tell you, ha?"

Three sardonic but obviously impressed men with passive, curious faces watched McClain, asked questions. McClain said nothing. He sat on the table, and Brother Mary took off the tape, and then McClain went into the shower, and Gerdy took the reporters outside. McClain came back in a towel and sat on the edge of the table, exhausted, and looked at Ravenel.

"I think I'll lay down for a minute," he said.

"Sure," Brother Mary said, patting him on the arm, "sure now. You just lie down, take it easy." He looked at Ravenel and grinned. "Dint I tell you? You got nothing to worry about. I *tole* ya."

Ravenel wanted to look at the eye. But it was not the time. And there was something which kept him away from McClain.

Brother Mary stepped back and looked down at McClain proudly. "Ah, he's a dandy. He's all sugar."

McClain's eyes were closed. His face had a curious haggard look. The eye was a mound of bluish flesh, black along the cut, the eyebrow black with dried blood.

"Hadn't you better work on that eye?" Ravenel said.

"Let him rest a minute. He's used to it. Listen, you know the thing that makes him great? The thing they don't none of them have any more? He's a killer. He goes in after 'em, you saw it yourself. Isn't he a dandy? And another thing, you notice something? He's thinkin' all the time. You hit him with one punch, and he says yeah,

I see, I see how you do it, and you never hit him with that same punch again. He *learns*, all the time."

RAVENEL drove him to the hospital, wanting to get a look at the eye. McClain lay with his head against the car window, watching the street lights go by like small silent shellbursts. Ravenel was silent. McClain was not aware of it. He lay seeing the fight and going over it, moving in again at just the right moment, feeling the punch hit, stop, and go through, watching him fall, the eyes turn up, half moons of white in the black face, knowledge of victory, hit him again, it was just exactly then, at that time, perfectly timed coming forward and moving right into it, and his face as he goes down, because that's the way he came in, right into it that last time, hit and go down.

The car swung out into open country. The moon rolled out from behind a looming black ridge. McClain saw the soft light on the open field, black trees, the mounded shadows of sleeping cows. In his mind he kept hitting the black face, saw it fall and go down, but the vision was receding. He was sleepy, expended. Arm raised in victory, rest now in peace. Arm raised in victory, all the faces looking up. But all that was weak. Victory. Over and done. And so rest in moonlight for a while. Hit him again, watch the man fall. Raise the arm. And rest.

Ravenel drove without speaking. McClain looked at him, tried to guess what he was thinking. Doctor Ravenel. Had worked all that day in the emergency room. He would be good at it. McClain wanted to see it. He thought: I'll ask him. I'd like to follow him when he makes rounds. To have those lives in your hands. McClain raised his own hand, the right one, the one which ached always, down inside the wrist, like a peat fire.

"How you doin'?" Ravenel said.

"Great," McClain said. His lips were puffed. When he got out into the light he would look pretty bad. Raise the hand in victory.

"Hey," Ravenel said suddenly. "I saw your old man."

McClain turned. He had to turn far enough to see out of the one good eye, the right one.

"Saw him early this winter. In the emergency room. He didn't recognize me. I didn't recognize him neither until I saw the name on the card. But he was your old man all right. Mean old bastard, ain't he?"

McClain nodded.

"Took about nineteen stitches in his face. He got in a brawl with somebody in a bar." Ravenel chuckled. "Runs in the family. Only *he* lost." Ravenel chuckled again. "It was your old man all right. I didn't know he was still in these parts. What's he do now?"

"I don't know."

"You haven't seen him?"

"No."

"You haven't missed much."

They pulled up at the entrance to the emergency room. McClain had not seen his father in more than seven years. He did not know what would happen if he ran into him. He felt an uneasiness, a bitterness; he did not want to think about the old man. He was too tired. Ravenel was chattering his way down a clean green corridor. A very thin nurse with exploded hair came forward, hands pursed together, like a chipmunk. Ravenel set McClain up in a room with bright lights, and the nurse hovered near, and then another nurse came.

Ravenel worked on the eye. His hands were gentle and confident. McClain looked up into his face, up close, the eyes intent, eager gray eyes they were, and the hair really much thinner now in just this one past year, and McClain felt a surge of gratitude. Charley Ravenel. There was that about Ravenel that could be relied on: he was imbedded in the world like a bright stone.

"It's all right now, but you know, goddamit, you can't take this crap—Lucy, get us some coffee—I mean this goddam eye ain't leather. Listen"—he stepped back and said calmly, solidly, in a profane but businesslike way—"you keep this up, Thomas, you could go blind."

"Well," McClain said.

"You *will* go blind," Ravenel amended.

"Not for a while yet."

"How much time do you need?"

"I don't know."

"How long are you going to stick with this?"

"Long as I can."

"Dumb bastard." Ravenel studied him.

"Hell, Charley, you know me. I've always been a little bit nuts."

"True," Ravenel said. He lighted a cigarette. "Let's say anyway that you are an original."

"You got to admit I'm good at it," McClain said.

Ravenel shrugged. "Amen. So what's to happen?"

"I need it, Charley."

"Sure. Until you go blind."

The nurse came in with the coffee. Ravenel drank silently, then gave him a pill for pain, a pill for sleep. The eye had swollen shut now, and McClain was hurting all over his face and down the back of his neck. They went out into the night, and Ravenel drove him home.

McClain floated. Streetlamps flared. It was good to be back with Ravenel. The pill for pain was working, and McClain began to float out of himself and out into the softness of the night, the black sweet folds of the deeper dark. He wanted to thank Ravenel for coming and at the same time he wanted to ask him if he was coming to the next one, because it was damned good to have him in your corner, because the bloody corner was empty, was always empty. But he knew Ravenel was very busy, all doctors were very busy, and from the look of his face he probably didn't want to come.

"I've got a big one coming next month."

"Oh," Ravenel said politely.

"First one for real money. Gerdy said it was all set." He mentioned the name of the fighter. The name meant nothing to Ravenel.

"Think you can come?" McClain said.

"Don't know, Thomas."

"Did it bother you? Tonight?"

"Some," Ravenel admitted. He turned, grinned. "Professional jealousy. Man, you tear 'em up worse'n I do."

"I didn't think it would bother you."

"You should see yourself. The look on your face." Ravenel was grinning carefully. "You're a sight to behold. I thought . . . hell, you scared *me*. You wanted to kill him. I thought you were trying to kill him."

McClain said nothing. It was nothing he could explain. It was a thing that happened and it was not a matter of trying. When the time came, it was there without effort, it all just came, it was all there waiting to be let out, like an animal but not like that, like a bomb but not even that, because there was not really any explosion or even a fuse. It was just there and it happened, as the water flows to a fall, and falls, and flows to another fall.

"Have you ever thought about that? What would you do if you actually did kill somebody?"

"I've thought about it."

"Well?"

"I don't know."

"I don't know either. I would have thought I'd know, but I don't. I tell you. . . ."

"What?"

"It's a hard way to make a buck."

McClain turned away. It would have been nice to have Ravenel in the corner.

"I'm trying to understand," Ravenel said. "It just seems like such a hell of a waste."

"It's the only thing I'm good at, Charley. When all's said and done, it's what they made me for. I'm a natural. There's where I belong. I don't know why. But when I fight, I'm whole. It doesn't even matter if I lose. Not right now it doesn't. But if I quit I'm in trouble, Charley."

"You'll go blind, kid." Ravenel said. "Or kill somebody."

McClain grimaced. He put up his hands helplessly. There had never been a future, and he had always known it.

Ravenel drove on down the road. "Well, in that case," he said slowly, "I guess we'll just have to rally 'round." He put out a hand and touched McClain's arm. "You poor bastard, you've been punched too much."

"Worse things can happen, Charley."

"I guess maybe so."

"Well, thanks for working on the eye."

"Hell. I'll take it out in trade. I may ask you to collect a couple of bills."

McClain grinned, floating, as they drove up the road to the cabin in the clearing.

"Hey. One more thing," Ravenel said. "I almost forget."

"What?"

"Congratulations."

"About what?"

"The fight. You won. Remember?"

"Oh, yeah. Oh, well, thanks."

"The pills are working. Go to bed."

"Right, doctor."

"Sounds funny, you know, coming from you."

"Don't mean it that way, Charley."

"Good night, kid."

Ravenel drove off. McClain stood alone in the dark feeling very fine.

TWO

MCCLAIN WAITED until a week when there was no fight and therefore no marks or cuts or tape on his face. He had a haircut and bought himself a new suit, and wore a white shirt and a tie. He went during the middle of the week because she would be busy on the weekends. He did not know what would happen; he did not expect anything. He was going through the world one day at a time. On a Tuesday in May he took that train back across that same river and arrived at the school in the late afternoon.

And so he came back to that same black railing and looked out over the trees and the town toward the chapel. The day was clear and warm, changeless as an engraving. He had a sudden blinking sensation, as if he had stepped off the world and it had revolved beneath him and come back under his feet. He stood for a long while on the platform. The sense of permanence faded. He had left in the dead of winter, when the air was gray and there was ice in the streets. Now it was spring. Everything was changed. The air was warm and wet, and the ground was bulging with live seed. He felt the summer ahead: lightning and rain. Ravenel would marry. Lise would leave here. A time of endings. He thought of her that day on the stone steps, at the music building, sitting timeless and warm on the gray stone, with the sound of *The Messiah* coming from inside, from out of the dark. Ravenel had said she was engaged.

She would be sleeping with someone now.

He thought of that, saw it in a sick luminous vision, shook his head, repulsed. Coming here was not a good idea. She would be . . . twenty-one. Quite grown up. Graduating soon, no longer the school-girl. Engaged. Time to go to bed. He did not want to think about that. But it was a strange thing. She occupied a place in his mind that was permanent and beautiful and almost untouchable. The memory of her was not even a picture, but one clean place, an area of joy, lovely, immobile. He wandered slowly up the hill, remembering. He delayed. He watched the girls walk by. They seemed younger. Bells rang, classes changed. God, it was a lovely day. He sat on a stone bench and surveyed it all dreamily, the bright young world. He no longer felt an alien here. He had his own place now: in the ring, with his hands. He remembered his own words to Lise: I'll come back, if I can.

Well, he was back. But not for long.

He began to feel restless. He got up abruptly and went into the nearest coffee shop and called her house. She was not in. He left no message. At that moment he began to think that he would play the chance as it came; that if she was not home now, that might possibly be a sign, and perhaps he should leave now and never let her know he had called. He drifted on out of the shop and walked slowly down the street near the statue, the stone path that led to the river. It occurred to him that he was afraid.

He stopped and sat by the statue. He had left her in fear. He looked into himself, testing. It was odd the way you could close your eyes and check yourself out, running a fine finger of mind down there into the dark, down along the dark places, probing, testing. There was fear there, all right. He remembered. You had to be very careful of feeling something for a very young girl, because very young girls are not reliable, and you yourself are not especially reliable, and you were trying to hold yourself together, and you couldn't take the pressure of her and your own weight too.

But he was different now. He was tougher. The probe found a tough place. Stay. Stay and see her. When she looks at you, old chum, there will be something in her face you need to know. If it's there, you need to know it, and if it's not there, you need to know that too.

He rose and went back to make another phone call. On the way he passed the library, and she was standing on the steps.

She was standing with two girls, talking to a boy. She was wearing glasses. She had on a green jacket and was cradling her books in her arms across her chest, smiling, relaxed, the long golden hair brilliant and liquid in the sun.

McClain felt a remarkable shock. He stopped and watched her. His face felt thick and foolish. He began walking slowly toward her. He had no idea what he was going to say. When he was about thirty feet away from her, he stopped. He did not want to talk to her with people watching them. He waited.

After a moment she saw him.

She stood up straight and looked at him. He made a ridiculous smile. She nodded. She stood there looking at him for a moment, and then he saw her excuse herself and start walking toward him. She had a strange set to her face; not happy. She was pale. She was not wearing any makeup. She looked exactly as he remembered her.

She said hello. They talked. He said something about trying to phone her. She said that she had read about him and knew he was back. He had not expected it to be this difficult to talk to her. Her face was white. That pleased him. But she seemed afraid. He suggested they walk. She nodded and fell in beside him, and he began walking back toward the bridge over the gorge near the music building. He looked down on the blonde head. She did not look up at him. Abruptly, she tugged at her glasses, took them off, tucked them in a pocket while cradling the books awkwardly.

McClain said he didn't remember the glasses. Lise said something about vanity. She smiled, but her eyes looked up at him in fear.

"I bought you something in Damascus," McClain said. He held out the package, the blue brocade.

"How are you?" she said.

"I'm fine. Can we talk?"

"Somebody told me you'd gone back to fighting. I read about you."

McClain nodded.

"I've thought about you a lot," she said. "I wondered how you were."

"Have you got some time now?" McClain asked.

"I have to be back soon."

"I know. But I won't be here long. I just. . . ." He did not know what to say. The truth. "I had to come see you."

"Why?" she said.

"Because," McClain said, stumbling. The lovely face, those extraordinary eyes. Because I love you. But he could not say that. "I wanted to see how you were," McClain said.

"I'm fine," she said. Her face was still very pale. She turned away from him.

"Ravenel told me you were engaged," McClain said stiffly.

She nodded.

"I don't want to know anything about him," McClain said.

"All right," she said.

They reached the bridge. He remembered the dark night, snow falling on the blonde hair, the fur of her coat framing the lovely cheek, the wide eyes of innocence. He wondered again if she was sleeping with this one. He looked at her body, her face, but he saw only the lovely schoolgirl. And then her eyes looked at him clearly, dark and wary, and, remembering pain, she stopped.

"I have to get back," she said. But she did not move.

"All right."

"You look different," she said.

"I am."

She watched him. "Are you really all right?" she said.

"Yes."

"Will you be coming back here?"

He shook his head.

"I didn't think so. I'll be going soon myself."

"Listen," he said. "Can we go somewhere and talk?"

"Why?" she said.

"I just want to talk to you."

She looked at him silently. He could not tell what she was thinking.

"I have to get back," she said.

"I won't be here long," he said.

"I know." She turned and looked along the bridge. A couple came strolling, hand in hand, the girl coy and laughing, the boy sad and gloomy. The boy passed McClain without curiosity, but took one long careful look at Lise, and the girl with him stopped laughing.

"Didn't mean to come here," McClain said. "Thought it best for all if I stayed away. I don't mean any harm. But there I kept thinking, you see, and every now and then, right at anytime at all, I would think of you, even when I didn't want to. And listen, I know I am not the best thing that ever happened to you, and I don't want to trouble you, but I did want to come by and say hello and tell you I wish it wasn't this way and that I miss you and maybe we can keep something warm, we can stay friends at a distance, you over there and me over here, just at least keep talking, because I don't want to lose that too."

She said nothing. In a moment now he would tell her he loved her. He controlled that. He stood silently in the gathering dusk with his hands in his pockets and the package tucked under his arm. He would not move toward her without a sign.

She moved back and sat against the railing. She leaned down and put her books on the walk.

"Charley Ravenel's getting married," she said.

He nodded.

"Are you going?" she said.

"Yes."

"I don't know the girl," Lise said. "I worry about Charley. How's your friend, Wilson?"

McClain told her about Wilson. First he told her he was dead, and then he told her how it happened. He took a long time to tell it, and while he was talking it grew darker and the lights came on on the bridge, and it began to be the way it all was that time ago.

When he was finished, she said: "I always wanted to meet him. I used to lie in bed at night after one of those long dead dull days and think of how it would be with you, sleeping out in the open on the way to Singapore. I used to wonder how he'd accept me."

"You would have got along fine. He never much trusted women. But I think he would have trusted you."

"I'm different now," she said.

"Do you love this guy?" McClain said.

She leaned back against the rail. "He's very nice," she said. "He drinks too much, and he's very bright."

"I won't like him," McClain said.

"No," she said. "No, I don't think you would."

"I need a sign," McClain said.

It was getting darker, and colder, and he wanted to be with her.

"Isn't it incredible," she said. "It's as if you left yesterday."

"Yes," he said.

"Isn't that absolutely remarkable," she said. "A year and a half. You'd think I'd have some sense. I never was very bright."

"Me neither," McClain said. She was standing back away from him with her hands behind her holding the railing, and her body was presented to him all soft and round and hot.

"No," she said. "No." She shook her head. She was beginning to cry.

He watched her face shaping into that crumpled unnatural agony. He moved toward her.

"No," she said. He stopped. She could not control the tears. She put out a hand to him slowly, and he took it and pulled her slowly to him against his chest. He put his arms around her and held her while she cried, and he felt a terrible mixture of triumph and pain. He held her but did not kiss her. This was what he needed to know. He had not expected it and did not know what to do. He stared sightlessly over her shoulder into the thundering night, the blossoming stars.

She stopped crying and backed away. "Well," she said. "How about that?" She wiped her eyes. He did not try to hold her.

"We can't do that," she said.

He nodded.

"Not again, Thomas," she said. She put both hands to her face. "It isn't fair to do that again."

"No," McClain said.

"You walk right in and walk right out. It isn't fair."

"No."

She had stopped crying. She bent over and picked up her books. "I have to go," she said.

He nodded.

"I shouldn't blame you," she said. "I know what it's like for you. But I just can't handle it, do you see?" She shook her head helplessly, and was about to cry, but she controlled it. "I'm sorry," she said. "Will you walk me back?"

They were going now. He walked beside her, unable to touch her.

"Listen," he said. "We've got to wait."

He stopped. He did not want to go away from the bridge. She waited for him in the dark.

"I didn't know this would happen," McClain said. "I didn't understand."

She waited silently.

"It takes me such a long time to learn things," McClain said.

"I've got to get back," Lise said carefully. She was poised now, polite. The schoolgirl was gone.

"I wish you the best of luck," she said. She put out a hand. It was very foolish, but it was the only thing to do. McClain took her hand.

"Thank you for the brocade," she said. "It was very nice of you to think of me."

He gave her the package. It had come from the other side of the earth, across the desert and over the mountains and through the Khyber Pass. It had survived Wilson and the sea and all that long winter and now was handed over formally and politely and would vanish into a chest somewhere to be taken out and gazed at from time to time with care, when no one was near.

"I'm sorry about Wilson," she said.

"Yes," he said. "Good night."

"Good night."

She began to walk away. At that moment he felt a violent sexual need. He could reach out and force her. The hands moved in his mind, but he did not move. She stopped and turned.

"Thank you very much for coming," she said.

He went back that same night on the train, back to his place on the mountain, but that was too lonely. There were girls in the city who loved fighters. That Friday he fought a Cuban named Rodriguez and knocked him out in the third round.

RAVENEL'S WEDDING was set for a Saturday in June. The night before the wedding McClain had a fight downstate in New York and so had to drive most of the night to get back. But the day dawned clear and warm, a very fine day, and McClain put on his best suit and patched up his face and went on down to see Ravenel face the preacher.

It was to be a formal wedding. The church itself was one of the oldest and therefore most formal and reliable in the country. It was a stone building, impressive, huge, very cold, and with great gray columns flanking a Roman entrance. The whole building was supported on columns; McClain stood between two, Samson-like, and nudged experimentally, and thought he felt a tremor. But people were looking at him, and he smiled foolishly and stopped nudging. He felt peculiarly lightheaded; he was suddenly foolishly happy. It was a fine day, and he was happy for Ravenel, but it was more than that—he watched the gathering crowd, which was dressed in elegant colors and formal white jackets and dignity. It was going to be a solemn occasion, and therefore he grinned. He had never in his life been able to attend anything dignified without a sense of absurdity. He remembered communion as a child; he couldn't believe people were serious. He remembered a sly wink at the minister, irrepressible giggles. The same thing happened in the Army, which was a place where damned near everything was ridiculous, but it happened most painfully in church. He had not been in a church in years—he could not remember the last time. He wandered along between the stone columns, memories beginning to blossom, memories from the bottom of the mind, the darkness of childhood. He remembered his mother kneeling at his side and praying. He could not remember what she was praying for. He saw a vision of the huge warm woman, dark beside him, on her knees, wearing black—the vision was gone, blotted in daylight, he could not call it back. He could not even remember her face. He stopped by the black iron fence, stood looking out over the adjoining graveyard which was church property. His mother was not here, she was up on the mountain—he would have to go there soon. The stones here were all very old, some of them dated back before seventeen hundred. He peered at the odd bleak cold shapes, crosses and angels, the writing in stone faded faint and almost smooth. The noonday sun was warm and soft, almost directly overhead, there were not many shadows. He saw a name: RAVENEL. He started, stared, chilled. But of course, there were many Ravenels here. He stood trying to see: Rachel? He could not make out the name or the date. He held the fence, was getting rust on his hands. He wondered if there were any McClains here. He thought of his own father, who was somewhere near, above the ground still. His father would be having a beer somewhere now.

He saw Charley Ravenel.

The little man was sitting by the back door, the door into the vestry, smoking a cigarette and staring out moodily into the graveyard. McClain grinned.

Ravenel was dressed in a bright white jacket and dark pants, a frilled formal shirt without a tie. He looked weary and disgusted.

He was sitting smoking a cigarette with a forlorn, doglike droop, the wind rippling his light fading hair. He saw McClain and gestured wearily.

"Hey, groom," McClain said. "How you bearing up?"

"I was just inside," Ravenel said with vast disgust, "and I was sitting there trying to clear the old brain and steady the nerves, and up comes the goddam minister, and you know? The silly bastard tried to talk me into joining the *choir*. The *choir*." Ravenel shook his head in bitter disbelief. "At a moment like this."

"He must not have heard you sing."

"True. That's what I should have done. I should have given him a fast chorus of 'Roll Me Over.' Hee." Ravenel chuckled.

"You want to be alone?" McClain asked. He was thinking that it was an important day, a private moment, and perhaps Ravenel wanted these last few minutes to think. And then he thought of how he would feel himself, on a day like this, and then he thought of Lise, and felt a soft pain inside him like a discovered pool.

"No. Hell no, really." Ravenel looked up at him cheerfully. "I see you been workin' on the eye again."

"How long will it be before you're back in action?"

"Jesus. You make it sound like I'm about to be badly wounded."

"No, I mean, you know. How long will you be away?"

"Two weeks. Maybe three. As long as the bread holds out."

"Sorry I couldn't make the stag party."

"That's all right. You didn't miss much. Too many goddam relatives." He peered cautiously around McClain. "They're all over the place, you notice? I got too many damned relatives. So has she." His face fell. McClain saw that he was thinking of in-laws.

From far within the church they heard the organ begin. Ravenel took a deep breath, blew it out gloomily, arose. McClain felt awkward, he held out his hand.

"I wish you the best, Charley," he said.

Ravenel nodded silently. "Gonna be a long day," he said. He started buttoning his shirt collar. "Where's my goddam tie?" He panicked briefly, then calmed himself. "This is all for the broads, you know. This whole damned thing is designed for the broads. So they can sit there and sob. I feel like the lead character in a soap opera, I do. I wanted to just get the hell out of here, but no, you know, all the goddam relatives." He finished buttoning the collar.

Glazed, gloomy, he looked wistfully out across the cemetery. "But she is a good broad. She is."

"I've never met her," McClain said.

"That a fact?" Ravenel stared at him sightlessly. "Well, we'll get together. Well, I guess I better go in." He gazed at McClain's cigarette. "Let me have one more of those, okay?" He took the weed and puffed. One more deep breath, and he shook McClain's hand again. "I wish I had a drink. Well. Here goes the last of the Ravenels." He went in behind the oaken door.

McClain went back around to the front of the church, saw that most of the crowd of people had already moved in. He entered himself, stepping into the dark, the organ music, the light of the stained glass windows. He was reminded of Jerusalem. He felt vaguely uncomfortable, like a poor man in the house of the rich.

There were flowers all over the front of the church. The organ music was soft and soothingly religious. There were a lot of elderly people there, but then off to one side he saw a flock of the young ones: the interns, the nurses, the fraternity boys. McClain found a seat at the back and sat watchfully waiting. He had not known it would be this elaborate. Two young and very beautiful girls came in and sat beside him: smooth knees next to him, under clean lace and a silken skirt. He felt, as always, the stab of desire like a conditioned reflex. Now more people came, and the girl moved up against him; he was forced to move further in, and the girl sat warm against him all during the ceremony, and he could smell perfume and feel her thigh, and it bothered him delightfully throughout the ceremony, although she wasn't more than seventeen. To feel horny in here, here below the chancel, with the organ music playing, was part of the absurdity of the whole thing, because it was natural to feel horny, it was human to feel horny. He grinned, thinking of how easy it would be to lay a hand on her knee, or to reach down and peel back the skirt, slowly, like a banana.

Well, he had better not stay in the bloody church for long. He looked for someone he knew, but there was no one, he could not even find Clawson, and so he bowed his head gravely and sat meditating the lovely young knees, and the white gloves folded primly, nervously in the lovely lap.

A girl sang. She was a fat girl, but she had a fine voice, and she sang something in Latin. After that the music stopped and everyone rustled, and then it began.

The heads all turned, the organ came down firmly with the familiar march, and the ritual began. Everything was lovely and solemn and beautiful: he heard small sobs. The girl appeared at last, Ravenel's girl. She was small, delicate, much younger than he had expected, not really pretty but fragile and doll-like, a sensitive face framed in white lace. Her hair was a dark auburn, coppery against the white. She seemed very pale. McClain watched, but formed no impression. All he could sense was a delicate quality, something pale and breakable. She moved down the aisle on the arm of a thin, sad man, who stepped out of the way, and there was Ravenel.

He had come out sometime earlier and was standing with the minister, looking grave and slightly haggard. The best man, who stood at his side, was his older brother, whom McClain had never seen. The brother was a lawyer, was tall and thin, looked nothing like Charley. Charley Ravenel had never been close to him, but this was a tradition that had to be observed. McClain sat watching it, feeling a mixture of absurdity and permanence all at the same time, and some sadness, and all the while he smelled the perfume and felt the sweet thigh against him. The ceremony was over very soon. The couple turned and came down the aisle. The girl was smiling, but Ravenel still looked grave and solemn, bowed by the weight of what had happened. McClain smiled at him, but Ravenel looked straight ahead and went on out of the church.

McClain filed out behind the two girls. Everyone in the crowd around him had someone to talk to; he felt alone and uncomfortable. There was still the reception to be held, out at a country place overlooking Champlain, but he did not want to go. There was no one to talk to. He thought he ought really to say good-bye to Charley, but that really didn't matter. Charley would be busy enough right now, and so there was nothing keeping him. He started to move through the crowd, and the people stepped aside, and there was Lise Hoffman standing with a group of girls. He went walking slowly by. She was smiling and chatting and looking back past someone into the church. She did not see him. She was wearing a dress of blue velvet under the blonde hair; she was stunningly beautiful, and many people were looking at her. He had hoped to see her, and now the sight was a bright silent shock. As a schoolgirl she had been lovely, but she was a grown woman now, and he had never seen her in quite this way: poised, smiling, at the center of the group. He stood off to the side and watched her. All the while he watched, he felt himself dissolving. He needed to be near her. He told himself that he'd better get out of there, but he didn't move. She was surrounded by several fresh-faced boys. One of them would be the one she mentioned. She would belong to one of those, the brightfaces. He began to feel how really far away he was. He got into his car and took his face from her and drove away up the street and out into the country. Then he turned west and headed toward the lake and drove to the reception. He parked a long way away, on the bluff above the lake, and he could see the couples already posing for pictures on the lawn.

The house was a stone mansion with several acres of lawn, and a view of the lake and the mountains that was magnificent. McClain walked alone across the lawn in the brilliant sun and looked for her, watched the girls go by in their bright-colored dresses, watched couples holding hands, saw the bridesmaids reunite with lovers. But was a long way away. They were all strangers, all but Ravenel. He felt that in some deep way he did not even belong here, and it would not really have mattered except for her. He could forego this world and all the bright people, and the stone houses and the quiet lawns and all the onward and upward life of goals and achievement and progress, but he could not forego her. He could not quite forget her. One more look.

He walked around the house. People strolled arm in arm on the lawn. He saw the fraternity boys gathering in the parking lot: there would be whiskey in the cars, and very soon now they would all be loudly drunk. He wanted a drink himself, but he did not know any of the boys. He looked for her, not knowing what he would say if he found her, knowing there would be nothing much to say except hello and good-bye.

He saw her at last coming up the walk that led to the main house. She was with two tall boys. He moved up by the front door so she would pass him as she came by. He stood there and people were looking at him as they passed, trying to identify him. She saw him. She smiled politely, doing it very well, that charming, gentle smile. He nodded. As she kept coming toward him, the smile wavered, her face began to show the strain. He didn't give a damn what his own face showed. When she reached him, she had stopped smiling. She stopped in front of him.

"I'm so glad to see you," she said.

He nodded.

Now there was no smile at all. She stared at him with great dark eyes. "I have to talk to you. Can you wait?" she said.

He nodded.

"I'll go inside. I'll be back out in a few minutes."

He nodded again. She went in past him, and the people went in with her, a whole flock of them stared at him as they passed, talking behind their hands. He felt himself suspended. He walked along the porch and stood looking out over the lawn and the lake, out to the mountains. His heart was beating very fast, he was not thinking. He knew something was about to happen. There were people in front of him; he realized suddenly these were the two girls who had sat next to him at the wedding. They smiled as they passed, pausing with obvious curiosity. He was supposed to say something; he nodded and tried to smile. They went away. He had forgotten about everything, the wedding, everything. There were no rules. No more arguments or reasons. There was only Lise.

After a while she came back out on the porch, alone. She took his arm and they walked out on the lawn.

She said: "I'm still in love with you."

He stopped walking, turned to look at her. She held his arm.

"I don't want to fight it," she said.

"I love you," McClain said.

She came into his arms. His arms went around her like hot metal. He backed and looked into her eyes.

"There isn't any future," McClain said.

"I know."

"I don't have anything to give you," he said.

"Let's not talk now," she said.

"Will you come with me?"

"Yes." She turned and looked back toward the house. Some of her friends were on the porch, watching her. If she went with him now, they would all know it, and her life would be changed irrevocably. For him nothing back there was real. There was nothing left now but her, the smell of her, the look of her, the touch of her. The earth was real that touched her feet, and the air was real that she breathed, and all else was real because of her, hot and real and living and lovely.

She looked back once, and then went with him.

THEY WENT BACK to his home on the mountain. They sat holding each other and watching the sun set, and then in the dark he made love to her. It was the first time in his life he had been to bed with a girl he loved: when it was over, he was not the same man. He had come apart, and the pieces were reassembling all that night. Some part of his hunger was soothed. Some raw place, red since birth, was whole again.

She was supposed to be staying with a girl friend. She called, awkwardly, on the telephone, and then spent the night. He awoke in the morning with a light rain falling and a mist around the cabin, and he looked up to see her coming to him dressed in a white slip, the blonde hair down over her shoulders. He made love to her in the daylight, in the gray morning, with rain on the roof, and they lay for a long while dreaming. After that it was all perfect: silent and warm and at peace. Every few hours there was the hunger, and he would love her again, stopping sometimes in the midst of it to talk to her, talking while still inside her, still loving her, moving unconsciously until the talk blended with the loving. And now he could talk. The words came out of him, drawn to her, exactly the right words at the right time saying the right thing, words going from him and falling into her eyes, as the snow flakes had fallen into the river that night on the bridge. He told her all of his life, beginning to understand more and more that he had perhaps never been really sane, and probably never would be, and all the while he could reach out and touch her—nothing mattered, none of the death or the pain or the bloody endings.

He awoke once in the night to find the moon bright in the room and the rain gone, and Lise sitting above him looking down. Even in the dark she still reached to cover herself with the sheet, now that he was awake, and he let her do that but moved his hands in under the sheet to hold her.

"Isn't this just marvelous?" she said. "Just absolutely marvelous?"

"I'm sorry I snore. My nose was broken when I was a kid. In a fight. I can't help it."

"Most people look defenseless when they sleep. Like babies. But you don't. Your face goes quiet."

He moved his hand to her breast. A cloud moved over the moon, and her face went into darkness, and he moved closer to her.

"You look so calm," she said. "It's strange. It's almost another face entirely. But beautiful, very beautiful."

She kissed him. He pulled the sheet slowly away from her breasts, and she let him, and he looked down on her and then lay against her.

"Charley Ravenel told me you could go blind," she said.

"Don't worry about that. Don't think about that."

"You're right. I'm sorry."

"Live now. Think of now. Feel me. Watch the moon."

"I have to learn to do that."

"Did I wake you with snoring?"

"No." She kissed the top of his head.

"Were you dreaming?"

"No. As a matter of fact, I slept very well. I didn't think I could. I've always thought I couldn't possibly sleep with somebody in the *room* even."

"That's true. I've thought about that. But it isn't awkward at all."

"Well, you must have had. . . ." She stopped. Her fingers were moving in his hair.

"No," he said. He shook his head. "Never this way."

She was silent.

"Not now," he said.

"All right." He moved away from her so he could reach up and kiss her on the lips. She lay back down and he lay above her, resting his head on his arm.

"Oh, God, you are lovely," he said. "You are the loveliest thing I've ever seen. You were lovely that night you came down the stairs in the gray dress with the pearls at your throat, and you were lovely on the bridge in the snow, and you were lovely on the steps at the music building, and there was always something about you to be afraid of. You. . . ."

"Afraid?"

"Oh, God, yes. There is too much . . . I'm afraid of you because I don't know how to handle this. I don't know what to do, and I'm out of control, and that's a thing I've got to watch. I'm in control right now because you're here, and it's very quiet and dark, but I don't know what will happen. Why is it that it has to hurt? When I look at you I feel something all the way through, all the beauty and the sex and everything, but always underneath there's pain. At the thought of losing you. At the thought of the coming of the morning. At the thought that someday you will look at me and that look won't be in your eyes."

She smiled at him silently. She shook her head and said nothing.

"I have never loved any girl," McClain said. "I've known a few and some I was fond of, but I never loved any of them even though I was in bed with them, and I never opened to them. I think I know myself pretty well, and I know this won't end. Not this inside me. It doesn't matter what else happens. We might fight, or I may go away, or even maybe go mad, which is something I am afraid of, frankly, but the feeling won't end. I think that's also a thing to be afraid of. It won't ever end. But it will have to. Because we sure won't go on this way."

"Don't talk about it," she said.

"I don't know what's going to happen. I don't even know what's going to happen this week, or even tomorrow. It's a strange thing, but you know, ever since that time in the war when I almost died, I stopped really making plans or looking forward. I don't think about next spring because there might not be a next spring. Do you know what I mean? I feel about everything that it is temporary. That each day is alive as it goes by, and you look into that particular day, but you mustn't make plans."

"Don't," she said.

"But that's not bad," he insisted. "Don't feel sorry for me. I've been happy this way. I only get into trouble when I try to plan. Because none of this has any point, and there's no purpose to the way we live. Well that's all right, it's all right if you follow your instincts. I just close my eyes and let go, and I'm all right. I was born to use my hands, and so I use them, and now I can lie in the dark with you at peace because I was born to you too."

"Yes," she said.

"And yet there's the other thing," McClain said.

She looked up at him.

"There is the feeling that even though there is all that silence, and stars just fall, and nobody's there to answer the prayers, even though the Commandments are a joke, and priests are obscene, and you

know all of it is as absurd as an Indian rain dance and not only
absurd, but tragic and terrible, even so, you think always in the back
of your mind maybe there is a point, maybe. Maybe. And then you
know for sure there's a point. You can feel it in the morning, in the
woods, in your arms. It's all too beautiful. But that's the bloody
trap, it's all *too* beautiful. And then you think if there's any point at
all, it's a terrible one. But you don't want to think about it."

"We won't think about it."

"All right," he said. "We'll lie here not thinking about it." He
rolled slowly over her and moved his hands down her and kissed her
breasts. She moved to receive him. Now he held her down. When
he made love to her this time, for the first time there was savagery
in it. The loving was a rape. He began slowly, sweetly, tenderly,
but it turned brutal, and he could not control it, and after a while
she did not want him to. That time he used her. That time she was
afraid of him. But the fear had nothing to do with the love. They
slept, and then again in the dawn he made love to her, and this time
it was different again, this time it was absolutely mindless, no thinking at all, just the pure feeling of the two of them together in timeless motion, flowing into each other and blending finally into one.

She was with him for three days. On the last day they tried to
become sober. He drove her down into town and she bought another dress, because she could not go back in the dress she had worn
to the wedding, and now the world of all those people was becoming real again. They walked in the woods beyond the house and sat
on a gray rock overlooking the valley. She was very practical. She
had been brought up to believe that there was no such thing as an
uncontrollable emotion; her father was a calm, hard man who believed that passion was self-indulgence and weakness. Now that she
had been with McClain she knew that it was possible for you to go
out of control and not through weakness and that there was nothing
rational about it. There was something in him that was enormously
more valuable than anything else on earth. She would be with him
for as long as she could, in any way she could, and she knew it
would not be for long. If she was careful she could prolong it, and
she knew instinctively that the only way it could be was the way it
had already been, she could go on expecting nothing and absolutely
without reservation, there to be loved, there to give as long as there
was something left to give. And, of course, it could not last. But

now was not the time for thinking. Maybe something would change. Maybe as time went on and the fire in them cooled there would be something permanent formed in the ashes, something that would endure. But McClain was outside the world. He was moving along toward his own end in some way she sensed but did not understand, she knew only that what he was now would not last.

She arranged to spend most of the summer with him. She had graduated and was undecided about the fall; now, she would spend the summer with him as far as possible and she would make no plans. She was going back to scandal, for by now everyone she knew would know she had gone off with him, and the boy to whom she had been briefly engaged would have to be faced. She would do whatever was necessary.

He drove her to Burlington on Monday evening. For the first few hours after she left he was still happy, there was the smell of her in the cabin, the warmth of her in the bed. But later in the night it became quiet and cold, and he became uneasy. He was alone. He went outside and stood in the dark staring at the stars. He felt a vast sense of cold motion. He expected to hear a voice, but there was the same starred silence as ever. He said aloud: "I love her." He turned to go back into the house. Then he turned, and to the silence he said: "Thank you."

THREE

ONE DAY McClain was waiting for her on the streets of Burlington, and he saw his father. It was a very hot day just after a rain; there was steam in the air, and water lay in pools in the black tar streets. McClain stood alone in under an awning and waited for her in the hot shade, the smell of her heavy and sweet all down his body under his clothes, the wetness of being with her soaking into him in the heat. The old man was a tall, black figure out of the heat: a big old man with a black hat and a red face. He came along in the hot air, moving slowly, black eyes sightless in the red face, moving like a soldier near the end of a long march. McClain saw him and nothing registered: an old man, a hot day, people, girls walking with wet skirts in the heat, the wet air. And then he came back to the old man, who was approaching now with huge round shoulders under a dirty black coat, and McClain looked into the face, and recognized the big man, his father.

His father had grown old. McClain had not seen the man in eight years. He stood watching the man come, unable to move, a curious silent twisting beginning to turn coldly uncomfortably in his stomach. The old man had fear around him. But an *old* man. The hair gray, shining like gun metal. The face weary or drunk or both. The eyes old, drawn inside and gone to water. And yet still dangerous, still a big hard silent man, black in a dirty coat. McClain stood there. The old man came on and went by. He did not look up, or look anywhere at anything; came by moving slowly, steadily, wearily up the road toward the park, and McClain watched him go and heard the voice calling him out of the past, the raw, red voice that was like the scream of a mad animal, calling him to come and be damned. And so, McClain stood on there silently, woodenly, unable to move or to call after him, not knowing if he could talk to the man or even if the man would listen or care, if in the long run McClain himself should decide it was worth it after all. And so the old man went out of sight, and McClain watched him go and never moved and did not know what he felt.

Later she came. She came in a white dress printed with scarlet flowers, her hair long and aglow in the sun. He held her, touching her on the arms, the lips, feeling her move in up against him and the dress fluttering against him and the light weight of her stroking him whenever she came near, with that marvelous smell, that perfume and soapsuds odor, that warm sweet girlish smell that he would transform later that day into the woman smell, the wet thick murmur of lust.

He started to tell her about the old man. Later he lay with her in the dark and talked into the dark, into her. But he found for the first time he could not tell her all of it. It was too dark and too long ago, and he did not want to live it over. And Lise beside him lay on one elbow on the warm sheet and listened, but did not understand. There was a violence in the old man which was not hate and not evil, had no meaning at all, but was as natural to the old man as fire is to coal, and McClain could not explain it to Lise, but he understood it. So when she asked him: what was it like to be with him, McClain said only: it was bad.

He did not talk any more of the old man. But he saw him again, on the streets of the city. He passed him three more times that summer and never spoke, and the old man did not see him. All the rest of that summer, that hot, wet, marvelous summer, while McClain fought steadily and won every time and was happy with Lise, the old man moved through the world near him like a distant storm, a darkness with soft thunder, and McClain was aware of him every day in the back of his mind, out of sight, ticking away like a hidden clock. He would not go to the old man. The old man would not come to him. But they would meet.

RAVENEL CAME BACK from his honeymoon with an air of vast new responsibility. He moved into a new house—all stone and glass, very modern, overlooking the lake—and took up private practice as a GP. He held a housewarming to which he invited all his buddies —a rare collection which included several doctors but no nurses, one drunken priest, a flock of musicians, one television announcer, a refugee from Hungary, two Cubans, one gorgeous colored girl, three flaming prostitutes, an Englishman named Rex, and a moody old woman named Sarah. At the party Ravenel made a long speech in which he renounced his misspent youth and dedicated himself to a lifetime of service to the sick and needy, and then he got royally, marvelously drunk and spent half the night staring with a glassy saintly stare at his wife: a shy, silent little girl who seemed impossibly young for Ravenel, and who spoke hardly at all that night, and did not drink, and sat staring with round eyes at the wild assembly. It was a moderately successful party. No windows were broken, and there was only one serious fight: a bald painter did a quick sketch of the moody woman, who was deep in Scotch and did not appreciate the likeness and struck the painter with a convenient lamp. Other than that, there was no real action. The affair degenerated into a drunken glee club singing college songs in the kitchen. McClain and Lise went back to the cabin on the mountain, and it was a long while after that before he saw Ravenel again.

In July, McClain signed to fight a man named Dover Brown. Now, for the first time, reporters were interested, and now people were beginning to drop by to watch him train, and suddenly now McClain had many friends. The bout was set for early September, and it was a natural, because Dover Brown had been around a long time and had a good name as a puncher. For the first time McClain became aware of a fight up ahead, really aware. Brown was one of the few names McClain remembered from before the war. He had been a top contender once and had fought all the big ones and beaten some, and McClain had seen him work and respected what he remembered. Brown was a local boy; he worked out in the gym near the hospital. One night in the summer McClain went down, to watch him train.

The gym was a gray brick building in the slums, known as the Downtown Athletic Club. It was one large room with metal girders webbed across the roof under large dirty skylights. There was only one floor, which was wooden, and there were usually three rings set up in the center of the floor, and seats stacked around, although quite often nowadays the rings were dismantled, and kids played basketball on the wooden floor. The building was a memory left over from the old days of club fights and cigars and political rallies, but there had already been a plan drawn up and signed that ordered the building destroyed, and there had been no fight to save it. There were few club fights any more, now that television was moving in, and the political rallies no longer liked the downtown atmosphere. Politics was becoming respectable, and there was something about the building that was old and smelly and disreputable, and also very cold. There were always old men in the building, old men lining the chairs and smoking and talking and dreaming, cold in the winter light in the vast smoky cold of the big room in the Vermont winter, and the same old men in the summer, sitting sweaty in shirt sleeves while a large fan tucked up in the roof plucked feebly at the thick air, the smoke, the sweat. Many kinds of men trained here: some pros but mostly amateurs, many young kids, an occasional fat businessman working away at melting off a paunch at the one form of exercise that seemed to offer at least some excitement—if you could afford to pay somebody to stand up and be hit and not hit back too hard. There were very many colored boys, and almost never a woman, although there were women waiting outside sometimes, and some of those women were quite well dressed. There was a track running around the walls of the building, just under the roof, above the seats, and there was usually someone running up there, around and around, dressed in a sweat shirt and sneakers, running away the unrunnable fat, and you got used to the noise of it, the rather comfortable noise: the thump of the feet above you, coming, receding, the slow sucking of the fan, the coughs of smoked lungs, the slick sound of sneakers on canvas, the dull sound of punches. This was McClain's world. He was at home here.

McClain came up the aisle between the stands. There were some men blocking the aisle, and he could see Brown's head above the hats: black, unmistakable, a round steel ball bobbing and gliding. McClain stood by himself watching, already beginning to feel conspicuous although no one had yet noticed him. He was not used to being noticed, to having the heads turn as he went by and seeing without seeing the people talking about him behind their hands, and sometimes he liked it very much and sometimes it bothered him. It took him a moment to get over it now: he had that tight, eerie, stretched feeling of knowing that people were turning to look at him—one glassy moment when you did not see anything in trying to appear as if you noticed nothing—and then he saw Brown moving large and black beyond the ropes above him.

McClain began to forget the crowd. Brown was an old old pro. His movements were calm and slow and graceful. He was thick in the middle but it wasn't fat; he would take a body punch well. He was older than McClain remembered; there were speckles of gray all over the black head, looking almost white against the black. And he was very black. There is one kind of Negro skin that is blacker than the rest, and when it is dry it is dusty, and when it is wet it is very smooth and almost silken black, and that was his color. McClain watched him, forgetting everything but the way he moved, that slow, easy, patient, almost lazy way of moving and riding along, eyes half closed and face expressionless as a rock, a black rock.

"Hey, man."

The voice at his elbow. He looked down into the whiskery face of Brother Mary.

"How's it go?"

"It goes," McClain said.

"Watcha think?"

"He's big."

"Yep. But he's slowed up a lot. You see that? He's got no real left hand any more."

Brown had been pushed away, cuffed rudely on the side of the face. He bent over, both hands in front of him, his eyes peeking over the gloves, softly, calmly, and came back with a slow hook that missed by a foot and made him look bad. McClain did not know what to make of it. The boy sparring with Brown moved in on him, and McClain, watching from behind, saw the boy's whole body shudder as Brown came up into him with the right to the body. There were several grunts of approval from the crowd.

"He was just foxin' him," McClain said. "He's still got plenty."

"Not with the left he hasn't," Brother Mary said.

McClain grunted. He had never heard anything like that. You didn't lose one punch at a time. When you lost it, you lost all of it. But then, maybe he had hurt the shoulder or hurt a muscle. Because Brother Mary knew his business, and the left sure didn't look like much, and it had been, he remembered, one hell of a left.

Faces were seeing him. Now faces were turning to him. He said to Brother Mary, to have something to say: "How would you fight him?"

"Stay outside. Use the long left and let him walk in on you, and then hook him high. Don't bother to hook him low. You won't hurt him down low, but he's at an age now where he has to be careful about the eyes. You don't have to worry about his left no more, but stay away from the right. Stay outside for four, five rounds. He likes to please the people, so he'll chase you. He ain't very smart. Also he's heard that you're a puncher, and he'll be planning for you to put it to him, so he'll be waiting for you to swarm him, and when you don't, you'll confuse him. I tell you, he ain't bright. If he had any sense, he could have been quite a boy. But you just take your time and stay outside and wait until his arms slow up and his hands start to drop. Then you take him."

"You make it sound easy."

"It should be. If you do it right. If you don't let him hit you."

"He's got a lot left."

"That's for sure. But he's stupid."

A little old man, tiny and frail in a dirty blue shirt and a grimy hat, came up to McClain and grinned toothlessly, birdnosed, and punched McClain feebly on the arm.

"You the boy, ha? You the boy fights the nigga?"

The word jarred him. McClain looked up to Brown, hoping he hadn't heard. The black head moved sightlessly in after the sweaty body before it.

"You can take him," the old man said contemptuously. "I gonna put my money on you. You beat the shit out of him. Dumb nigga."

McClain looked at the old man, and the old man backed away.

"Watch the left," Brother said. "You see that? He uses the left to find the range. He paws, and then he hits, you see? Now a smart fighter, a smart fighter could really use that to foul him up. That's what Maxim did."

"Joey Maxim?" McClain said.

"Yep."

"I didn't know he fought Maxim."

"He put up a pretty good fight. But he didn't belong in there. Like I tell you. He's too goddam stupid."

And that I'm not, McClain thought. He watched the black man move, trying to gauge it from a distance to see what he himself would do, how he'd handle it. You couldn't tell about the weight of the punches from here. You never could tell that until you were right there, because sometimes from a long way away the punches seemed slow and soft and easy to avoid, and then you got in there and it was as if there was lead in the gloves, some extra unseen invisible power, so that the slow soft punches came on in and hurt, really hurt, and although they seemed slow, somehow you couldn't avoid them. And then there were other fighters who seemed so fast and so clever that you wondered how you'd ever catch them, and then after a while they weren't fast any more, you were moving at their speed, and what had seemed cleverness was only speed, only motion. There were many things you couldn't tell until you were right in there with them. About the only thing he could tell for certain right now—McClain sitting calmly, silently judging him, Brown, McClain's mind toting facts together, compiling and analyzing without any emotion at all—was that Brown could be hit, and hit pretty easy. There were many, many openings. Brown invited the punch, in order to counterpunch, which was part of his style. McClain thought: I'll take him.

At that moment Brown moved in and clinched, hanging on for a moment to rest, and looked over the boy's shoulder and saw Mc-

Clain. Dark eyes inside the headpiece looked down and registered. McClain was feeling the new knowledge inside him; turning it over like a discovered gem: I can take him, all right. Brown hung there for a moment, large and round and dark, his head a black mound with the gray shot through it like flecks of gray silk; he looked at McClain and nodded. McClain nodded back, instinctively. It was suddenly as if they were the only two people in the room, exchanging between them an enormous secret. McClain felt a startling kinship, a fondness for the black head. The dark eyes blinked, moved back into shadow. McClain thought: he's not very bright. Watching the black man move steadily, slowly, instinctively, McClain felt pity. All the years of punching. Close to the top only to lose, never quite knowing why. And you could train and train, but you'll never learn. Too old now and still punching. McClain tried to see the dumb silent eyes. A flawed man. Never to know why. Flawed as I am flawed. And never to know why.

"He's a mean bastard, Brown is," Brother Mary said. "You be careful with him."

McClain said nothing.

"Even meaner than most," Brother said. "Ain't got a friend in the world, the bastard."

McClain smiled.

"They're all mean, when you get right down to it," Brother said. "You know? I get goddam tired of all this goodhearted crap the papers hand out. If a man's a mean hard son-of-a-bitch inside the ring, he's a mean hard son-of-a-bitch outside it, and all this Sunday pictures crap with the champ with his kid on his knee. . . ." Brother spat. "They're mean and that's good. Let's keep it that way. Give me a cold mean son-of-a-bitch every time."

"Like me," McClain said.

Brother looked up at him. The eyes had a calm look, as if he was taking a picture. "Yep," Brother said.

A man behind McClain was talking about the fight game. He said the trouble with it was too many niggers. McClain left the gym and went out into the bright heated air.

He walked slowly back uptown. He felt useless and strange. Lise was coming that night, and he needed her; he walked with visions and memories of her clouding his head while he thought. Dumb nigger. The black face with the unseeing eyes. He felt the kinship between him and Brown, a kind of peculiar fondness. He wished the fight was soon, and over. He would have no trouble punching the black face, once the fight started. Dumb nigger. Goddam people. Goddam the blind old men. He began to feel suddenly angry.

He walked up the hill and saw rain clouds. Very hot. But on the mountain tonight, it would be cool, and she would be warm and moist in his arms. He shivered, alone. He would fight, and he would win that one. He was certain of it. He would take the old man, Brown, all right. Because he could take anybody he could hit, and he could hit Brown, and so he would move on to the next one. He was moving on. He felt a strange cold inevitability about all of it, as if he was imbedded in a glacier moving unalterably down the hot slide of summer. Lise.

He stopped at the top of the hill, shook his head. It was not yet time to think about it. He had this one summer when he would win the fights and lie with her afterward. And the summer was half done. And she was coming tonight, and tomorrow they would walk in the woods up toward the peak. So the only problem for right now was to figure out what to do with the rest of the day. He ate dinner by himself, and then he called Ravenel.

RAVENEL was still at the hospital, making rounds. McClain waited for him in an empty coffee shop, just before visiting hours. He sat peacefully alone, thinking of all the beds upstairs, all the people waiting. He had never felt uncomfortable in hospitals; he rather enjoyed it. He had restful memories of lying by the window in a dark silence gazing out to sea. He sat thinking of that other hospital and those days: Kashka: I work. He smoked a cigarette and watched the nurses come in and out, a bright little flock of candy-stripers, plump and innocent as partridges, and he thought again of Lise, felt the hot rolling iron turning in his loins. He saw her face as she made love. He closed his eyes, then there was Ravenel.

"Hey man." A thump on the arm. Ravenel, gaunt and tired, fell into a chair and flagged down a waitress. "Man, a long day." He rubbed his eyes; the waitress approached with a foolish grin, but Ravenel was too tired.

"Hit me one time, Pearl." Ravenel held up a bony finger. "Black."

"Yes, sir, Doctor Ravenel."

"Use the clean cups," Ravenel said. He looked at McClain, took a weary breath, grinned. "Hey, man, how's it go?"

"You look beat."

"Don't use that word." Ravenel glanced around, "I've got to be goddam respectable nowadays." He breathed again. "But I sure am working. Listen, after you get out of the office and make all the house calls and then make rounds over here, you know what the hell time it is?" He went on complaining. The waitress brought the coffee, holding her rear carefully, obviously, away from Ravenel. The waitress was a snaggletoothed woman in her late forties. Ravenel did not notice the joke: the waitress went gloomily away.

"Had one die today," Ravenel said. "You know?" He looked up for understanding. McClain nodded.

"Woman of seventy. Came in last week complaining of leg trouble. So yesterday had to take her leg off. Just below the knee. When you're that old, it's rough. But I really thought she'd make it. Nice old lady, you know? They called me last night, because the stump was bleeding, only I got here at about two ayem, and it wasn't bleeding and there was no temperature, it was just oozing a bit, sera, you know? And so I go home, and then it really does bleed, and I come back, and from here I go to work. Jesus. But I called over here today, and she was all right. And I thought sure she'd make it, but they went in just after her visitors left, to bring her the supper, and she died. Just stopped beating. I really thought she'd make it."

"Old friend?" McClain asked.

"Yep."

"Close friend?"

"Not really. Just a rather nice woman who lived about a block away when I was growing up. She told me a long time ago that if I ever got to be a doctor I could treat her. Friend of my mother. Quiet. Shakes you up a bit. You know?"

"Think you'll ever get used to it?"

"This? Oh, this isn't bad. Listen, when I was in the emergency room, they died like flies. The worst is the kids, of course. Well, you know. I'm used to it now, I guess. The woman was seventy. What the hell. Nothing you could do. But it does bother me." He drank the coffee, gagged. "Jesus," he said in disgust. "Let's go get a snort. No, wait. I've got a couple more people to see."

Ravenel talked. He was very good at it; he would have been a good teacher. He used ordinary language and the stuff obviously fascinated him, and it also fascinated McClain. It was something McClain had never been able to get clear in his mind: the picture of the body as a machine. Even after the war, even after the blood spilled out like the water emptying from a dead battery, and the sight of bones under the skin, a red and white scaffold, and the loops of intestine like dirty gray sausage, even now there was still something miraculous about the way all these things ticked and pulsed inside him, lighting the fire of his mind. In the hospital you could feel it: tick tick tick, a wet pulse fluttering in every room, a small heat. When Ravenel talked it was all so clear and mechanical: you could see him bending over a patient with a wrench. It was all so clear. McClain thought, wouldn't it be nice if you could unscrew the scalp and reach in there and tighten things, or flush it out, or even just shine the light in. But Lise. All bone and blood inside. Yes. But such a beautiful machine. And thinking of that he thought of the movement inside her, himself moving into her hot and wet.

Ravenel said: "How goes it?"

"Fine."

"How's the little broad?"

"Fine. She's coming tonight."

"Tonight? Great. Maybe she can join us later. Listen, my little broad sends the word—she wants we should get together, maybe have a picnic. Take off some weekend and go up the mountain someplace near your place. Okay?"

McClain nodded, delighted. "I wasn't sure about that."

"About what?"

"Your wife." A new sound: wife. It rolled oddly in his mouth.

"What about her?"

"Well, I didn't know how she'd take to me and Lise. I thought she might be a little bit . . . *scandalized*, you know. She's just a kid."

Ravenel looked at him, made a strange face, blinked.

"But how's the Hoff? Listen, what we'll do, we'll have a brew."

They were approached by a round, white nurse with a sparkling bubbling smile. Ravenel looked up.

"Doctor? The Father asked for you."

"The who?"

"Father O'Flaherty. He's up on Four. Can you come up?" The

nurse smiled with clean fat geniality. McClain saw that she was concerned.

"The Captain? Oh." Ravenel looked at her. "Oh, all right. I'll be along. Four, you say? In the interns' lounge?"

The nurse nodded.

"You remember O'Flaherty," Ravenel said. "You met him at that blast of mine. Let's go up."

McClain remembered the priest vaguely. A boyish face, gray hair at the temples. The white collar. McClain had avoided him.

They stood up and walked to the elevator. McClain saw the stethoscope protruding from Ravenel's pocket. The walls around them were in icy dingy green. There was that hospital smell in the air: that tight strong smell of washed floors and medicine. McClain felt interested, a part of all this. He was curious now.

"You never did get to talk to him," Ravenel said, alone with him in the elevator. "He's a strange duck. But a very nice guy. He used to be a chaplain in the Army, and now he's out in private life and has a small parish and doesn't know what to do. I think, really, he's just beginning to grow up. And isn't that a weirdo thing to say of a priest? But this one's rare. In some things he's a boy. I meet him here all the time. He comes to give last rites, all that jazz. You know, Shall We Gather at the Liver. Comfort the sick. I see him all the time. Got to notice he was squashed a lot. Them priests. . . ." Ravenel shook his head. ". . . they really booze it up, you know? When I was a kid, I never knew that."

McClain thought: at communion, grape juice. A wafer. This is the body of Christ. It was ridiculous, even then. Warm grape juice. When I was very young, I believed it.

They went out of the elevator and down a pale green hall in soft lights. There was a small room in a dark recess, and they entered it into darkness. McClain saw light flickering against a wall: a TV set was on. A tall intern in a white suit lay on a bed watching the set between stockinged feet. He said hello to Ravenel, gestured into the next room. Ravenel went on, and McClain looked over his shoulder and saw the priest.

He was a tall man sitting with his head in his hands. There was a night lamp on the table by the bed, and he was turned into the light and had his hands over his eyes. When Ravenel came in, he took his hands away from his face and blinked and took a long deep breath, trying to come back from where he had been. His face was thin and wet.

"Hey, man," Ravenel said softly, kindly. "How you doin'? How you getting along? Listen, here's my old buddy, ole Tom Mc-Clain. You remember ole Tom. He hits people. So how you doin'?"

Ravenel's voice was gentle and very fast. The priest nodded at McClain. He seemed embarrassed, but Ravenel chatted on, oblivious. Then Ravenel had his hand and was taking his pulse.

"You ought to watch it with the sauce, man," Ravenel said cheerily. You ain't old enough for that stuff. Hey, Thomas, I want you to get to know this man. He's a good man, for a priest. We do a vaudeville bit around here, I heal the body, he heals the soul. Hallelujah. Right, man? Hey, listen, you've got a fast heartbeat, you been running anywhere?"

"I'm all right, Charley." The priest nodded at McClain. "I've seen you fight. I've wanted to talk to you." His voice was breathy, like the voice of a man in pain. In the soft light McClain could not see his face clearly, but it seemed that he needed a shave. He was older than Ravenel, no doubt of that, but his face had a youth in it, an open ingenuous look that was defenseless. McClain, without knowing why, felt compassion.

"Let's go on down and get a cup of coffee," Ravenel said.

"I'd rather not. I'd rather just sit here. Damn. Did they go down and get you?"

"Um." Ravenel nodded.

"Damn." The priest shook his head. "I'm sorry."

"That's all right. Listen. What happened?"

The priest took a deep breath. "Well. Same thing. One died."

Ravenel nodded. He looked briefly at McClain.

The priest took another deep breath. His face began to tremble.

"A little girl," the priest said.

"Yep," Ravenel said. He grimaced.

The priest began to cry, slowly, soundlessly. Ravenel waited. McClain felt appalled.

"Four years old," the priest said. "I had to talk to the mother." He paused, wiped at his face. He went on talking. "You know, Charley, I just can't do that."

"I know," Ravenel said.

"I just can't say what you are supposed to say. . . ." He paused, gulped, wiped his face. "I don't. . . ." He shrugged, bewildered.

"But of course it's my *job*," the priest said.

"Don't let it worry you."

"But it's my job."

"So you can't handle it. Some people can't. Let it go. There's nothing to say anyway. You're trying to bring them something you don't have."

"But it's my job," the priest said. The tears were slowing. The priest coughed, shook his head quickly. "This is disgraceful," he said. "Not even in the war. I was in the Korean War, you know. I could take that all right. A lot of them died and that really wasn't bad. It wasn't. But this. I don't seem to be able to handle this."

He went on talking, trying to explain himself. McClain was embarrassed. The priest stopped talking, composed himself.

"Come on, Frank," Ravenel said, taking him by the arm. "Let's get out of here."

"I could use a drink," the priest said.

"All right."

The priest stood up, swaying. He was a foot taller than Ravenel. He said to McClain: "I'm sorry to meet you under these circumstances."

McClain smiled. There was nothing for him to say. They went down in the elevator, and everyone they passed said good evening, Father, and the priest was well composed, but everyone knew what had happened.

They went to a local bar and proceeded to get drunk. It was one of those evenings when they were all ready for it, almost exactly ready and each almost to the same pitch, as travelers converging on the same oasis from different directions. They all recognized the unspoken need. They sat together, and for the first hour there was little conversation. The bar was an ancient place which dated from before the Revolution. There were low-beam ceilings and panelled walls and one genuine white-bloused, big-busted barmaid. They drank. McClain began to miss Harry. He began to miss Lise. He listened as the priest began suddenly to explain himself. This was something Ravenel tried to stop, but the priest found it necessary.

The priest had led a very sheltered life. McClain listened to all this with compassionate numbness. There was something about parental obligations. Then the priest had taken orders. He was nearly thirty when he became a priest, and right after that he went into the service, and he had stayed in for almost ten years, counting the war, and it was astonishing how far away you were from reality in the Army.

"Amen," Ravenel said.

McClain—as always when he drank—began to float off into his own world. Remembering between the priest's words his own war, his own Army, the fighting there at the end and the way it felt to wake up deaf and alive in a silent world. He wanted to ask the priest if he had ever heard from God. He was not drunk enough to do it yet, knowing it was a foolish drunken question, but at the same time he had never had much to do with priests, and he had a genuine curiosity. He wondered if priests heard voices telling them what to do. He wondered what happened when they prayed, and how they knew exactly what God wanted. He supposed it was all in the books. They learned it by rote as you learned everything in the Army: gentlemen, our course today is in the nomenclature of the M-1, this is a semi-automatic, gas-operated . . . if you lived forever, never to forget that. Nor the way it was to wake up deaf and see the mouths move soundlessly, you not quite aware yet that you were alive.

He watched the priest. A man of kind heart. It had not occurred to him that priests could weaken in this way. He felt a new friendliness, an awkward kinship. And thought of Dover Brown. My other buddy. The dumb nigger.

Good old Dover Brown. Will put up a hell of a brawl. Here's to you, Fuzzy wuzzy. Come one, come all. McClain was beginning to feel very good.

Ravenel had leaned the pinched face forward on a bony hand and was listening with a pursed and brooding mouth.

"Can't think that way, goddamit," Ravenel said suddenly. "Excuse me, Frank, but you got to let it ride. What you've got to face is you don't solve nothing. You just fight a holding action till you get older, that's all."

"But what if you. . . ."

"Listen," Ravenel said. "The big problems you don't solve. The big tragedies remain the big tragedies. You just get older, and they don't matter so much. I have spoken. Have a brew."

McClain wandered off to call Lise. She would be checking in with the girl friend in town, and he left word for her to come by and pick him up. He came away from the phone in dreamy sugary love, and touched the barmaid as he passed—a gentle touch which startled her: she twitched like a squirrel—and he apologized, and she looked at him with weary, gloomy eyes, and moved away into the dark. But he felt loved and warm.

When he got back to the table they were talking about Irish wakes. Ravenel was arguing that the Irish custom of celebrating the death was a marvelous idea, and he was slipping in and out of an Irish brogue that was hilarious coming out of the small pinched leprechaun's face. O'Flaherty was weakening, chuckling; he began to giggle. Ravenel looked up at McClain with an expanding joy.

"Broads, broads, broads," Ravenel said happily. "Jesus, that's a lovely broad you have there. No offense, of course. But a man should surround himself with the good things of life, do you know? She's coming now? Good. Ah, good. Listen, Frank, here cometh a girl will tickle your cockles. Excuse me, no offense. I really have very bad manners. Apologize."

"'S all right," O'Flaherty said happily. "No 'fence."

"I confess I see no harm in it," Ravenel said. "Got to have broads. Lovely, lovely broads. You know I love broads. I love the look of them and the smell of them and the touch of them, and I even love to hear 'em talk, even when they say godawful stupid things, they're lovely, lovely. Um." He stared sadly across at the billowy barmaid, who moved across his horizon like a full-rigged ship. "What a charmin' prow," he said.

"And you a married man," the priest said.

"There is no such thing," Ravenel said haughtily, "as a married man."

"Why don't you call the little girl? Your wife."

"What. Her? Here?" Ravenel looked around the room with gathering apprehension, then sniffed. "Not proper, old boy. Not on your collar. No bars for that broad." He paused, meditated. "Well, that's all right. One's wife should stay out of bars. Out of the company of boozed fighters and potted priests. For shame." Ravenel drank.

"Why don't you call her, Charley?" the priest said.

"Well, I'll tell you." Ravenel put down his drink. "I've worked hard of late, and have accumulated a sadness. And I feel no need for dignity. And she is a good lass but somewhat stiff, do you see? And while that's an excellent thing in a wife, and necessary, and even lovable, there are times when 'tis inappropriate. Do you follow me? Then follow me." He drank.

But the priest was melancholy. He was getting very drunk. McClain began to feel a gathering numbness himself. He still wondered if the priest heard an occasional voice.

"I have often wanted to ask somebody," McClain began, then he paused, feeling ridiculous.

"About what?"

"About Joan of Arc," McClain said.

"What about Joan of Arc?" Ravenel said.

"I don't know," McClain said honestly. "I just wanted to ask somebody about her."

Ravenel stared at him. He blinked, then stared again. "Oh," he said. He considered the subject. After a moment he said, decisively: "Nuts."

O'Flaherty stared at him.

"Talk about a nutty broad," Ravenel said. "But on the other hand. Listen here, Frank, ole buddy. You're the authority. Think ole Joan was a nut?"

O'Flaherty weighed the proposition, then came out slowly, incoherently in favor of sainthood.

Ravenel disagreed. "Bloody church ought to read up on the subjeck. People hear voices, they're in one special kind of deep trouble."

"My point exackly," McClain said.

"The case was examined with great care," O'Flaherty said, but he said it sadly, without real faith.

"You got to admit that if you personally started hearing voices, it would come as something of a shock," McClain said.

"Oh, not necessarily," Ravenel said. "Your real nut, to *him* the voices would be perfectly real. He wouldn't even question 'em. Have you ever seen one? Creepy. Had one t'other day. Was sitting there talking to God." He cupped his hand to his ear, stared upward. "Yes God? That right, God? No kiddin', God. I swear, God, I didn't know. Yes, God, right away, God. It was weird."

"But you do listen, every now and then," McClain said to the priest.

"Um."

"I think everybody listens, really," McClain said. "Which is kind of strange. Ever since I was a kid, I've been sort of half expecting it. A voice to tell you what to do. But at the same time, if you hear it, you know you're nuts."

"You don't need a voice," O'Flaherty said. "The messages come in many ways."

"Yep," said Ravenel. "Get messages all the time. A fever. A boil. A bloody tumor."

"All the same," O'Flaherty said. "Her case was a strange, strange case, and many famous men, and also, there was something undeniably saintly about the girl." He was less drunk, thinking. "And you *do* wonder as to what it was she heard."

Ravenel gazed at him sympathetically, affectionately, and patted him on his drinking arm.

"Just so long as you don't start hearing it," Ravenel said.

O'Flaherty smiled. "Oh, I don't know. It might be very interesting."

McClain sat warmly drinking in the flowing dark, intensely interested, and there was Lise. Ravenel rose to greet her with shark-like joy, enfolding her in his arms. She was wearing her hair long and loose above a soft gray sweater, and the sight of her put a sharp thrust into him and at the same time a sweetness, a blooming sort of silly tenderness that troubled him and weakened him, and he smiled foolishly, and she sat down next to him with that wondrous smile, that lighted cheek, and kissed him. There was one small shadow of worry in her eyes—she looked at the drink and then into his eyes watchfully, quickly, and he felt himself looking at her with a sad silly smile, and suddenly he was feeling very good, and he held her hand and grinned drunkenly, but with a molten warmth, loving her. O'Flaherty was looking at her with his mouth open, his face radiant and innocent, eyes like foggy diamonds.

"But she's a lovely girl," O'Flaherty said in awe. "A lovely girl."

"Goddam right," Ravenel said dreamily. "I'm sorry but I got him drunk. But you notice he's carrying it all right. Taught him that when he was young, to hold his liquor. You won't know it to look at him, but he's drunk clear out of his mind."

"Are you?" Lise asked happily, cautiously.

"Exackly," McClain said.

"Shame on you," Lise said.

" 'S terrible." McClain grinned.

She kissed him suddenly, on the tip of the nose.

"For God's sake, don't slobber," Ravenel groaned. "Ugh. Disgusting. Can't stand these public displays of affection." He put his arm around O'Flaherty's shoulder. "And how goes it with you, Frankie me darlin'?"

"Don't let me interrupt," Lise said, settling down. She put a cool hand under the table and touched McClain's thigh, and he reached for her hand and held it close. The bosomy waitress blossomed above him, looking down on Lise with vast suspicion. Ravenel reassured her with a coy smirk, and Lise took Scotch. Ravenel stared after the departing waitress with deepening gloom. He said suddenly to McClain:

"Jesus, Thomas, remember old Harry? Old Harry's bar?" He chuckled and hiccupped.

"Good man, Harry," McClain said in stately judgment.

"Yessirree," Ravenel said.

"What were you talking about?" Lise said.

"Oh, God." Ravenel bowed his head.

"About Joan of Arc and about what you do if you hear voices," McClain said.

"You are absolutely beautiful," O'Flaherty said, gazing happily at Lise.

Ravenel sighed. "I look at her, I hear voices."

"Me too," McClain said. They drank. In a moment she was part of the group. She fit in without question, and McClain sat back and watched her, marveling. He began to feel very strange. He was drunk but he felt no despair. He was filled with this extraordinary gentleness, as you feel when you hold a baby that is clean and fresh and belongs to someone you love. He remembered holding someone's baby, a long time ago. He looked at the priest—never to know a woman. Oh terrible, a terrible thing. He was filled with compassion for the priest. He focused on O'Flaherty: the wide eyes of innocence. The priest was talking about insanity. He said it had taken him a long time to understand that we were all a bit crazy, every blessed soul.

"Amen to that," McClain said. "I'll drink to that."

"Goddam right," Ravenel said. He looked from Lise to McClain and back again to Lise. "Thass beautiful," he said sadly. But he was not that drunk. There was something in him that was quiet and watchful.

"What's your diagnosis, Charley?" Lise said.

"Of what?"

"You were making a diagnosis."

"Was I?"

"Um."

"I don't mind," McClain said. It was odd how you could drink this much and not feel the sadness. He felt a spasmodic joy, as if he had heard unremembered good news. "I know I'm gone," McClain said cheerfully. "I don't mind 'tall."

"You?" Ravenel said. "Hell, no. You ain't crazy. Your average nut, now, his problem is he's out of touch with reality. *Your* problem is too goddam much reality. No. I don't think you're nuts at all. Dangerous, yes. To yourself. Yes. But crazy?" He paused. He cocked his head to one side. His face wore a distant smile. He looked at Lise, reached out, and touched her.

"Tell you what. I *did* think he was nuts. For a long while. But now I'm not so sure. If you want the diagnosis. Drunk as I am. Maybe he's crazy, but there's a peculiar logic in it. A long time ago, something very, very bad happened to him, or maybe he just grew up into it slowly, but things around him stopped making sense. The world around him turned into a nightmare. You can see it in his face. It really doesn't make sense, you know, if you think on it, so most of us don't think on it. We go on. But he doesn't. He's aware all the time. I think he sees things I don't see, and feels things I don't feel, and you know what? What he sees is really there. I don't see it only because I've taught myself not to think about it. Old Frank here is beginning to see it now, aren't you, Frank?"

The priest nodded dumbly, obediently.

"It's a bloody world," Ravenel said. "We sit here, and a few feet away the bodies of children. Ugh." He shook his head. "Jesus, what brought that on? No more of that."

They drank. It was getting very late, but none of them wanted to go. Lise put music in the jukebox, and McClain danced with her. Then they came back and talked some more and drank some more, and then McClain was on his feet showing them how to throw a left hook. Ravenel followed that with a scientific discourse on how to deliver a baby, with gestures, and the priest followed with a lecture on the finer points of delivering a sermon, or a Mass, which began as something funny but ended as something deeply religious which stilled them all, because the priest was doing penance. Gradually they gathered an audience, because Lise danced, and they were a rare group: a stewed and penitent priest, a drunken fighter, a small scrawny doctor, a beautiful blonde girl.

Into the dark night, holding Lise. Good night, good night, good night, my friend. Lise drove. I love you, McClain said. It was a marvelous night, with lightning in the distance, her body near, a warm breast, the smell of flowers, her voice in his ear, and through the window, the black of heaven.

FOUR

BROWN WENT DOWN for the first time in the seventh round. Until then it was a good fight. Brother Mary was right: the black man was old and slow and made too many mistakes, took too many punches, but he was still very tough, and McClain had to be careful. So he wore the man down, going for the belly early in the fight, hooking time after time to the body, while the black man came in after him with dull black eyes, always coming in. He hit McClain one good punch early in the fight, and it was as hard as anybody had ever hit McClain; he came away at the end of that round with a blasted, silent, windblown feeling as if nothing around him was quite real, and then he woke up and was careful, and in the seventh round he caught the black man with one good left hook to the side of the jaw, and the black man went down, and that was the beginning of the end. The man got up with silence in the dark eyes, looking straight ahead at McClain as if nothing had happened, not even bright enough now to cover up and heal the wound, but he moved in dangerously feinting a right, and McClain measured him and dropped him with the right, and that was the end of it.

McClain was pulled into the center of the ring while handlers dragged Brown to his corner, and there were flashbulbs going off and many people beginning to crowd into the ring, and Gerdy was saying: "We're in the big time now, the big time." Normally, Mc-Clain did not go over to the other corner after the fight, but this one time he went across the ring and pushed through Brown's handlers and shook his hand to show his respect. The black man looked up at him with no emotion, sightless, still partly unconscious, off in his own private far-off galaxy where sounds came dully from a long way away, and the noises and the roars and the dreams made no sense, and everything was light and filled with motion and actually very warm and comfortable.

Lise was waiting back at his dressing room, along with Ravenel and O'Flaherty. It was the first fight she had ever seen. She stood off to one side, round-eyed, remote, beautiful: he could not tell what she was thinking. Nor could he go near her because he was too messy. He sat watching her over Brother Mary's shoulder while the Brother worked on his hands and Ravenel worked on his face, and Ravenel was delighted and Lise smiled tightly and McClain could not tell how she had taken it. He had trouble seeing, as usual, and kept blinking to clear his eyes, which was becoming a nervous habit, and he saw her staring at that, and he tried to smile and thought that he'd have to remember not to blink so much.

Ravenel and the priest were both overjoyed. They had both become fight fans. Ravenel explained confidentially that after the second round he'd thought McClain was through, and the priest agreed, and Brother Mary grunted with vast superiority, and in the background Sam Gerdy talked about the future. McClain tried to see Lise through all of them, but then the doors opened and there were too many people.

He wanted to get a chance to talk to her but he couldn't. There was a party that night at the home of a wealthy local man who was now Gerdy's friend. McClain was to be the guest of honor—there was brightness in the air around him, the hot, clear brightness of victory—and many strange and beautiful people were there. McClain was swept up along with Lise and Ravenel and the priest and a number of people he knew vaguely, and so went numbly, happily, into the dark and out onto somebody's stone patio, where white-coated servants were delicately passing booze to beautiful women.

Lise stayed by him, but they had no chance to talk. Ravenel moved in and and out like a pinball, lighting what he touched, and O'Flaherty, conspicuous in his collar, stood talking most of the night to a succession of painted girls. McClain's lips were puffed, his eye had swelled. It was late and he was tired, and it was increasingly obvious that Lise wanted to talk to him, but he was meeting important people: a senator, several very big politicians, a TV announcer, a writer, a covey of local hoods, and some of the most beautiful women he had ever seen, most of whom were dressed in glittering fantastic clothes. Leather and diamonds. McClain was propositioned twice. One of the women was plump and very rich. The other was quite young and dewy-eyed. McClain enjoyed it all numbly, vaguely, and through it all, he was feeling very good. He watched Lise and held her hand, and occasionally fondly patted her butt when no one was watching, which scandalized her, because she was perhaps the only even remotely innocent guest in the place, except for the priest, who stood speaking gently, quietly, kindly, to three gorgeous prostitutes and had no idea they were anything other than three rather overdressed but unquestionably charming little girls. Then Ravenel moved in with a moody look and said, hey, and took McClain by the arm.

They backed off to some glass doors. The night outside was clear and cold, and from the glass doors you could see down over the city and the rows and clusters of colored lights. Ravenel said: "Hey, listen. They took Brown to the hospital."

"They did what?"

"He collapsed in the dressing room. They had to call an ambulance."

McClain blinked, waiting.

Ravenel looked up into his eyes. "That's all I know. Fella just told me."

"Oh," McClain said. After a moment he said: "Well, that's too bad."

Ravenel frowned. "I didn't see anything. He looked all right to me."

"Me too," McClain said.

"Well, I thought you should know."

McClain nodded. He thought: I caught him one hell of a punch. His mind went back to the last moment: hit and go through. Down he went. And he was through then, no doubt about it.

McClain shook his head.

"Honey?" By his arm, Lise.

"Yep."

"Let's get out of here."

"All right." He started to move, then turned to Ravenel. "Listen, is it bad? How do I find out? Maybe I should go over."

Ravenel was watching him. "I don't know. I tried to call, nobody there I know. I'll try again. But I wouldn't go over there right now. Wait a bit."

McClain nodded. Lise went off to get her coat. McClain moved toward the door and people said: going so soon? and thrust wet champagne glasses at him. He drank one and smiled, trying to be polite, the public figure. People crowded around him and called him champ, and he noticed many hands touching him carefully, sensuously, and there were strange looks on the faces: a delicate caution, polite restrained fear, as a man looks down on a tiger on a leash. McClain stood by the door. Then he noticed on the far side of the room, a pool of quiet. A wild-haired head babbled in front of him, holding high a champagne glass, and waves of perfume steamed up McClain's nose so that it twitched, and he nodded, smiling, looking for Lise, and saw heads beginning to turn toward him, odd looks on the faces, and the five-piece combo blazed off into "A Shanty in Old Shanty Town," and there was Ravenel, his eyes dull, the scrawny face looking grave and old. He took McClain by the arm.

"Let's go."

"Lise," McClain said, pointing. Ravenel looked around. Somebody had cornered Lise across the room—McClain could just barely see it—a curly blonde head bent over her, smiling suavely. McClain felt a flush of rage. Ravenel still had his arm. The group near Lise was looking at McClain: all of them looking silently with curious flat greedy expressions. The priest came up. O'Flaherty, blissfully drunk, a champagne glass in his hand. Drinking made him a handsome man. The pretty head in front of McClain turned to the priest.

"Are we goin'?" O'Flaherty said sadly. "And all this free booze?"

"Listen," Ravenel said. He strained his neck to see Lise. "Listen, go get Lise, will you? We got to get out of here."

McClain, looking down, felt something register. He looked into the side of Ravenel's face and began to understand. Ravenel did not look at him. Another group had fallen silent across the room. The priest looked at Ravenel.

"He just died," Ravenel said.

The priest looked without comprehension.

"I just called the hospital, and they said he was dead." Ravenel glanced briefly at McClain, then away. "I guess it was a blood clot."

The priest's mouth opened. Silence was spreading slowly across the room. The band thumped a tinny finale.

"There'll be reporters here in a bit," Ravenel said. "Let's get out of here."

Lise came. Her mouth was set in a firm, hard line. McClain stood numbly, wondering. Ravenel took his arm. They opened the door and went down a stone walk into the cold, and the door opened behind them, and somebody called. Lise came from behind and took McClain's hand. Ravenel told her what had happened. She said something McClain did not hear. They got into the car in the dark.

"You're sure, now," O'Flaherty said.

"I talked to Hutchinson," Ravenel said. "He pronounced him dead about twenty minutes ago."

"God in Heaven," O'Flaherty said. He crossed himself.

McClain sat in the back seat holding Lise's cool hand. He looked at her vaguely, and she looked back at him, but it was the face of a pretty girl a long way away. He felt nothing. He did not know what he was going to feel.

"Where do you want to go?" Ravenel asked.

McClain shook his head.

"Reporters'll be out looking for you. Listen, you ought to keep away from them. Tonight, anyway. You know how they can be. Just keep away."

"Well, he can't go home then," O'Flaherty said.

"No. Nor a motel either. Listen, I'd put you up at my place, but they'd come there anyway, and besides, I don't know exactly how the bride will feel."

"What did he die of?" McClain asked.

"Can't tell yet. Head injury. There'll be an autopsy. Could be an old injury. No way to tell. Let's not talk about it." Ravenel turned into a bright street.

"You can have my place," O'Flaherty said. "I'll go stay with somebody, and nobody would look for you there. The little house behind the church."

"But I'm going with him," Lise said. McClain looked at her.

"Is that all right?" Lise said.

"Well, of course," O'Flaherty said. Then he understood. McClain watched him and smiled. O'Flaherty had turned and was facing into the back, one arm over the back of his seat. McClain saw his eyes widen.

"You could get yourself in a lot of trouble, Frank," Ravenel said.

O'Flaherty chuckled. "That's a fact now, isn't it. Well, you're welcome. Really, there'll be no fuss. And who's to know?"

"I can't do that," McClain said.

"Sure you can. I'd take it kindly."

"Frank," McClain said.

"All I'm doin' is helpin' a friend. Head there, Charley. I've got a bit of the bubbly there, we'll have a quickie."

"You know what you're doin'?" Ravenel said gloomily.

"Sure I do. I'm helpin' a friend."

"I don't want to hide," McClain said.

"No," Ravenel said. He hunched forward over the wheel. "That's for damn sure. You won't hide. You'll get it right between the eyes. You won't hide from nothing. But what are you going to do?"

"I don't know."

"I mean, are you going to give it up?"

McClain said nothing.

"Are you even going to think about it?"

McClain blinked. He was trying to think, but he had put up a strong fight and had been hit hard, and he had had a lot of champagne. He was very tired, and his mind was a fuzzy, floating, weary silence.

"You'll be all right, legally. I'm pretty sure of that. There was a guy killed here about two years ago—remember that, Frank?—and it was legal. So that won't be a problem."

McClain closed his eyes. He felt the pressure of Lise's hand. He remembered suddenly that other fight a long time ago. At the party. Where that tall, dark, handsome boy was standing, bored, grinning, and I hit him and she saw. He opened his eyes and looked at her. She was gazing into his face with innocent compassion. He looked away and shook his head.

He thought: Death follows me.

But what a very bad break. What a bad, bad break. Black face, dumb eyes. I hit him as hard as I could. Too old. Thirty-five. By that age he should have known more. Never learn. Down he went.

Hit him as hard as I could. This time I wasn't even mad, I was just fighting good and hard and carefully. What a bad, bad break. Wilson. His death alone. Tony Wilson, as he looked with vomit on his beard. No.

McClain again shook his head. He looked out the window at moving street lights.

"What a hell of a break," he said.

No one said anything. They came to the church. It rose out of the dark like a black wedge. They got out of the car and went around the big building and down a path through some bushes to a small frame house in the rear. O'Flaherty unlocked the door, and they went into the cold and the dark, and O'Flaherty bustled, lighting lights and turning up the thermostat. It was a small room, dark and quiet. There was just the living room and the bedroom and a small kitchen. There were many books and a large fireplace and a statue of Jesus.

McClain sat on the couch with Lise. Ravenel sat across from him while O'Flaherty got a bottle.

"I'll have to get back," Ravenel said. "Long day tomorrow."

"You go on. We'll be fine."

"How do you feel?"

"I'm all right."

Ravenel started to say something, stopped. O'Flaherty came out with four glasses of brandy. They all drank. McClain sat back again, and there was a long silence. O'Flaherty told them to make themselves at home, showed Lise where everything was.

Ravenel was watching McClain. Lise went with O'Flaherty into another room, and Ravenel said: "What you goin' to do, Tom?"

McClain shook his head.

"You all right?" Ravenel said again.

"I'm fine."

"Don't mean to bug you," Ravenel said.

"That's all right."

Ravenel stood up. "Got to buzz off. The bride'll be spastic." He whistled for O'Flaherty. "You take it easy. Finish off the bottle. We'll think tomorrow."

"Don't worry, Charley."

"I'm not worried. Not about *you*, anyway. You're goddam near indestructible. I must admit, though, that I worry about the little broad."

Lise came back with O'Flaherty. Her face was gentle and grave.

"Come on, Moses," Ravenel said. "Get your coat."

"You're sure this is all right, Frank?" Lise said.

"'Tis my pleasure. I want you to relax here. And listen, if you don't mind one small commercial. That door there leads through a hall and into the church, and if you've a mind, well, go right ahead. Nobody to see you anyway. But feel free."

"Frank," Ravenel said. "You're beginning to embarrass me."

"Oh, excuse me. I just meant . . . well, you make yourselves at home. And no one will bother you."

"We'll use Frank's car," Ravenel said. "I'll leave mine here in case you need it."

"I don't have to tell you . . ." Lise said. McClain did not move, but she saw them out the door. Their faces looked at him from the door, unjudging, warm. The priest could give no words, so he gave his home.

Lise closed the door.

When she came back he was afraid for a moment that she wanted to talk. But she said nothing. She came to him and kissed him, and they lay together on the couch, and then she turned the light out, and they lay there in the darkness.

"I'm sorry you had to see that," he said.

"Never mind."

"I'm always saying I'm sorry."

"Don't talk now."

"We'll have to talk."

"I know. But not now. Rest now. Close your eyes and hold me."

He lay back in the dark. He was enormously sorry, but he said nothing. He did not move. He lay in the rolling dark, which was around him like black folds hiding a body, and then he was asleep.

HE CAME ALIVE suddenly in blackness. He jumped; she moaned. Her head was on his chest. He lay for a moment in the desert of his mind, and then memories blossomed. He saw Dover Brown go down. The eyes dulling and turning upward. Lying now under a sheet. The eyes open in the black face.

McClain grimaced. He moved carefully, delicately, out from under her, and she slept on. He stood in the center of the silent room, dizzy; he almost fell, and then he sat on the floor. He was in the dark in a strange room. His head and face hurt, and the muscles in the back of his neck—from the last punch *he'll* ever throw, dead Dover Brown.

O'Flaherty had drawn all the curtains, there was almost no light at all. McClain struck a match and lighted a cigarette and saw Lise's face, asleep. Young, so very clean. She was curled up, her feet tucked in under her skirt. The match went out. But he had seen the door leading into the church. He rose carefully and groped his way through the black to the door, opened it, moved out into a cold hall.

There were glass windows down a long narrow corridor, and there was light coming from streetlamps. He could see: he stopped. The corridor ran straight to the church. He had never in his life been in any church alone: the dark door ahead plucked at his brain. He was drawn to the silence.

He moved down the cold hall, opened a heavy door, moved out into the dark vaulted room. There was a night light above the altar, soft light on the flutes of the organ. He saw candles burning on the far side. He stood smoking a cigarette.

For a moment he had an eerie looming sensation of motion, as if the walls were moving, as if he dreamed. But he could smell wax, and dust. His feet moved on a thick rug. He felt himself smiling in the dark. But he felt very strange. Very light and strange.

A good place to think. A quiet place to think. He walked cautiously along the rows of pews, listening. The house of God. There was no sound. He looked toward the front of the church, wondering if the door was locked. Probably not. He half expected somebody to come in. But it was very quiet. He could not even hear anything from outside, any trucks moving, or birds, or any of the city sounds. A good quiet place. He picked a pew near the front and sat.

It was not very comfortable. He slouched. Looked at his cigarette. Dover Brown.

Is dead.

Yep.

He took a long puff on the cigarette. Dumb nigger. You're a long time dead. Well. And what do you feel?

I don't know.

I'm sorry.

But how much of it was your fault? He was in the ring a long time. A lot of people hit him.

Don't think like that. You hit him. He died. That's the truth.

Yes but—

Don't think like that.

All right.

So I killed him.

He's not the first, after all.

No.

McClain closed his eyes. The war. Man standing in waist-high grass. Bullet hits high in the chest, puffing dust from the coat with the impact. Man falls backward, and when you see him later he has open mouth, very bad teeth.

McClain shuddered.

So. So now. What's the point?

No point.

What does it change?

Nothing.

Ravenel wants you to quit. Will you quit?

No.

Why not?

Because there's nothing else I can do. Because if I was made for anything, this is it.

Were you made for anything?

Apparently. Apparently to kill Dover Brown. . . .

Thinking was becoming more difficult. McClain got up and walked to the altar. He was aware of the enormous silence. Candlelight glowed on the organ flutes.

Be practical. You could quit.

Yes. Quit and do what?

Quit and go back to school and learn something useful. That would make her happy.

I know. . . .

He put his hands on the railing. There was a statue of Jesus, yellow in candlelight, hand upraised in benediction. The face looked down in lifeless repose. Many people came here and knelt here and believed in this. McClain blinked, shook his head.

I can't quit.

Why not?

If I quit, I may come all to pieces.

You may do that anyway.

Yes. . . .

He turned away from the altar. If you could pray. I wonder how many pray. For forgiveness. Do you need forgiveness? Yes. Because of the death of that poor black man.

Many people helped you.

True.

But you can't take all the responsibility, and besides, what does it matter after all? What rule did you break? What commandment in which you don't believe did you break, and what do you need forgiveness for if you break no rules, and how can you break rules if there are no rules to break, and who did you injure except Dover Brown, and go apologize to *him*, go, ask forgiveness of him, and see how much of it he hears, or cares, or ever will again.

. . . and yet. I didn't mean to kill him. . . .

McClain sat down again in another pew. He was beginning to feel very bad. He looked up again at the altar, and saw the face of the statue, and thought suddenly of the toothless orderly who had bent over him those early days in the hospital after he had been wounded, back before he could hear, and the orderly's grinning, toothless mouth moving, only no sound, and he had wondered if he were deaf forever, or in a madhouse.

. . . and so I came back. Back, then they wouldn't have me. I thought they weren't ready for me. I thought there might be a point. . . .

He got up and walked to the door. His cigarette was burning down. He stood by the door and realized that he was crying. Have to stop that. He opened the door and threw the cigarette out and wiped his face.

. . . you know what? All you were saved for was to kill Dover Brown.

No.

That would seem to be the way it is. Old buddy.

No.

He looked back at the altar.

I have never quite accepted . . . I have never been able to believe . . . in absolutely nothing. . . .

At that point he suddenly stopped thinking. It was easy.

. . . and what about Lise?

I guess that's over.

Yes. That's over.

I won't last much longer, and I don't want her to be around for that.

And why won't you last?

Because I won't accept it. I will never accept it.

And that's the truth.

SHE WOKE just after dawn. He was sitting in a chair by the couch, watching the light come over her. He was trying to understand what it was exactly that he loved. She was very beautiful, very beautiful, but it was not that, and not the sex part either. He did not know what there was in him she could love. The more he thought of it the more of a mystery it was. He looked down on the curve of her thigh beneath her skirt, the round hip rising full and heavy and warm above the smooth belly, and he had the memory of her eyes, black and smudged like coal as he loved her; he thought of all the joy she had given him, and he felt a stuffed feeling in his chest, a weighted pain. There were too many mysteries. What would happen now was a mystery. He was very tired of mysteries.

She moved. She rolled over on her back and stretched and yawned, and he watched the light cloth of her dress tighten over her breasts as she moved. She saw him, smiled.

"How long have you been up?"

"Not long."

"Did you get a good rest? Oh, my gosh, it's morning." She sat up and looked at the bright windows. "I slept all night." She was astonished. She put out her arms. He held her and kissed her; she complained fastidiously about the state of her mouth. They lay together on the couch. He ran his hand down her body and between her legs. The movement did not rouse him; he wanted just to hold her there, to feel the possession of her. She tucked her face into his neck.

"I could sleep all day."

"It was nice of him to give up his place."

"Wasn't it? He's a sweetie. You're a sweetie. Um."

"Go on to sleep."

"No." She pulled back. "I ought to get up and fix you something." She put cold fingers on his face. He had not shaved. She started to smile, and then suddenly her face clouded. He could see the memory come over her. She ran her finger along the edge of his swollen eye. "You were up all night," she said.

He shook his head.

"I should have stayed with you." She grimaced.

"I don't think we ought to stay here."

She studied him. "All right. But let me make you some coffee."

"It would be better if nobody saw us here."

"It won't take but a moment. He told me where everything is."

She got up and went into the kitchen, running her hands through her hair. He sat on the edge of the couch and watched through the door, and she moved back and forth and smiled at him. The pale light of dawn was in the windows; the cold gray glow was in the room. Under a sheet lay Dover Brown. She came back into the room with hot coffee, and she sat on the floor next to him and rested her hand on his thigh.

"You've got to stay away from me for a while," he said.

She nodded silently. She looked sleepy and warm and very young.

"Don't know what I'll do now," McClain said.

"It was very bad luck," she said.

"That it was."

"And that's all it was."

"Yes."

She studied him. He looked into her eyes, and that thing passed between them that was inexpressible, and he turned away.

"I have some money of my own," she said. "Enough to go away for a while."

He began slowly lighting a cigarette.

"Or if you don't want to go away, we could take a place back in the valley and you could stay there and you wouldn't have to do anything. I could get a job, and you could study."

McClain said nothing.

"Do you know it's been almost two years? Since I met you? I was thinking of it last night. That night on the bridge was two years ago. You know what some of my friends used to say? That it was hypnosis. That you had some power over me."

McClain looked at her. Her mouth was touched with a soft smile.

"You know I wondered about it. I wouldn't be at all surprised if there was some truth in it. I'd look at your face, and I'd have no will. Except to be with you. I used to wonder if it would wear off. You did too. But I don't think it will, now."

McClain stared at her.

"But you can't quit, can you?"

McClain shook his head.

"I didn't think so," Lise said.

McClain said suddenly: "I don't like what I am."

She reached anxiously for his hands.

McClain said: "I don't want to be what I am."

"You shouldn't say that."

"But there's something in me that won't give up," McClain said. "I wish I could kill it. I wish I knew how."

"Don't talk that way."

"You know what's strange? Last night, after he died, I thought you'd all look at me . . . because I did it. I thought everybody would look at me as something horrible. But nobody did. Isn't that strange? I don't understand that."

"Darling," she said, "darling."

"I need some time to think," he said.

It was time to go. He stood up. She watched him, then she rose and got ready. Before they went out the door he stopped and took her in his arms.

"It was only bad luck," she said.

"Listen," McClain said, looking into her eyes. "One thing I want you to know. Of all the things that ever happened to me, in all my life, you are the best."

She gazed back at him with those wide marvelous eyes. "Take care," she said.

"I will."

They went out with great care, pausing and hiding between the high bushes, so that no one saw them go. He drove her to the train station and said good-bye and watched her go away.

FIVE

MCCLAIN STAYED ALONE in the cabin on the mountain. No one came out to see him. He did not call Lise, or go into town to see Ravenel. He needed time, a silent space. He carried the death of Brown with him like a cold pool in his skull. He wanted time to think, but he wound up not thinking at all. It was the most beautiful time of the year: there was wild color everywhere, and the autumn light all red and gold, turning the world soft in the afternoons, clear and clean and smelling of burned leaves and winter. There was snow on the mountain peak and snow on the peaks far off in New York, and then in the second week the first snow came down in the valley. It was very pleasant to sit in the house alone with no sound but the crack of boards shrinking in the spreading cold, and the sigh of the snow falling steadily all down the valley. He liked to walk back up the mountain in the falling snow, and then find his way back—it was a mindless thing, all quiet and alone, walking in the snow searching for your own tracks, coming across the tracks of birds, rabbits, bobcats. He had remembered a trick from his youth: There was always a hollow space under a pine tree, a space that was empty of snow. The tree was like an umbrella, and the snow slipped down the pine needles and built a wall until it reached the lowest limbs, and one could break through the crust and find a warm hole down inside next to the bole of the tree, the hole all matted with pine straw. He liked to take his rifle and let himself into the hole, and then cover the entrance with snow, all but one small peephole, and he could lie warmly all afternoon looking out at the half-buried orchard, where deer came often to nibble at the leaves of the trees. He could not shoot the deer. Once he saw a buck, the most magnificent buck he had ever seen, tall as a man at the shoulder, gray-backed, standing with that clean kingly indescribable grace just below his tree. He leveled the rifle on that one, but he could not shoot it. There would be no point in that. He did not even shoot a bobcat, or a fox. There was life all around him in the white woods, life burning in the crystal cold. He came upon scenes of small deaths: tracks of a rabbit ending in a wild flurry in the snow, bits of torn fur, flecks of dried blood like dried brown crystals, tracks of the bobcat leaving. Every day, every moment, something died. Jaws were moving, moving, chewing, killing. He lay in his hole watching the squirrels move: forever alert, forever in tension, and tails curling like rippling wire, heads forever jerking around to see, to see. That was almost the only thing McClain thought about while lying in the hole, that things were dying around him. Everything was eaten. Frozen to death or eaten. He thought about that, and also about the unutterably beautiful sight of the snow falling on the trees, on the rocks, on the cold silent ground.

The first week in November brought the first of the really deep snow. It piled deep between the pine trees, and when the crust hardened he could walk among the smaller trees and touch the tops, they were buried so deep, and it was no longer possible to find a hole underneath.

Throughout most of that time he was relatively clear in the mind. He knew he was in trouble, and so he set himself to wait it out. He had been in enough of these times to know that sometimes the worst thing you could do was think. He was increasingly tired, and it never was any good to try to think when you're tired. What came out then was despair, and there was no more time for despair. The best thing to do was just take it very slowly, and keep your eyes on the outside world. If he let his mind alone, it would tell him what to do, sooner or later. The trouble was that every now and then he suddenly got violently restless, and then he had terrible dreams. Sometimes at night the walls moved. Dover Brown would not down. If his death did not matter, then nothing mattered at all. When he began to think about it, McClain looked beyond it, and now for the first time saw something like an opening into something very bad, something indescribable, which was everywhere in the back of his mind, a black wind, a curtain, a hole. Once he had run away from it, now he was fighting it, but he was tired. So he held on.

But it did not pass. One day he got very restless, and he went in to see Ravenel, but Ravenel was too busy. He did not call Lise. He was not ready for her. He went to the gym and saw Gerdy, and there was a fight lined up for him at the end of the month: a very big fight for a lot of money. Many people would pay to see him now. That did not matter. McClain went back alone to the cabin, and then there was a letter from Lise: a short note in round letters on blue paper wanting to know how he was, and when she should come see him. That same day he lost several hours. He was sitting by the window in the night listening to music, a record of Lise's, and he was looking at the lights in the valley, and suddenly there was a thump, like a blow to the head, only without the pain, and just a slight dizziness, his eyes out of focus, and there he was out on the porch, sitting in a chair, half frozen, and the lights were out in the valley, and the moon had come up and was high in the sky.

He went on sitting. He could not understand what had happened. He did not remember coming out on the porch. He went back inside and saw Lise's letter on the table, and had a moment of white fear, thinking he must be going out of his mind. The clock on the mantel said it was nearly three A.M. He did not even know what day it was. He drove all the way in to town to make sure he had lost only a few hours. He got back in the early morning and finally slept. He thought about telling that to Lise, or to Ravenel, and decided not to. But he knew that something was going to give soon.

The next day his father came to see him.

McClain had been out in the woods in the late afternoon, and when he came back around the last bend and in sight of the house, he saw an old black car. He did not know who it was—no one had been up to see him in a long time. It was a gray day, windy and cold. McClain came down the road feeling a sudden hunger to speak to somebody. A black figure got out of the car, and he saw it was his father.

McClain stopped, paused, came on. The old man stood tall by the car, holding his coat to his throat against the wind. McClain felt his heart thumping in his chest. He had not spoken to the old man since before the war, even before that, since before school. He felt frozen; ice in his chest, ice in his mind.

The old man nodded. McClain looked into his eyes, watery blue eyes, eyes blinking tears against the wind.

"I come to see you," the old man said. His face had a strange stiff look. His eyes were watchful, cautious, like those of a weary animal. McClain stopped a short distance from him.

"Can I come inside?" the old man asked.

McClain nodded. He went up on the porch and opened the door and then went in himself first, letting the old man follow. McClain went over to the fireplace and began stoking it up. He did not feel anything, not fear, not anger, not anything. He turned and the old man was standing uncertainly behind him, rubbing bare hands.

"Don't mean to stay long," the man said. There was still a touch of the Scotch tongue there, the halting, nervous, biting sound that in itself, unbidden, rang raw echoes in the back of his mind.

"Sit down." McClain pointed to a chair. The old man nodded again and moved to the chair, and McClain saw that he was a little drunk. He was dressed in an ancient black overcoat and a dusty black hat, and when he opened the coat, McClain saw that he was wearing a tie: a red tie on a blue shirt, with the collar of the shirt rumpled but clean, as if it had been washed but not ironed. He had shaved, too, and his skin was fresh and clean under the watery eyes, but he was drunk all right. He blinked and sighed and rubbed his nose.

"I didna' come for money," he said. "You rest easy abat that."

McClain shrugged.

"Although," the old man said seriously, "if you've a bit of the hard around, I will take that kindly. As it's cold, you know. Bitter cold. And you live in a cold place up here. And that dirty damned car has not a heater."

McClain stood silently, then moved over to the cupboard. He was not drinking much any more, and there was still a full bottle of Scotch. He poured the old man a long drink. The old man asked for a bit of water with it, and McClain took it across the room to him and put it down next to him, not looking into his face, while the old man thanked him politely, and took a very long drink, nearly finishing what he had.

"I should not speak badly of the car," he said, wiping his lips. "I had to borrow it from a friend in order to come on up here. It's a long time since I've driven and Be Jesus, I was off the road twice, once into a deep, fierce, bloody snow bank, and do you know, I haven't a license. I haven't a license since, oh, for ten years anyway. But it worried me somewhat. It's hard to get around, do you know, in this country, without an automobile."

McClain watched, listening, waiting.

"Well," the old man said. He took a sip of the glass. He looked out the window at the gray sky. He said, off-handedly: "Well, how've you been gettin' by?"

"Fine," McClain said. Ten years. In a moment.

"I heard about the fella who died."

McClain said nothing.

"I would have been there, but I couldn't afford it. Things don't go that well, as you can see. But I don't complain, I don't complain. I did see you fight once. Cuban fella. You were very good. I didn't know you were that good. Sorry about the one who died. I wanted to talk to you about that." He blinked, rubbed his eyes. "I wanted to come several times, but, do you know, I hadn't the nerve."

He finished the drink. He looked into the glass and smiled. He looked at McClain and winked. "Lot of guts there. More guts in that little glass than in whole bloody armies."

McClain went wordlessly to the counter, got the bottle, brought it back, and set it down by the old man.

"Kind of you," the old man said. He poured another one and sat and looked at it and said nothing for a long moment. McClain looked down at the gray head, the iron hair. He was now—how old?—fifty-six.

"So how have you been?" the old man said again.

"Fine," McClain said.

"You didn't want to see me, anyway," the old man said gently, "or I would have come."

McClain said nothing.

The old man shook his head abruptly. "Never mind that. Never mind that. Doesn't matter." He drank. "Very nice place here. Very quiet. I was surprised when you came home."

"Me too," McClain said.

"Why'd you come here?"

"I was tired of wandering."

The old man looked at him, trying to understand.

"I should have left here myself. Long time ago. Should have taken you. But you know. I just wasn't up to it."

McClain bent over, worked on the fire. He was beginning to feel very tense. He wanted to say something, but he did not know what it was.

"I was never up to a hell of a lot," the old man said. He sat back softly. His voice was calm, flat, with no emotion in it. "Funny how you can be so strong in some things and so weak in others. When I was a boy I could break men in my hands. I could go overhand up a rope straight up into the sky. Never feared dying either. Don't fear it now. Don't fear anything now." He broke off, looked at McClain. "Am I bothering you?"

McClain shook his head.

"Don't mean to bother you. Old man. That's what I am. Too old. Done too much wrong. No time to talk about it now. When you are old enough, maybe you will look back on it and forgive some of it, but, Christ, I do talk, don't I? Listen, I just came because I'm going away for a bit, and I wanted to see you this one time before I go."

The fire caught, began to burn. Paper tucked under the logs caught and flared high: McClain felt the heat.

"Where you going?" McClain said.

"Well, the winters are too cold, do you see? I went to see a medical friend, and he suggested a change in climate, as if I were loaded and not an old drunk, which in itself is a compliment of a high order, if you think on it. Anyway, he thought there was something redeemable here, or that I should at least make some small effort to hang on to what's left, and he suggested for the sake of my lungs I should go south, so I know some people who know how you do these things, and I'll be movin' on."

"How bad is it?"

"Oh, it isn't bad at all, not bad at all, just a spot, do you know, a small spot no bigger than the memory of a pint."

"Do you need some money?"

The old man sat still. After a moment, he said, "I did not come here for that."

"All right."

The old man started to rise.

"I just came by to say good-bye. Now I'll be moving on."

He stood up. McClain said nothing. He didn't want the old man to go, not until he had said something, but there was nothing to say.

"One thing," the man said. "Have you been to your mother's grave?"

"No," McClain said.

"Well, I try to keep it up. Her birthday is in January, you know.

Well, if you would do me this favor? If you would go there on her birthday with some roses. It's a custom I fell into. It would please me if you would do it. I've done it every year—Jesus. Twenty years."

He waited. McClain said: "Sure."

The old man stood, took a deep breath. "Twenty years," he said. He shook his head slightly. He began to move toward the door.

"Why don't you finish the bottle?" McClain said. The old man stopped and looked at him. McClain felt something giving in him: there was a surge of appalling affection. The old man looked at him and something passed between them.

They stood for a moment, and then the old man said: "Good-bye, kid."

"Good-bye." He wanted to say more, but nothing would come. The old man said: "Do you remember her at all?"

"Some," McClain said.

"God, she was beautiful. There was something . . . she was what I wanted, do you see? There are some things a man can't handle, do you see?"

McClain nodded.

The old man put a hand to his eyes. "Well, it's all done now, I couldn't accept it and now it's all done. So now I am what I am and it's time to move on. Good-bye, kid. Listen, will you shake my hand?"

"Sure," McClain said. And looked at the old man's face and knew that this was the last time, that the old man was going off somewhere to die, and so end it all, even the possibility of any life between them, or healing of old wounds, and in that moment he understood that he loved the old man and always had and always would, even along with the hate and the silence there was still that inevitable, enormous love, but it was so huge it was inarticulate, and there was some halted frozen thing in him which even now could not speak, not even now, in the face of death and the end of it, the fadeout into the long silence.

He held the man's hand. The man looked at him and then went off. McClain sat alone that night and drank the last of the bottle and remembered his mother, who had died before her time. But he could not remember her face, or anything she said, and he could not even remember what it was like to be with her, because it was all too long ago.

ONE DAY, just before the fight, there was Ravenel. A gaunt blue-cold face, damning the climate.

"How the hell you doin'? Jesus. Thought for crissakes you'd run off. Let's get out of here, go get a drink."

They drove back to town. McClain had not really trained, and so he drank. He had no need of training. He walked in the woods and far up the mountain and slept long hours and he was ready. He had no need for whiskey. He was quiet and sleepy inside. Ravenel drank heavily. He had been invited to join a group of doctors, and he was considering it. He did not especially admire the people involved, and he hated giving up his freedom, but there were advantages. There would be people covering for him on weekends and at night, and besides that there were social advantages that would please his wife.

"The bride takes that stuff serious," Ravenel said. He drank. "That social jazz, that means a lot to them women."

"True," McClain said.

"I'll tell you one thing. I'm makin' money by the potful."

"That so?"

"Yep. All goin' into the house right now. But one of these days, going to buy a boat. Sloop. White sails. Sail it on the lake. This bloody goddam climate. Gets you to thinking of sand beaches and tan broads. Ah. One of these days. Just get up and take off. Hey. I saw your old man."

"Me too."

"He ain't well, you know," Ravenel said.

"What's the matter?"

"Lungs. Booze. He'll be around for a while yet. But thought you should know."

McClain had known it. It would have taken something like that. He told Ravenel about the visit.

"A bit late," was all Ravenel said.

They drank. They were in a smoky tavern, and it was very cold outside, and McClain could feel the cold creeping in along the floor and up around his ankles.

"Had one dream all my life," Ravenel said fondly.

"What's that?"

"Go around the world on one of them four-masted schooners. Ship's doctor. I swear," he insisted. "There's this boat, full-rigged sailing boat, goes around the world once a year, and you go along for cheap, as part of the crew. Everybody works, helps sail the thing. Costs you practically nothin'. I was plannin' on it, I really was. Once in your life, you know, just take off and go to hell and back, go all the way around, see it the way it really is. Before they blow it the hell up." He brooded. "I mentioned it to the bride, as a matter of fact. I believe we have there what you might call a source of friction." He drank. He peered up suddenly at McClain. "You've already been, haven't you? You lucky bastard. You just picked up and took off." Ravenel stared at him admiringly. "Got to hand it to you. At the time I thought you had a loose screw, but when else does a man get the chance? Tell me about it." Ravenel drank wistfully.

McClain told him about Jerusalem, and the filth, and the girl there, and gradually he got into the telling of it and went on to Afghanistan and the death of Wilson. He told that slowly and accurately, reliving it, seeing it again, the narrow road in front of the car, the mountains sheer and black with ice in the ridges, vomit on the beard . . . write me a letter . . . the black *thing* that was there in the corner, waiting. He took a long time to tell it. Near the end he had the stunning creeping sensation that the same black thing was waiting for him outside, in the black cold, now. He did not tell that to Ravenel.

"Sounds like meningitis," Ravenel said absently. He squinted at McClain. "You are a very lucky man. Amazin'." He shook his head.

They sat silently in an empty bar.

"Got to be up early tomorrow," Ravenel said. But he did not move. McClain was reluctant to go outside.

"You are a very strange man, Thomas," Ravenel said.

"Not so strange," McClain said.

"You baffle the hell out of me."

"Very simple," McClain said. "I got this one problem. I just can't stop believing. That's what's strange. I know there's nothing to believe in, but I can't stop believing." He picked up his glass. He was looking into himself and seeing something inside that was indestructible. "Isn't that strange? In all this world there are no signs and no miracles and nobody watching over and nobody caring. But I believe anyway. I've been followed by death, all my life. I see no meaning in anything. I can't forgive them for the death of my mother or for the death of Wilson either, or for teasing me with Lise, although I know at the same time that nobody did any of that, that it was all meaningless bad luck. I believe. I would do what they wanted if I knew what they wanted. I can't help the belief. I can't help it. I tried to run away from it and that didn't work, and I tried to fight it and that didn't work. I really don't know what I'm going to do. I wish to God. . . ," he broke off.

Ravenel said nothing.

"You know what?" McClain said. "The old man wasn't such a bad man after all. You know that? He was just weak. And you know, I don't hate him any more, and I don't even know if I ever did. Isn't it amazing? You go on loving and believing in spite of everything. That's me. You know what? I love the old man. I do now. I can't forgive him, but I love him."

"He's gone now," Ravenel said.

"Yep," McClain said. "And soon he'll be dead." He looked at Ravenel. Ravenel nodded. "And so that's over," McClain said. "You know what? I'm tired."

They moved out into the dark. McClain had thought that talking about it would make him feel better, but he did not feel better.

"I think of them sometimes," Ravenel said suddenly. "All those guys that died in the war. They rot. I'm here. But there's no answer. You can't think on it. You just do your job, and sail boats, and make love."

"You going to be at the fight?" McClain said.

"No." Ravenel turned his face away. "Wanted to tell you about that. Can't make it."

"Oh," McClain said. "All right."

"Well. Might's well make it plain. Look, kid. It was all right for a while. It was kind of fun, Roman gladiator type jazz, I enjoyed it. But the guy died, do you see? Listen, I don't want to trouble you. But I don't want to watch you any more."

McClain nodded.

Ravenel touched his arm. "Every time you hit him, I'd be worried. Do you see?"

"Sure," McClain said. "Forget it."

"Do you want to get killed?"

"That would sure answer a few questions, now, wouldn't it?" McClain smiled.

ON THE DAY OF THE FIGHT McClain hunted up through the woods toward the peak. He came out in a strange bare place, a place he'd never seen. He moved silently in the soft snow, mindless, expectant, but nothing moved. There was no wind and no sound, and the gray ceiling of cloud was just above him, smoky and still, caught in the tops of the tall pines. It was warmer now: here and there a branch bent slowly under the weight of the snow, and slowly further, and then the snow fell and the leaves swished upward. He did not see any birds. It reminded him of the war; he found himself moving with stealth from tree to tree, expecting. But there was nothing, not even any tracks. He expected at any moment that something would come down at him over the snow; he imagined seeing a man behind a tree. It was eerie. But he was alive and alert, he could see very clearly. He could see the snow mounded slightly over the hidden rocks, and he could see the grain of frozen bark under glazed ice, and he could see the edges of the rough cloud hanging along the tops of the trees. He stood alone for a long time. Looking out across that open snowy glade, he felt an odd sensation of size, as if his mind could not quite contain what it saw, and then he realized that this place and this moment were enormously beautiful.

Later that day he slept, and when he awoke there was a wind up and snow was blowing against a black window. He dressed, and ate, and could not shake the sleep, and drove to town.

He went toward the fight without any emotion; as a businessman goes to a dull but necessary meeting. He was not due at the arena at any specific time, and so he wandered for a while, had coffee in a quiet place, walked a long distance alone. He was quiet in the mind, he thought about nothing in particular. He thought once about Dover Brown, but it was only one quick memory and not a sharp one and made no impression. He began wondering idly but without interest if it was good to be so uninvolved going into a fight, but he did not worry. It would be there when he needed it.

The involvement was inevitable; it came the first time they tried to hit you.

He came to the arena and there were police around the door. It was a large crowd. McClain recognized some of them and said hello peacefully and saw respectful nods and one cold raw look from one of them: an unmistakable anger. McClain slowed, looked. A man with black eyes and a thin white face looked at him with contempt. McClain did not know why, did not ask, he moved on. Inside the arena he thought: Dover Brown. Well. Somebody at least gives a damn.

It was cold, as always. But there were reporters now, lining the cold halls. There was Sam Gerdy, resplendent and fat in tight pants and a broad yellow tie, looking like a sort of corrupt Pickwick. There were many questions, and McClain, who felt dreamy and sleepy, said nothing, and let Gerdy shield him and try to answer. Reporters surrounded him and moved with him into the room where Brother Mary was waiting with another man, a new handler, a thin man with a black moustache and an excited, idiot grin. McClain took off his coat, and they were asking him how he felt about going back in there tonight after the last time, after the death of Brown, and Gerdy answered that, and McClain thought about it. He did not know how he felt. He did not feel anything. The reporters pushed in on him, looking at him with flat unseeing eyes, as if he was unreal. He was irritated: they saw it. He knew from now on they would not be friendly. One fat one peered at him through thick, thick glasses, face assuming a nasty, virtuous expression. McClain thought: Killer McClain. It was absurd, a scene from an old, old movie. None of this was real. He looked at the fat man, who was mouthing an unheard question, and grinned. Headline: killer of Brown hilarious as he faces new opponent. But none of it was real. Gerdy shooed them out, finally, and McClain forgot them.

"Well," Gerdy said. He came to McClain dramatically—McClain was just then getting out of his pants—and took him by both shoulders and stared dramatically into his face.

"Well, Tom," he said, and his breath was awful, hot with whiskey and garlic. "This is it. This is what we've worked for, all these months."

"This is what?" McClain backed off with disbelief, almost tripped over his pants. It was incredible.

"I know you give it all you've got, all the time," Gerdy said soulfully, "but this time, this one time, you've got to give it something special."

McClain blinked. He turned to look at Brother Mary. The Brother grinned and shook his head.

"You could be one of the big ones, boy. Do you hear me? One of the big ones. I've done all I can—from here on in, it's all up to you. I know you'll do it. Just stay loose and calm and follow what we tell you."

There was a bit more of that, and then Gerdy left.

"Now what the hell was *that?*" McClain said, amazed.

"You know what?" Brother Mary said. "I think this time, for the first time, he bet some money on you."

The other handler, the thin man, giggled with meager joy.

"Yeah, but man, you take this guy, you're in the high cotton. He's got you there, you bet. You win this one, you got it by the short hair."

"This is Cueball." Brother Mary introduced the thin man. "He ain't got no smarts, but at least he's sober. Come on, Cueball, fix 'em up."

McClain dressed. He had an air of brittle unreality: if he closed his eyes, it would all be gone. The Cueball chatted. Brother Mary went on patiently, lovingly, working on McClain's hands. He had always worried about the hands; he worried now. The hands had come this far only because of him, and he knew it. He started telling McClain how to fight this one, talking slowly and calmly with no apparent care that McClain would even listen, and every now and then he would talk about the hands, which were not the hands of a fighter, too small, really, and too brittle. He explained to McClain how you must take care of a pair of hands, how the tape must go, and he explained it also to the thin man, who flitted about the room like a demented moth.

"What do you hear about Dover Brown?" McClain asked.

"What do I hear?" Brother Mary looked up. "I don't hear nothing." He squinted at McClain. "I hear they buried him, as a matter of fact." He chuckled, a high breathy, feathery noise.

"I didn't hear anything much at all," McClain said.

"You won't. The cops can't do nothing. Nobody in the game will bug you. Listen, it's the breaks."

"I thought there would be talk," McClain said.

"Nah. Listen, you can't let this one hit you like some of the rest of them bums. This one can hit, so you got to be careful. In the early rounds he'll go for the belly, and then when he gets you there, he'll give you a good shot up high, and then you'll be in trouble, so what you do, you. . . ."

McClain listened, but his mind was not on it. He was weary; he relaxed and took a rubdown. It was very strange. He had killed a man not so long ago and hardly anyone had spoken of it, and he had not really thought much of it himself, except that one night, and even now he had trouble thinking of it, it was almost as if he felt a duty to remind himself of it. It was a strange world. Everything that happened out there did not seem to matter. But he could see the black face. And yet one part of him slept on, serene, untroubled, silent. And now he felt sad. He felt really remarkably sad. Which was not at all the way to feel in the dressing room before a fight. He got up off the table. There was screaming above him. Somebody had been hit.

"How you feel, kid?" Brother Mary said.

"I feel all right."

Brother Mary nodded, but he was watching him.

"You're a shrewd man, Brother," McClain said.

Brother smiled, nodded.

"Why do you stay in this racket?"

"It's my racket," Brother Mary said.

"Why?"

The old man made a gesture with delicate hands—a broadening wave that took it all in: the dirty bricks, the pipes, the roaring from above, the grinning fool with the towel and buckets, McClain himself, standing taped and ready.

"Because it's true," Brother Mary said.

"Right," McClain said. He understood.

"One other thing," Brother said.

"What?"

"This is the only game I know—as long as you asked me—where the best man wins."

McClain smiled. "Not always," he said. "And even then, not for very long."

He went out to fight.

All the way down the aisle, he tried to wake himself up. The crowd turned to see him, curious now to see the killer. A woman yelled something over and over. He walked through a tunnel of smoke and light, stepping over candy wrappers, cigarette butts. It was very cold. The best man always wins. The phrase resounded in his brain. He reached the ring and went through the ropes and stood there, feeling chilled and strange. There was a dullness in his brain. May the best man win. There is no best man. He looked out over the pale faces, the hungry eyes. He was alone. Ravenel was not there. He felt strange hands: the giggling Cueball. He sat.

Across the ring: a handsome black face. Another black man. This one good-looking, businesslike. The big time. May the best man. . . . There was an announcer long ago who used to say, "and may the better participant emerge victorious." Absurd. But now it was not absurd. The black man sat motionless across the ring from him: relation to Dover Brown. And are you afraid, my friend? My good old friend crouched in there like a mad animal?

No. I am not afraid of anything. But I am very tired.

He looked clearly at the black man. The black man carefully avoided his face. McClain tried to see. One more fight. Here I am again. All my life, coming into a ring. All my life, I put my head down and go forward. In the war I had the same feeling. I have gone as far as I will go.

He felt suddenly very nervous. He did not like the way he was feeling. Be businesslike now and get this one over. He stood up.

"Sit down. Goddamit," Gerdy hissed. "You got time."

"I don't need it," McClain said. All my life I been coming to these things. May the better man. . . . He looked down at the faces. Why do you want to see me? What do you want to see me do?

He took control of himself. Brother Mary had once said: you are the best natural fighter I ever saw. McClain remembered that now. And remembered at the same time with appalling clarity the clear and open snow that same morning, and then suddenly for no reason, the sight of Lise in gray coming down the stairs, the pearls at her throat, that long, long time ago.

Now he did not feel like fighting. He wanted time to sit back and think about it. But they moved him to the center of the ring. This time for the first time in his life he looked at the man facing him: a clean face, had not been hit. Handsome man, slight moustache.

McClain looked at him and felt nothing, absolutely nothing. He wondered if this one had known Dover Brown. Be businesslike now. He looked into the handsome face. This one was a creamy color, a golden coffee. Are you the better man?

He went back to his stool. He was not ready. He looked back over the faces. Maybe she had come, after all. Maybe Ravenel had come. It would be so much better if somebody was there. Up toward the back of the room he thought he saw the old man, but it was too smoky and the face was too far away. And then the bell rang, and he turned and moved out into the ring.

I do not want to hit this one.

He covered and moved slowly to his right. The black man came after him. The black man moved with an oiled grace: be careful. McClain's body took over, and instinct moved his feet, his hands. The black man came in after him, and McClain's body covered up and McClain retreated inside himself. His body went on fighting. He was hit once in the stomach very hard, and then there was daylight. The black man went away. McClain was aware of noise. He blinked, watching, but it was as if he was watching from a long way inside himself. He ought to get going any moment now. The black man came in again, and McClain took another hard one on the side of the head, but the body moved for him, fought for him. The round ended.

He went back to the corner and Gerdy talked to him. McClain sat absently listening to the noise and the buzzing, letting cool water come over his face, noting that even now his feet were cold. He studied the handsome man across the ring. Yes, he was good. It did not particularly matter. You could lose this one. Yes. That did not matter either. There was the bell, and he was up again.

He had always been a slow starter. He knew that pretty soon now he would begin to function, to plan. Until then, he was careful. The trouble was that it did not really seem to matter. It was more than that. There was no weight in his arms. He had no feeling of power in his arms. It was like one of those dreams where you dream you are hitting someone as hard as you can, but the punches land like powder puffs, and the man you are punching laughs at you. He knew suddenly that he could not hurt the man facing him. He had not the power. He backed off, blinking. The black man came after him and hurt him.

In the corner Gerdy warned him. McClain sat dreamily, patiently, on the stool. He thought again of the cool open snow of the morning. A big buck in the stillness. Danger. He saw himself with a rifle in the woods. And then Lise smiled.

They pushed him out again. He blinked, trying to clear his head. He was hit once very hard, went back into the ropes; for a moment he floated, the world all white lights and rosy mist. Then he saw the black man coming, the eyes like black diamonds, and he held on. Better get going soon, he thought. He pushed the black man away and aimed a weak punch and missed, and was caught in the side twice and pushed back into the ropes. He felt no pain, just the numbness, the shock. Then he took one on the jaw, and he was back against the ropes and in trouble. He felt himself rising and coming up over the edge of a black hill and beginning to fall over the other side, but he made an effort and held on, and then hands were helping him back to his stool. He could hear the screams. He tasted the salt blood in his mouth. Gerdy was saying words. McClain felt a stab of anger. The Brother was there, soothing his face. McClain thought: I am in trouble.

He rose and went out again. But the black man was cautious and stayed away. That was a mistake, because McClain had been in trouble, but now his legs steadied and found the ground, and the world came back to normal, and he could see again and knew what was going on, and began to care, in a dumb animal way, to care only to keep from getting hit any more. The black man saw something in his face, and so bided his time.

In the next two rounds the black man began slowly, systematically, to destroy him. McClain knew exactly what was happening. He took it. There was still no power in his arms, and without the power, there was nothing he could do but take it. Because this colored one really was good, this one had everything, speed, punch, brains. The one thing wrong with him was that he was not a killer, he did not have the finisher's instinct; he did not know how to come in where the damage was and finish his man, and he had not the feeling for it. He hit and hurt and moved back. He was very good. And yet, and yet, McClain thought: if I ever get going, I can still take him. If I can only hit him. Let's see how he takes one.

But he did not hit him. The black man hurt him. McClain's left eye began to go, and then he couldn't see and had to turn his face slightly, and that one time the black man hit him, and McClain was on his back.

He saw the lights and the smoke. He rolled over and watched blood drip from him onto the dirty canvas. He was amazed. There was that same dull, steady screaming, like a great flow of water. He was down. He heard the numbers counted. His pride arose: No! Get up! He had never been knocked off his feet before. He got up, hardly hurt at all, but the world was soft and rolling under his feet. He looked around for the black man, and he felt fear now, not of the pain, but fear of being knocked out. He did not want to be knocked out. He looked for the black man, and all the while he could feel the screams of rage from his injured pride, from the mindless animal below that was beginning at last to roll over and hate. He saw the black man coming and tried to be crafty, but it was late, and his arms would not really move any more, and he could not see out of that left eye. He was hit again, but did not feel it, worried only about going down, tried to hang on, and then the incredible brilliance of the lights again, and he was down.

And so at last the rage woke him up. There was hate left after all. Enough hate to clear the brain. He was on his hands and knees, and all that was human was gone; he was stripped to the hate alone. He rose, alive, and looked for the black man, and the black man saw him coming and avoided him carefully, picking at him, waiting for an opening, and would not come in. McClain went after him, hit him once, just once, and the black man carefully went away, drifted away like black smoke. McClain could not touch him, the black man drifted before him, and in the last desperation of his own last terrible rage, McClain beckoned to him, come in, come in, and I'll kill you.

But the black man did not come in. McClain weakened. The floor began to move, and he could not see. He could feel himself fading, the light going inside his head as the light goes at sundown. The black man hit him again and again, and he was on his hands and knees, still trying to rise, when the fight ended.

He still had something left. He rose by himself and went back to his corner. The black man said something to him, and faces were gathering around him, but he was not wholly there. He looked out through the narrow opening of his right eye, found his way up the dark alley and back to the room.

He was almost completely exhausted, but there was something left. He was near the end of the road. There was more rage, even now. Fingers worked on his face, on his eye. Pain shot through his eyeball and up into his brain. He tried to think. But he could remember nothing but the punches, the feeling of the black man hitting him again and again. A hand sponged his raw face, water eased his dry lips. He tried to see who was there: it was Brother Mary. Little white hairs sprinkled all over his face like silvery straws. But McClain could not see clearly. He tried to say something. His lips were thick. He felt another spasm of rage, like a red fountain bursting up through the floor of his mind. He could feel the black man still hitting him.

They worked on him silently. There was no one else in the room but Cueball and Brother Mary. Cueball left and there was only Brother Mary. McClain did not notice when the Brother was gone. He sat alone in the dark. The last of the hate faded like the dying sun. He was near the end. He thought: I've been hit too much.

He began to clear in the mind. He began checking himself for damage. It was possible to be punched into queer street and not even know it, and he was certainly in strange shape now. It was more than weariness. He was very near the end. He wished Ravenel was here. Ravenel would know if he'd taken one too many. He got up.

He could walk all right. He put on his coat. He put his hands to his face and traced the damage to his eye. It was very bad. But that did not matter. What mattered was the mind. He was not certain the mind was working right. You had to be careful now, because the mind was rearranging itself. The mind was like a cave with loose timbers, and something had been knocked loose and the whole thing could go. Which really would not matter either, in the long run. He was done. And wasn't that a fine thought? He opened the door into the dark hall and there was no one there; there were sounds from down the hall, but his world here was empty. He turned back and looked at the black room and the table where so many had lain and bled. He said aloud, suddenly: "I am never going to hit anybody. Ever again. And nobody is ever going to hit me."

He went out the back way into the alley. He did not want people now. He walked to his car and drove slowly down the street. He thought he could go to Ravenel, but now he did not even want that. He did not want to disturb Ravenel. It was good that Lise couldn't see him. He began to drive poorly, because he was dizzy. Every now and then he could hear music, soft music. He drove out of town, and back up the long narrow road to his house on the mountain.

He lay down and tried to rest. But his mind was rearranging. Something was happening. He got up and made himself a drink and drank all of it. No more time for rest. No time to think. Time for action. He had some fight left. But there was nothing to hit. He went to the window and sat looking out at the night, but there were no stars. There was a soft snow falling, and it was very beautiful.

He sat for a long time. He knew it was true: he would never hit anybody ever again. The need for it was gone. With that knowledge came a sublime peace. He sat resting in that for a while, and then the restlessness came back. Time for action. He walked around the room. He was still dizzy and he had trouble standing. There was something more to be done. He did not know what it was. He began to remember odd scenes: Wilson in the war, tripping over a pebble, falling flat, giggling foolishly. Kashka and the nurses, the day they gave him the medal. One night with Lise when a star fell. One long, cold spark against the black. Her face in moonlight. It was all beautiful. The morning was beautiful. Sunlight coming over the peak.

"I will never hit any man," he said aloud, "ever again." He began putting on his coat. He felt very good, but very tired. Now he would go out and walk. He pushed open the door and walked out into the snow.

It was not cold. The snow was good on his face. He knew his way up the road, and it was not long until dawn, and soon now the sun would be up. And he was all done. It was marvelous to feel the weight all gone. He wanted to sit on a peak and look at the morning.

"You'd better talk to me now," McClain said. "If there is anybody anywhere, you'd better say something now."

But there was no sound but the crunching of his own feet in the snow. He moved on up the road.

"I guess you're really 'round the bend now," he said. "I guess so." He walked slowly, waiting. He knew that there was something ahead. He began to feel that there were mines in the earth, explosions in the earth, that if he stepped on the wrong place, the whole world would go. He tried to walk with care, but he was too dizzy. He knew he was no longer quite sane, but that was all right too. He thought: don't hold on any more. Just let it go. It doesn't matter, nothing to be afraid of. He wandered along.

"If there is any God at all," he thought, ". . . if there is anything to say, say it now."

But there was no sound. And yet he could still hear music, not wild music or anything to fear, but the kind of soft, almost tuneless music you hear when you are humming to yourself and not quite aware of it. And the music was in the back of his mind and quite pleasant. And he knew that he was very near the end, the end lay ahead somewhere near the peak. If he could find that one open place.

He wandered in the woods. He expected someone to say something, he expected someone to appear. He knew someone would appear. Because he knew he had come as far as he could.

He could begin to see light. The snow had stopped. He moved on up over the soft snow, hunting. I am not a madman, he thought. I only have to have somebody talk to me. I need somebody to help me. And then he heard a voice: "Thomas. You be careful now. You'd better rest now."

It was the voice of his mother, coming from the back of his brain.

He knew she was not there, but it was almost as if she was. And he thought of that: Will I see her ever? Is she lost forever?

And there was more silence and he went on into the light.

He knew now that it was impossible to disbelieve. If there was no one here now and nowhere to go and all this was emptiness, then he would lie down and let it go. But there was no sound. The day was coming, soundless and bright. He stopped in a cleft below two rock walls and saw the light coming, flooding the sky above him. Now something was coming. His mother's voice said again: "Thomas, you take care."

But he said: "It's all right, Mom, I'll be all right."

He watched the light flood morning through the trees, and something was coming, something was happening. There was light boiling in the ground, light blooming in the rocks and the ice, light beginning to warm him and blind him. He said aloud: "I'm sorry." All his life he had hated. He was sorry. Now he was near a Presence. He had either gone mad or there was someone here. But there was no sound. He saw the light on the peak, and the light in the sky, and he felt the mortal beauty of the white earth. He began to give up. He had fought all his life, but now he was coming home. He went to his knees. He knelt on the breast of the earth, in a moment of incredible tenderness. He said again: "I'm sorry." He could feel his mind giving way, and then it gave, and he shuddered all the way down to the black bottom and beyond that into the bright hell below. He was alone forever and ever. There was nothing forever and ever. There was no one to meet him. Beyond the light there was nothing. There was nothing. He tried to pray. There was no sound. But he no longer needed a sound. He was no longer himself. Things were dying in him: questions died like small candles in a great wind. He felt unutterable beauty, and he gave in, and he was alone in the enormous wild light of the morning.

RAVENEL WAITED FOR HER in the physicians' lounge at the end of the hall. He looked in on McClain several times, but McClain did not regain consciousness. Ravenel went through the doctor's private horror: he knew what there was to fear. If the pulse began to slow, if the respiration began to slow. . . . Once when Ravenel checked the pulse it was perceptibly slower, and Ravenel got worried. If McClain were bleeding badly enough inside his head, he would go on bleeding until he died. Ravenel waited, and the pulse slowed, and Ravenel knew he was dying, and then the pulse steadied and held, and the heart went on beating and McClain had a good chance to make it. You could be sure of nothing. Ravenel had seen too many die who had no business dying and too many go right on living who should have given up. But the pulse was steady and the heart went on beating, and Ravenel talked to McClain silently, coaxingly, angrily, in the dark room, and the pulse beat strongly. Then Ravenel went back to the physicians' lounge to smoke and steady his nerves and listen to music.

Lise came in the early morning, just before dawn. Ravenel smelled cold air and perfume. She was wearing a silver gray fur under the marvelous hair, and Ravenel felt a throbbing of traitorous joy at the sight of her.

"How is he? Can I see him?"

"He's all right. Sit down. Sit down for a minute."

"I read about the fight this morning. I didn't know what to do. He didn't call. How is he?"

"He's asleep now. He won't be awake for a while."

"Can I see him?"

"Sure. But he won't be awake. I want to talk to you."

"I thought I ought to come up. I drove all the way out to his house and the car was there, but he wasn't. I was afraid." She looked at Ravenel, wondering if Ravenel knew what there was to be afraid of. "I looked all over for him, but I couldn't find him."

She was trembling. Ravenel stared at the loveliness of her, the youth, the softness. His mind said, audibly: *ah.*

"How is he?" she repeated.

"Some hunters found him. I tell you, his luck is incredible. He was in bad shape; apparently he'd been wandering around. When they got him here, he was unconscious. The people downstairs knew him and called me. I came right over." He raised his hands in a gesture of helplessness. "He is really damn lucky. He could have laid out on that damn mountain until spring."

"But how is he?"

"Well, now listen," Ravenel said calmly. "I don't exactly know. He's been hit too much. You'll have to be careful when you talk to him."

She looked at him with round eyes.

"I took an EEG, and it wasn't normal," Ravenel said. "There's been a brain concussion. I don't know how bad that is, but you've got to watch it, of course. He woke up once and talked, and I had trouble making any sense out of it. Listen, don't get shook yet, wait till later. It may not turn out to be bad at all, and anyway he'll need you. Take hold. Right?"

"Right." But she was afraid.

"One thing you won't have to worry about. He won't be fighting any more." Ravenel grimaced. "He broke his hand someplace. Didn't do it in the fight. Looks like he did it somewhere against a rock. Did a very good job. It's broken for good and all. Compound. It'll never mend good enough to fight with."

She nodded. She was composed. "Is that all?"

"No."

She waited, her hands tight together.

"It's possible he will have trouble with his vision, or with his walking. Can't tell. Thing you have to face. He may have some memory problem. He may be a while getting well."

She nodded again. "Is that all?"

"Yes."

"You're sure?"

"All I can say right now."

"What did he say?"

Ravenel closed his eyes briefly. He saw the broken face, the bleeding eyes. There was a look in the one good eye that you get when you look too long at a very bright light.

"He just mumbled. I couldn't make it out except one thing. He said he'd made peace."

"Anything else?"

"No. Just that he had made his peace. He said it several times. An optimistic thing to say. Listen, I don't want you to worry, but I want you to be careful. He's been hit too much and pushed too far, and he should have it easy for a while. He has a right to be a little strange. Hell, he's been strange all his life."

"Don't worry. Can I see him?"

"Sure. But what are you going to do now?"

"Do?"

"Are you going to stay? Or are you just here for a visit?"

She rose slowly. She was looking at him with those huge, blue, injured eyes. "I didn't leave him, Charley."

"I know, I know. Forget it. But he's going to need somebody to take care. What are you going to do?"

"I'll take care," she said. She said it automatically, just slightly bewildered, as if he had momentarily questioned the rising of the sun.

"You know, I could get fond of you," Ravenel said. "Only in a sexual way, of course." He grinned, but he put out a hand and touched her arm.

They went together down to McClain's room.

He was sleeping in the soft light of the night lamp. His face had been treated and bandaged, and he looked much better now than he had that afternoon. Lise went to him and sat by the bed. Ravenel came in behind her. Something in McClain's face touched him. He stood by Lise as she held McClain's one good hand, and he looked down at the torn and darkened face, and suddenly he felt tears in his eyes.

"Can I stay for a while?" Lise said.

"Sure," Ravenel said.

"He might wake up," Lise said.

Ravenel nodded. He started to back away. He did not want her to see his face. He suddenly wanted very much for them to be happy. At that moment McClain stirred and his eyes opened. Ravenel was amazed.

McClain looked at Lise, then around the room. His eyes saw the hospital night stand, and Ravenel in the dark, and he smiled, an odd, quiet smile.

"Well, here I go again," he said.

Ravenel did not understand.

"Tom. How are you? How do you feel?" Lise said.

"I'm all right," McClain said. His face had a strange, soft look. He looked like a man on drugs, but it was more than that, it was the look that had worried Ravenel.

"Hey, Charley," McClain said.

Ravenel nodded.

"I made peace, Charley. Went up on the mountain and talked to them, and made peace."

"Sure, kid."

McClain closed his eyes. "Be all right, now," he said. After a moment he opened his eyes again. "You know what?" There was something grave and boyish about him, something young and filled with wonder. "You know what? I am never going to hit anybody. Not ever again."

"That's wonderful," Lise said.

"Never again," McClain said. "I've made my peace."

It was time for Ravenel to go. He backed away and went out the door and down the long hall. He left them alone in the soft light of the early morning and walked downstairs aware of all of it, all the newborn, all the dying. He did not know what was going to happen now, but he had been born an unbreakable optimist. One more day. He came out onto the steps and stopped and looked up at the night sky and the light in the east. He thought: what strange things we are. What wonderful things we are.

Ravenel went home.

About the Author

Michael Shaara was born in Jersey City, New Jersey.
He has been a paratroop infantry sergeant, a police
officer, and an amateur fighter, and like his main character Tom
McClain, has traveled widely in the Middle East. Mr. Shaara has
had more than sixty stories and articles published
in The Saturday Evening Post, Playboy, *and other*
leading magazines. He currently teaches literature
and creative writing at the University of Florida
in Tallahassee, where he is also at work
on a second novel.